PAWNS ON THE HUNT

ALEX J FISCHER

For my Family and Friends

1
***

Luke placed the now empty mug into the dishwasher, closing it before pressing a button, and the machine roared to life. He turned and saw the crowd in his boss's newly renovated business, which was back to its former glory. He looked over at Dale, writing bets on the chalkboard. "I miss George," he said.

"Don't tell me you're with my daughter on that," Joe grunted behind him. "I'm not changing my mind."

"He was too nice to work here anyway," Luke said. "How's it going, Joe?"

"Another day, another dollar," the older man said, coming up and standing shoulder to shoulder with Luke behind the bar. He rubbed his bushy brown beard with a grunt. "Do you think Dale's ready for his own collection runs yet?"

"Dale?" Luke ventured a glance over at his friend. He shrugged. "I guess it depends on who you send him after. He's gained a rudimentary understanding of collecting over the past few months, but I'd say he needs a little more mentoring before he's ready to go after anybody big."

"His God damn wife has been calling me recently. Did you know that?" Joe asked.

"Excuse me?"

"Yeah," Joe said. "She's been calling every week or so. She goes on these rants about how I need to give him a safer job and to have that mean guy, Luke, do the dangerous jobs."

"The woman is insufferable sometimes," Luke said. "Her heart's in the right place, if I'm honest though, boss."

"You think so?" Joe said, turning to Luke, his eyebrows raised.

"She just wants her husband safe. He's a gentler soul than I, so it makes sense." He grabbed a glass and filled it with the customer's preferred alcoholic drink before handing it off. "Her methods may annoy, but she's being a good wife."

"He'd better not be too gentle of a soul," Joe said. "That's why I'm having you mentor him. Shy men do not get us our money if they're too cowardly to lay the pressure on."

"I understand," Luke said. "I'm teaching him everything I know, boss."

"I know, son." Joe looked left and right in the crowded room. "How's everything going with you and Vickie?"

"She's been busy. She gets home late and won't tell me much. I guess it's to be expected when you work for who she does. They are holding us over her head, after all. She can't say no."

"Just be there for her," Joe said. "Let her know you're always there. She'll talk to you when she needs to. Trust me on that. Whenever something big happened, she always ran to me and told me all about it if she couldn't handle it on her own. She'll do the same for you. Just be ready for whenever it happens. By the way, have I told you about the night before prom when you two were in high school?"

"I don't believe so," Luke said. He took an order from a nearby patron sitting on a stool, grabbing a nearby shot glass and the appropriate bottle before opening and pouring it. He set it on the bar and took the money he offered. "Why?" He turned to Joe with a smirk. "Did she tell her dad all about how I asked her out?"

"Maybe," Joe said with a chuckle. "Don't tell her I told you this." He gave one more quick glance around the room to confirm his daughter wasn't in the room. "She was a nervous wreck and didn't know what to do. She was babbling on and on about how she couldn't do this, and you were an idiot for even asking her. I just smiled the whole time. I could tell she wanted to go with you to the dance, but she wouldn't admit it to herself."

"Is that why she cussed me out when she said yes? What did you do, old man?"

"Who are you calling old?" Joe's voice was sharp. He paused, staring at Luke's indifferent face before busting out laughing. "Fine, maybe I am. Yes, I told her to suck it up and just say yes before the dance, or she'd end up not going or going alone. She didn't fancy that. She just wanted a good excuse to say yes to you. She's a complicated one."

A nearby door opened behind them, along with some footsteps. A feminine voice spoke. "My ears are burning. My two favorite men aren't gossiping about me, are they?"

"You bugged my phone, didn't you?" Joe asked.

"Maybe," she said. "I need to know where you are in case anything happens."

"There used to be a saying in this country, sweetheart," Joe said. "Anyone who would give up personal liberties for security deserves none."

3

"That was said by Benjamin Franklin," Vickie said, sticking her tongue out. She leaned on the bar. "It went 'Those who sacrifice liberty for security deserve neither'. If you're going to quote it, quote it right."

"Aren't you in a fine mood tonight?" Joe asked.

"You just revealed an embarrassing story. Did you think I'd be all sunshine and rainbows?"

"Aww," Luke said. "It was cute how you said yes the next day, though."

"Be quiet," Vickie said. "I don't want to hear that right now."

"Maybe later then," Luke said, a knowing smile on his face. "Did you get off duty early tonight? Not that I'm complaining. You are my favorite visitor here, after all."

"You're still not good at sweet talking, honey," Vickie said. "Leave that to the professionals, though the attempt is appreciated. Yes, I'm off early tonight, but there's a hitch which I cannot speak of here," she looked at the man drinking his whiskey in front and to the side of her, "for obvious reasons."

"Luke, you head into my office with Vickie. I'll take over the bar for now."

"That's not necessary," Vickie said.

"Just humor an old man," Joe said, nudging Luke to the side. He pointed at the back office. "Go on then."

"Alright," Luke said as he backed up and ushered Vickie over. "Come on then."

"Fine." Vickie followed Luke into the small office. She shut the door behind her and turned to face her boyfriend. "You were never supposed to know about the prom story."

"I already knew that anyway," Luke said with an enormous smile.

"Really?"

"You're not as slick as you think you are sometimes, sweetheart. Now how was work?"

"Oh God." Vickie sat down in one of the two seats in front of her father's desk. "Don't remind me of that shit right now."

"That bad, huh?" he asked, while he took the seat next to hers. "A spy's work is never done."

"You're telling me." She rubbed the sides of her head. "It gives me a migraine just thinking of the job they tasked me with today. Speaking of which, I'll have to head out tonight and get on that."

"Head out? Is it that big of an assignment?" Luke watched as Vickie gave him a blank stare. "Alright, dumb question. Surely you can at least tell me what the job is then? I've already gone with you on one spy adventure. You know I can keep my mouth shut and am pretty good backup."

"That's the thing," Vickie said. "I never said you weren't coming with me. In fact, I was going to talk to Dad about getting you out of here for a bit."

"They want me to go with you?" Luke asked.

"Madeline does," she said. "You proved yourself, and it turns out my father made quite the impression on her. Ew," she shuddered. "Yes, I was instructed to get you to come along by any means necessary, since it's on domestic soil."

"At least you're telling me up front this time," Luke said. "I appreciate that instead of what happened last time." He reached over and laid a hand on her shoulder with a warm smile. "I'll go to keep you safe. It's what boyfriends do."

"I don't think normal boyfriends help bust international spies at war with this country."

"That just means I'm special." He used his other hand to gently poke her in the nose as he spoke. "Seriously though, it's only been a couple of months. What have you been doing since?"

"Paperwork. I had to verify that you did all the physical work on our soil, since technically we're not allowed to operate on domestic soil. Not that rules matter to those people."

"What's the job?" Luke asked. "Are we to track down another spy?"

"Kind of."

"What does that mean?" he asked.

"It's Zhang's partner this time."

"He had a partner?" Luke asked.

"Apparently so," Vickie said. "He's been lying low before and since Zhang went to Guantanamo. We've only got wind of him in the past few days. He's been spotted in Iowa."

"Iowa?" Luke asked. "Who the fuck hides out in Iowa? Is there anything of substance in Iowa?"

"Food production," Vickie said. "What better way to take the wind out of the sails of U.S. armed forces than to take out our food production? An army marches on its stomach after all. We're thinking the partner's going to take out several food processing plants."

"Surely that wouldn't impact our food production enough to matter?"

"One or two? Probably not," Vickie said. "If we leave him unattended, it won't be just one or two. It'll be eight to ten or even more. You get it now? At least that's the working theory of the higher up suits. They could be wrong. They often are, though they'll never admit it. You never heard that from me."

"Of course," Luke said. "I'll ask Reese to see if he'll go with us."

"Reese? You think he'd go?" she asked. "He said he wanted to be done with this the last time I heard from him at the bar party we had."

"He'll go," Luke said. "I know he will. There's no way he's going to allow a foreign agent to fuck with our food supply that's going to his brothers-in-arms across the pond."

"He could have been called back into service, you know," Vickie said with a smirk. "How are you so sure he's not?"

"I..." Luke paused. "I'm not."

"You are lucky your girlfriend has connections," she said. She reached into her purse, which was sitting in her lap, and handed Luke a folded-up paper. "Take a look at this."

"What is this?" Luke unfolded the paper and started reading. He looked up at Vickie every few seconds before returning to reading. "You're joking."

"I am not. I got him out of going back overseas and fighting in the trenches to do something that is much less dangerous."

"I'm sure he's going to be overjoyed to hear he's going spy hunting again in a state none of us have been to." Luke handed Vickie back the paper before she stuffed it back into her purse.

"He'll do what he's told. He's an army grunt. That's what they do. His superiors have already been informed of this, and he should be here any minute now." She held up her left hand and looked at the watch attached.

"You didn't," Luke said. "You did?"

"Setting things in motion is what we do," Vickie said. "Don't tell me you're surprised. Besides, compared to the harsh reality of organized warfare, this will be a cakewalk for him. He has a wife and a kid. I figured they'd want him doing the safer option. Right?"

"Probably," Luke said with a tilt of his head. "He's going to be pissed though. You mark my words."

"I doubt that." Vickie waved off his concern with a move of her hand. "He'll be thankful - you watch."

"You want to bet?" Luke asked.

"We're going to share our money soon enough, so sure," she said. "Why not?"

"Share?" Luke's eyes darted across the room until a look of realization dawned on him. "Aren't you forward? The answer is yes, if that was a question."

"It wasn't. I'm old-fashioned, remember? That's up to you, and you'd better do it right."

The door behind them opened to reveal Reese. He entered and shut the door behind him. He didn't speak a word. Instead, he sat on Joe's desk and crossed his arms. "You know," he started, "when I woke up today," he kicked his legs out toward the wall, "I expected to be hauled halfway across the world to continue the fight. Imagine my surprise when my CO wakes my ass up and yells that I'm reporting here tonight. CIA pull is strong to get that pain in the ass to do what you want. Why am I here?"

"He didn't tell you?" Luke asked.

"They're not real big on giving details ahead of time unless it's their operation, and even then..." Reese shook his head. "Why am I here? Vickie, was it? I assume it was your doing. Luke here wouldn't have that kind of pull."

"You'd be correct," she said. "You were such a help last time that I figured you'd want to come along on this next job."

"Were my words about not wanting to be involved with you guys not hint enough?" Reese fired back.

"Would you rather be playing the good soldier getting artillery lobbed at you along with small arms fire, or would you rather be playing a glorified game of hide and seek with deadly consequences? I know which I'd prefer."

Reese remained quiet and looked away before redirecting his attention back to her. "Am I going to go back to the front line after this?"

"I can make it so you don't," Vickie said. "You don't want to spend years away from your wife and daughter, surely? I'm trying to help you."

"By making me help you," Reese said. "I see how you CIA spooks operate now."

"Mutually beneficial arrangements are not a bad thing," Vickie said. "We get your expertise, your family gets you back quicker, and the country benefits from stopping a terrorist from destroying our food supply. Which, by the way, is going to affect the troops overseas. You're still helping them out by ensuring they won't go hungry."

"I'm not arguing," Reese sighed. He leaned back and rested his hands on the desk behind him. "There's no point. We're hunting another Chinese spy, was it?"

"Zhang's partner, actually," Luke said. "They think he's going after food processing plants in Iowa."

"That makes sense. Iowa is one of the states that produces the most food," Reese said, bringing a hand up to his chin. "Tell me we're at least getting equipped this time around. While I know your boy toy here is a beast with those brass knuckles, we need better gear."

"You're going to love this then," Vickie said. "I don't have the stuff here, but there are perks to working with us on official missions like this. We'll have access to all the CIA toys I can get, which a lot. This mission is critical, so we're getting the green light on anything we need."

"It's a start," Reese said. "What about you?" He turned to Luke. "What do you think about this?"

"I'm in shock," Luke said. "I heard about this just before you came into the room. I was just getting used to going back to collecting from bad and stupid gamblers."

"Whatever," Reese said. "It's not like I wanted to be dragged across the ocean to go back to that hell on earth. This saves me from having to get shot at."

"Don't get carried away," Vickie said. "We have plenty of time for that."

"Delightful," Reese said. "When are we headed out, and how much intel do we have on this partner of Zhang?"

"Good question." Luke looked over at his best friend. "How about it, sexy international lady of mystery?"

"Don't call me that," Vickie pointed at Luke and said in a stern voice. "It's technically wrong. I haven't been out of the country yet. It's more national woman of mystery."

"Thrilling distinction," Reese said, his voice full of sarcasm. "Answer the damned question already."

"Isn't somebody uppity today?" Vickie asked. "We'll cover that part later. For now, focus on getting everything you want to bring and be here." She reached into her purse and placed a piece of paper on the desk beside Reese. "Do not be late."

"Lady, I'll be there half an hour early," Reese said. "My superiors would have my ass if I was late. Knowing you, you'd tell them too."

Luke got up and leaned over to read the paper. "My place? Why meet at my place?"

"It's a secret," Vickie winked at him. "Now be there tomorrow morning at six am. We have ourselves a road trip, gentlemen. Do not be late. Be prepared to hunt. Bring anything you think will be useful. I have some devices we can use, but we're not stocked with an armory."

"Come to my place really quick, and we'll get all the weapons we'll need," Reese said.

"You replenished that stockpile from before?" Luke asked. "There's no way the walls are full again so soon."

"Not full, but they're getting there." Reese's frown turned into a smug smile. "You want to see?"

"Boys and their toys," Vickie said. She rolled her eyes and got up from her chair before slinging the purse's strap over her shoulder. "Let's head there then and get everything before we head to bed. It'll be one less thing we have to focus on tomorrow morning."

"Right now?" Reese asked.

"What?" Vickie asked. "Did you two want some more time to catch up?"

The pair of men turned to look at each other and back to Vickie. They both shrugged in unison.

"Fuck it," Reese said. "Let's go."

The two men slid past her and opened the door out toward the crowded gambling den.

"You've got to see the newest rifle I got last Sunday, man," Reese said to Luke, walking at his side. "See, I always get a new piece after Sunday services."

"Sounds mighty American right there."

"We're on the same page then."

Vickie slammed her father's office door shut as she watched them move around the bar and toward the front door of the establishment. "If I wasn't so confident he loved me, I'd be jealous right now," she muttered to herself.

"Ha," Joe to her side laughed loudly. "No need," he said. "That's just two men who've been through hell. Nothing to be jealous of."

"I didn't ask your opinion." Vickie walked past her father and tried to catch up with her subordinates.

Joe continued working, watching the three exit his place of business with a laugh. "It does an old man's heart good to see his daughter in love with a good man."

At Reese's house a little later…

"Come in, please." Angela was in a skirt and matching blue shirt. She was standing next to the now open door and was waving the group inside.

Evangeline stood beside her mother, waving at the group getting out of their respective cars. Reese got out of his car in the driveway and walked toward the two, his arms held out at his sides. "I've got good news and bad news," he said.

"All of you get in here," Angela called out, ignoring her husband. "You can tell me everything once we're inside, where it's nice and cozy."

Reese approached them and picked up his daughter before giving his wife a peck on the cheek and heading inside. Luke and Vickie climbed the steps leading to the door and quickly got inside so Angela could shut the door behind them.

"Now then, I am not arguing, but I did not expect to see you so soon, honey bunny." Angela took a seat beside her husband and daughter on their couch in the nearby living room. "Come have a seat." She gestured toward the second nearby sofa.

Luke sat on the end with Vickie sitting beside him in the middle.

"As I was about to say earlier," Reese cleared his throat, "I have good news and bad news about that. The good news is that I'm not going back overseas to fight the Chinese directly in close quarters combat."

"Thank God Almighty," Angela said. She traced the outline of a cross over her chest. "What's the bad news then?"

"The bad news is that I pulled some strings, but it doesn't come without a price," Vickie said. "I got him to help me and Luke with a job hunting one man, a spy, to be specific."

"Uh," Luke looked at her at his side. "Are you allowed to tell civilians this? Won't that get you in trouble?"

"Nonsense," Vickie said. "She helped us find Zhang. I assume your husband told you all about that afterward?"

"Of course," Angela said. She felt her husband snaking a hand around her back and gripping her side. "We never hide anything from each other. He mentioned the..." She looked at Evangeline before returning her attention to them. "He told me about the bad guy he helped you find. That's the only thing he has to do? Hunt one guy?"

"To put it in simple terms," Vickie said, "yeah, that's all we need. We believe the one we're hunting now was Zhang's partner. He's trying to sabotage our armed forces' food supply overseas. Our job is to stop him by any means necessary and secure our win on the battlefields. When I was given this mission, my first thought was to recruit your husband for his expertise."

"You have my blessing then," Angela said. "I'd much rather you go after one dude than face those horrible days over on Chinese land."

"Ever since they made headway into Chinese territory, I've heard it's been especially rough," Reese said. "From the stories I've heard from some of the boys, it makes me understand the eternal question - what's the price of a mile? The answer seems to be a lot of dead bodies."

Angela elbowed Reese in the ribs. Along with that, she gave him a dirty look.

"What?" Reese asked, bringing a hand to nurse his side.

"Dead bodies?" Evangeline asked.

"Uh..." Reese was visibly flustered.

"Sweetie, go upstairs and play some video games. I'll come get you when we're done," Angela said. "Now please, sweetheart."

"Okay, Mom." Evangeline got up off the sofa. "It was nice to see you again, Luke and Vickie." She ran over and gave them a quick hug before sprinting off up the stairs.

"Sorry," Reese said.

"You've always been insensitive. I'm used to it. Sorry about that, you two," she said, turning back to her guests. "You no doubt know how he is."

"Some would argue he's not as bad as his initial brusque impression makes," Luke said. "He just has a way about him is all."

"You are very polite, Mr. Simpson. If only more men were like you."

"We need to get some of my guns from out in the shed. That's one reason we're here," Reese said. "Apparently, the CIA is more of an intel gathering agency and doesn't have the guns they need."

"We prefer not to shoot if we can," Vickie said. "Sometimes it needs to happen, and then we find what we need."

"Apparently by recruiting me," Reese said. He tilted his head toward the kitchen and backdoor. "Shall we go get what we need?"

"I should let you all get to it then," Angela said. "Just

don't go off on a long diatribe like you tend to about your guns. They're not interested, sweetie."

"Actually, I..." Luke was cut off by Angela.

"Trust me when I tell you, Mr. Simpson, you don't want the entire speech. But on your head be it if you entertain my husband's eccentricities. I'll go see to Evangeline. Make sure you all get everything. I won't have you all leaving unprepared." She stood and reached up, grabbing both sides of her husband's face. She turned him to face her. "You make sure you've got everything. You get me?"

"I'll be fine, sugar," Reese said, leaning forward and stealing a kiss. He watched her move past him and up the stairs after Evangeline. "Now let's get everything while she's busy. We'll be here all night if not." He quickly led the group out the back of the house and toward the familiar shed.

Luke and Vickie watched as Reese undid the lock on the small building and opened it. He reached up and pulled on a nearby cord, illuminating the small shed's interior. Rows of junk lined the shelves of the shed. Toolboxes, tackle boxes, and anything else one might need were on these shelves. A familiar handle and square shape sat in the middle of the room's floor.

Reese knelt and gripped the handle on the floor before lifting it up with a loud high-pitched noise and climbing down. "Come on in," he said. "I revamped the place a little since you were last down here."

The pair walked over to the hatch and looked down to see a blue filled room. "What in blazes?" Luke asked before lowering himself to get onto the ladder. He climbed down, facing down all the while. He heard Vickie above him climbing down. He hopped down to the room's floor and saw the cause of the glow was some lights that Reese had installed all along the walls. He moved a few feet away from the ladder, standing next to Reese.

He put his hands on his hips and watched as his girlfriend climbed down. "Why blue for the light?"

"It's relaxing," Reese said with a shrug. He turned around and bent down under a nearby workbench. "Take your pick." He pointed up at the row of rifles. "Handguns are behind you on the desk. The ones above you are semi-auto. Fully auto is at the end of the room." He pointed over toward the far end. "In this box is every kind of modification you could ever want. Take your time. I recommend the iron sights if you're getting a rifle."

Vickie brushed past Luke and reached up to the array of nearby weapons. "These are nice," Vickie said with a smile. She pulled back the slide of the semiautomatic rifle and brought it up to aim down the sights. "I notice that some of these modifications are not exactly legal."

"Seriously?" Reese asked. He pulled out a red dot scope and tossed it over to Vickie, who caught it with deft grace. "Nice catch. Does a spy girl know how to use one of those? I thought they taught how to lie, manipulate, and not much else."

"Weapons training is one of many things they train us in," Vickie said. She removed the attached scope and replaced it with the red dot scope Reese tossed her. She turned the scope on with a hushed electronic sound. She aimed again, this time a red dot pointing where she looked. "I like this. I'll take this one."

"Good choice," Reese said. "A little generic, if I'm honest, but it'll get it done." He turned to see Luke staring at the selection of handguns. "You want my recommendation?"

"I'm not a gun guy, so sure," Luke said.

"Get a semi-auto," both Reese and Vickie said simultaneously.

"She's right," Reese said. "They're less likely to jam and easier to reload. You're more of an up close guy, so I was going to suggest a shotgun if you wanted something a little more daring. It doesn't require nearly as much precision either."

"Good plan," Vickie said. "Go with the shotgun. We may need something more powerful this time than our little peashooters."

"It's just one guy," Luke said.

"That we know of," she said.

"Point taken," Luke said. "I'm familiar enough with the system, but I'd like to at least fire the thing a few times before someone else is shooting at me."

"I do love the shooting range," Vickie said with a gasp. "We can make it a date. When do they close?"

"Not until like three a.m.," Reese said. "Go to the one off Main Street. Tell him Reese sent you. He'll give you a discount. Oh, and grab one of these before you go. These are top of the line." Reese leaned down and threw open a large case by the wall. Numerous vests laid nestled inside. "You'll thank me later."

"Noted," Vickie said. "One more thing. All this is in your name, correct?"

"You're asking if they're legal?" Reese asked. "Most of them. Does that matter?"

"I need to know for the paperwork. If we play with the fun toys, it changes which forms I have to fill out so the higher ups don't have a conniption. Are these two that we've selected legal or not?"

"Those two are," he said. "This one," Reese reached up to the one above him and took it off the rack, "this one is not, and this is what I was going to use. Does that change anything? I was also going to carry a grenade or two. You never know when those will be useful."

"That's all I needed to know. As far as grenades, go for it. I doubt we'll need them, but if it makes you feel more secure, go for it. Now we should get out of your hair. Do remember to be at that address by six tomorrow morning."

"You're the boss of this operation," Reese said. "Yes, ma'am."

2

_____

"This place reminds me of home, but kind of not," Luke said, stopping at the red light. To the right of their car was a green sign that read 'Welcome to Shelby County'. "You said the town's up ahead?"

"According to this map, that's right," Vickie said. "We need to set up a base of operations before anything else."

"I assume you have a plan for where that might be?" Reese looked over his shoulder out the rear window. "We're going to stand out to the locals wherever we go."

"Who cares about the locals?" Vickie asked. "So long as the other outsiders don't notice us, we're good. Speaking of which, we could use some of the local populace to help us out if we play our cards right. Turn right," she said.

Luke followed the direction and kept his eyes on the road while he spoke. "Is there a reason we're entering town by going through what passes for a ghetto?"

"What better people to gather intel for us than those who live on the streets?" Vickie asked. "I'm taking you to the local motel. We'll use that as our first stop. We'll change motels every single day we're here. I suspect our target will do the same."

"Speaking of our target," Reese said, "I assume at some point we'll get a name - hell, a face would be nice. Something to look for. Anything would be nice. I keep seeing faces on the sidewalk, and for all I know, we've passed the dude already."

"I doubt a foreign agent is just taking a stroll down this kind of neighborhood," Luke said, his voice stoic. "I'm more worried about the looks we're getting. The thing about small towns is that everybody knows everyone."

"You think he had the same idea?" Vickie asked.

"I would, wouldn't you?" Luke asked. "Get as much information as he can and then execute his plan. He wouldn't want to cause waves with the locals, so paying them off makes sense to me. He'd have a decent amount of cash to use, wouldn't he?"

"More than enough," Vickie said. "We're committed now. Keep going. It'd cause a scene if we pulled a U-turn now. As far as anyone knows, we're just passing through their little town on our way to bigger and better things."

"We're getting two rooms," Reese said. "I ain't sleeping on the floor."

"Privacy would be nice anyway, but we'll have to share one for planning," Vickie said. She looked down at the phone in her hand and pointed ahead. "At the end of this street on the right is the motel we're staying at. Pull us in there, and Reese will get us two rooms."

"Me?" Reese asked, kicking the passenger seat Vickie was sitting in. "Why me?"

"Because you're on loan from the army. I outrank you, and I'm giving you an order is why."

"She enjoys screwing with you is all. She does it all the time to me too," Luke said.

"Then you can go in with him. You're both brothers in arms, then you should suffer as he does too."

"Me and my big mouth," Luke said, his face a dour frown. "We'll need food too. Hopefully, this dump of a town at least has a pizza joint."

"Worry about bigger things than food," Vickie said. "You remember that wad of money I gave you this morning? Use that to pay for our rooms. Do not give your real names. We don't need your real names out there. It'd be too easily connected for news stations to put together after this is all over."

"That's why you're sending me. So you're not on the camera systems in there when they look." Luke pulled into a parking spot directly in front of the motel's office. "Come on, soldier boy. We've been voluntold our next duty while our better plans this all out."

"Yeah, sure." Reese undid his safety belt and opened the door, as Luke did the same for the driver's door. He took a deep breath and slammed the door shut behind him. "It gives us a chance to stretch our legs anyway."

"Come on then," Luke said. "Let's get this over with." He took off at a brisk pace toward the door. "Follow my lead. I don't want this to get any more awkward than it has to."

"You go in by yourself, big man. I'm going to scout this place out. See what kind of security we're dealing with here should worst come to worst."

"Just don't be obvious. We're trying to keep a low profile - not draw attention."

"I'll be fine," Reese said.

Luke went inside and booked the two rooms without incident. He paid for them and came back outside to see Reese turning the corner and approaching him. "Come on. Let's get everybody settled in and get this shit started." He held up two keys. He tossed one to Reese, and the pair walked back to the car. Once he got there, he knocked on the window, jolting Vickie from her reading. He backed up and let her exit.

"You got the rooms?"

"Right here." Luke held up the remaining key. "It's right over there." He pointed toward a nearby room. "Ours is room 107." He pointed toward the one directly in front of them. "Reese's is this one on the right."

"I'll get settled in after. I want to get this party started and know what we're dealing with."

Luke took the hint and walked forward to unlock the room. He pushed it open and stood to the side, gesturing inside. "Ladies first," he said.

"Thank you," Vickie said, taking his offer and entering first.

"What are you waiting for?" Reese asked.

"You're a regular comedian," Luke said, entering next and holding the door open for Reese. "Get in here, funny man. We'd like to shut the door sometime today."

"Yeah." Reese stepped through into the tiny one bedroom. "Where are we setting up?" He pointed toward the nearby double bed. "On the bed? The shitty little table over here won't do." He looked at the tiny table that supported a variety of amenities that the establishment offered below the television mounted in the corner of the room.

"The bed is fine," Vickie said. She sat on the side of it and placed her purse down. She reached inside the large bag and pulled out a manilla envelope. "Here's the intel we have," she said. "I've scoured this thing page to page all morning. See if you can find a lead I haven't."

"A fresh perspective can do wonders." Reese sat on the opposite side of the bed and reached over to grab the envelope. He opened it and took out a paper before handing another one to Luke. "Here, bud. Look this one over."

"This is so far outside my realm of expertise, but I'll try," Luke said while he studied the document.

"We're looking for a 5'4" Chinese woman?" Reese lowered the paper in front of his face and looked at Vickie. "Seriously?"

"Don't tell me you're sexist now, Mr. Hilton?" Vickie's question was not loaded, but more joking from her tone. "Who would suspect a cute little lady to cause such a thing, after all?"

"If you ask me," Reese said, redirecting his attention back to the paper, "we should have done what FDR did when this war started. It would have solved this shit before it started."

"Good old forced-relocation camps," Luke said, the disdain evident in his voice betraying his words. "What was that for? Weeding out spies?"

"Precisely," Reese said.

"Of which none were ever found, if I'm right," Luke said.

"They were there. They just couldn't make a move. Times are different now," Reese said. "Everyone's so damned sensitive, and look where that's got us. We're afraid to offend spies by putting them all in one place so they can't damage us."

"All my page has is her past sightings," Luke said. "She was in Kansas before this and Nebraska before that."

"Both prior states had food processing plants destroyed too," Vickie said. "You see why this is a priority now? Food supplies are already running low for our troops. We cannot allow another one to be blown up. We can't let our forces go hungry and cede land."

"If this chick was Zhang's partner, what was he doing? We never caught him going after any food supplies," Reese said.

"You never heard of it," Vickie said. "We were trying to keep it out of the public eye, but we believe Zhang was responsible for a couple of plants blowing up. He was trying to make ends meet when you met him. He'd gotten cut off from his resupplies and had to make money however he could. She is just continuing the work they started. This time, though, the public is aware of the factories blowing up. We can't keep a lid on it anymore, and there are all kinds of theories online, ranging from billionaires to some secret global cabal to Chinese agents. Guess which one's correct, why don't you?"

"We're in war. It's obvious." Reese tossed the paper down on the motel bed. "So, boss, what's our first move? I'd assume it's finding her?"

"What is this woman's name?" Luke asked. "My page doesn't show that. That's a good place to start in my experience."

"It says her name is Ai Xiao."

"Let's just call her Ai," Luke said. "That's easier to remember."

"You'd be correct," Vickie said. "Finding her is our first order of business."

"Easier said than done," Reese said with a scoff. "If she's planning on blowing a local factory up, she's going to be hoarding or trying to acquire powerful enough explosives. Either she'd have smuggled enough in when she got in the country, or she's buying them somewhere in the country."

"It wasn't smuggled in," Vickie said. "She's been here

since she was a teenager. She had to source it locally, which is why we're going to go pay the local big man a visit."

"Big man?" Luke asked. "What's that mean?"

"There's only one man in this Podunk country town that has access to such wares," Vickie said.

"How could you know that?"

"You underestimate how much overreach our intelligence agencies are willing to commit," Reese said. "You violated his fourth amendment rights, didn't you? You listened to him in his own house? Stop me when I'm right."

"War times are special circumstances," Vickie said.

"I don't think that's how rights work," Luke said.

"Shut up. Now they do. Are you two really going to argue when I got us a lead before we even got here? I saved us time. Time is one thing we do not have. We don't know when she'll blow the local processing plant up. It could be tonight, or it could be next week. We don't know. All we do know is she's been spotted here."

"So, who is this big man?" Luke asked. "I assume he's not someone we can just walk up to on the street and chat?"

"He's a local arms dealer. He goes by the name of Dutch Morgan. He's one of the only arms dealers here, as a matter of fact. This town's dry when it comes to that, aside from the gun stores, that is. He specializes in things those places don't carry."

"Explosives, illegal modifications, and the like, no doubt," Reese said. "I'd like to meet this guy. I speak the lingo; I'd be the best shot."

"Do we even know where the guy is?" Luke asked. "Or are we going to have to find him too?"

"We have his address," Vickie said. "Now he doesn't do walk in appointments, so that complicates this a fair bit."

"I'm sensing this won't be as simple as you made it out to be," Luke said.

"We do know one of his regulars and where he frequents. We can convince him to get you a meeting."

"Convince?" Reese asked.

"You heard me," Vickie said. "Now, to convince him. I'm sending you two. Take this." She handed Luke a piece of paper with their newest mark. "Go to this address and get the introduction we need."

"How much leeway do we have to get him to talk?" Reese asked.

"Any means necessary," Vickie said. "I do mean any means. Is that understood? This is a matter of national security. Do not pussy out. Our servicemen and women cannot afford it."

"We've got this." Reese reached over and tapped Luke's shoulder. "There's no time like the present. Let's get going.

"Call me when you're done," Vickie said. "I'll be here planning our next step while you two boys take care of it."

Luke and Reese got up off the bed. Luke folded the paper and stuffed it in his pants pocket. "Anything we should know about this guy?"

"He buys guns from the black market when the legal alternative is sitting a few blocks away," Vickie said. "Think about what that means. He's not a nice man, to put it mildly, sweetie."

"Stop overthinking it." Reese grabbed Luke's arm and dragged him toward the door. "We'll be fine. You've got me to watch your back."

"See you soon," Luke desperately tried to say over his shoulder before Reese slammed the door shut behind them.

"I'll drive this time." Reese held out a hand toward Luke in front of the motel room's door.

Luke handed him the car key. "I still wonder where she got this car. It's nice."

"We're on the official payroll, my man." Reese walked over with Luke toward the sports car. "They gave it to her. Don't question it; just enjoy the perks."

"If you say so." Luke got into the passenger seat while Reese got in the driver's seat. The engine roared to life, and the car pulled out into the busy traffic.

"Any means necessary, huh?" Luke asked as Reese drove. "Does that mean we have a license to kill?"

"Probably not a good idea to kill the guy who can get us in contact with the guy who'll lead us to our quarry," Reese said, focusing on the road. "It means that we can torture him if we deem it necessary from what I caught. That's your department," he said. "You're the expert there. I'm more of the homicide expert - you're the info collector."

"Just what I wanted to be known for in life," Luke said. "I'm that guy who can make people talk. Just call me Vinny, why don't you?"

"Vinny?"

"Apparently it's a reference you didn't get. Never mind," Luke said. "It was a character that tortured people for information."

"Don't get your panties in a twist," Reese said. "Besides, the last time we tortured someone, I was the one leading the charge. Don't forget that. I'll be there as back-up. You'll be fine. We're not killing the guy."

"She never did say what to do with him after we're done, so I guess we let him go," Luke shrugged. "How do we know he wouldn't run off to warn Ai or Morgan?"

"That's a good point," Reese said. "Call your girl and talk in code."

"What does that even mean?" Luke asked while pulling

his phone out of his pocket. "I'm not a superspy, you know. How do you even ask that in code that she'd understand with no prior prep?"

"Fuck, man, I don't know," Reese said. "Maybe something like 'Hey, sweetie, what do we do with our guest after our visit if he insists on talking to his boss?'"

"That's real subtle," Luke said, sarcasm evident. "Fine. She did tell me to call this number if I ever have any questions on this operation. That's why we brought that huge bag of burner phones."

"Get on it then."

Luke dialed the number and lifted the phone to his ear. "Yeah, no, we're not there yet. We just had a realization."

"Yes, sweetheart?" Vickie answered. "You just left. Why are you calling already? Did you forget something on your way to your appointment?"

"We just realized we did not know what to do after we show our friend around. What if he's a workaholic and wants to get back to it? We're trying to get him nice and relaxed."

"If he insists on working after your day out, then do whatever you have to in order to convince him not to. Any means necessary. Remember, he just moved out of his parents' house. He wants to make a good impression and show off." The phone cut out with those last three ominous words.

Luke hung up with a shake of his head. "I think I know what that means, and I don't like it," he said. "She said to convince him not to by any means. She emphasized any means."

"Guess we have the green light if it comes to it then. She can't blame us with vague ass wording like that," Reese said. "We're going after a customer anyway. I doubt he'll run to the dude. Now Morgan himself may be a different story, but that's not who we're after. All we're doing is getting a recommendation from this guy to meet Mr. Morgan."

"I'd really rather not end a civilian if it comes to it," Luke said. He stared out the side, his voice even. "I'd rather not kill anybody if the truth's known."

"Aren't you just a big old softie?" Reese asked. His tone wasn't mocking, it even broached something nearing understanding. "Neither do I if the truth is known. We do what we must. That's what they teach you in the armed forces. You never know what you're truly capable of until the meat meets the grinder. That's where you see the mettle of a man. You know what they don't tell you?" Reese asked.

"Go on," Luke said, watching the buildings pass by without turning to Reese. "That we're all stronger than we give ourselves credit for or some other Saturday morning cartoon nonsense?"

"The opposite actually," Reese said.

This drew Luke's attention. He snapped to look over at Reese. "What do you mean?"

"Do you know how many men I've seen panic and freeze on the battlefield? Everybody claims they teach you how to turn off your emotions, and to a degree they do; but you can never erase one part of a person. That primal need to survive by any means necessary. Some men it manifests in barbaric rage, wanting to kill each and every enemy, but that's rare. More often, it turns men into cowards. They freeze up and dig into their cover extra hard; rarely, if ever, sending any rounds downrange."

"Really? I always pictured every army grunt as being ready for a fight."

"No sane person enjoys fighting, dude." Reese turned right as he spoke. "If you ever meet someone who claims they love fighting because they get a combat high, run the hell away as fast as your feet will carry you, because that person is a psycho for real."

"That's..." Luke paused. "That's quite informative."

"My point of this was to tell you I've seen your mettle in a fight. You're not a coward. If I had to be drug along on this hunt, at least I know you have my back. Don't doubt yourself. Doubt leads to ruin."

"I think that's the closest thing I've ever received from you that approaches encouragement," Luke said. He chuckled at the dour face he saw Reese making. "Now, don't be mad. It was nice. You just better be careful, or people might think you have emotions."

"Fuck you," Reese said. The words did not match the meaning conveyed with the smile on his face.

"I appreciate it."

"Now let's cut this pussy shit out and get to work. We're almost there. When we get there, how do you want to do this? This is your turf. If you want info out of a guy, how do you do it?"

"I always want money, not info, but I assume it's similar. Right? Normally I'd do it myself, but with your combat experience, I can use you much more effectively than I did someone like Dale. I had him stand at the back door and let him tackle the dude running."

"I don't think he'll run," Reese said. "We'll be lucky if he'll even open the door and talk to us. He doesn't know us from Adam. I never open my door to people I don't know unless they have a mail man uniform on or something."

"I think you can rent those," Luke said.

"You're joking?"

"I am not. Now all we'd have to do is get something big,

rent the costumes, and we'd have a way inside, away from prying eyes."

"Something big?"

"We have shit tons of money, man. We say something like they've won a giveaway they entered, and we're here to deliver their free chair or something. We can even offer to put it together at no cost if they're reticent."

"No one would believe that," Reese said with a shake of his head. He pulled off the main road and into a nearby store parking lot. "No one enters giveaways anymore."

"My point is, who turns down free stuff? We make it clear we need no documents, money, or anything. Who's turning down a free chair? They could resell it and make a profit if you want to get cynical."

"True enough. That gets us in the door, and we can get what we need without causing a huge fuss. There's no guarantee he won't call the police afterward."

"Which would get squashed by Vickie working her spy agency magic. I don't think he would, anyway. What is he going to say? That two guys came in demanding a meeting with the local arms dealer that he frequents illegally?"

"Good point," Reese said. "We'll do it your way. I hope you're good at acting." His voice took on an exaggerated and quite bad attempt at a French accent. "We can't allow them to find out what charlatans we are, oui?"

Luke didn't verbally respond, choosing instead to shake his head with a sigh.

3

———

"Let's pray this plan of yours works, chief." Reese helped Luke take the large rectangular package out of the back of the truck.

"Just let me do the talking. We don't need your textbook charm this time. You'll have your day." Luke led the pair toward the house, backing up as he went. When he reached the top of the steps, he gave Reese room to climb the final step before the pair lowered the package down onto the porch. He turned to the house and pushed the button beside the door. A muffled chiming joined the symphony of engines that acted as the area's white noise.

They waited for what seemed like minutes until they heard a nearby thumping approaching. The door swung open to show a man in what was obviously his nightwear. He was adorned in boxers and a tied robe. "Who are you, and what do you want?" he asked.

"Hello," Luke said. "We're here to deliver this package."

"I don't remember ordering any package," the man said, scratching his armpit with a snort. "What is it?"

"I do not know, sir," Luke said. "Shall we place it inside

your house for you? We can also assemble it, should you choose, at no additional cost, as part of the promotion."

"You're not the normal package guy," he said.

"No, sir," Luke said. "We're trained in assembly. It just so happened you live nearby, so you got us."

"Hm, alright then," the overweight man said. He opened the door wide and stepped to the side. "Assemble it then. You can do it here just inside. I'll move it later."

"It's a lovely home you have," Luke said as the pair moved it inside the residence. He set the box down on the floor and knelt. "There's just one more thing before we get started," he said. "We need to ask you just one question." He looked at Reese and nodded.

Reese cracked a knuckle before rushing over to the homeowner and grabbing him by the collar. He slammed him into the nearby wall, knocking the wind out of him in the process. "We need a favor, pal," Reese said. "Dutch Morgan - you know him."

"What the fuck?" The man gasped for air, desperately trying to fill his lungs.

"I'd answer him if I were you." Luke stood up and wandered to within a few feet of the pair. "See, ever since he was born, he's had a bit of a short fuse. His mother would always task me to watch out for her baby boy. Trust me when I say do what he says, or things will get painful quickly."

"What about Morgan? What do you want, you crazy ass?"

"We need a meeting," Reese said. "You're going to set one up for us. You will mention nothing about how we convinced you, if you know what's good for you. That's all."

"Then he releases you, and you get to keep your new

furniture and can pretend this all never happened," Luke said.

"If I refuse?" the man asked. "What then?"

"Then he gets creative," Luke said. Luke strolled around the foyer, taking note of the pictures hung on the wall. "Cute kid," he said. "Is she yours?"

"Fuck you."

"That's a yes. I take it the woman behind him and beside you is your wife?"

"If I set up a meeting, he'll punish me for whatever you two do. Do you understand that?" The man gasped, gripping Reese's hands around his shirt collar. "He'll kill me."

"You have approximately two minutes before you pass out, give or take." Luke kept gazing at the various knick-knacks perched on a nearby table as he spoke. "My friend here is very good at keeping you conscious enough to answer, but if you keep stalling, even his skills may be put to the test. I hear brain damage occurs after enough time without oxygen. Let's hope that's not detrimental to your career."

"Just let me breathe, and I'll tell you."

Reese lowered him to the ground, allowing his target to gasp some breaths into his lungs. "At the end of the day, you're just a small cog in a giant machine here. Tell me, friend, do you love this country?"

"What? Of course I do."

"Good," Reese said. "Then you know your arms dealer friend deals with some less than savory types. Types that don't love America. Do you get my drift? I can't tell specifics, but you'd be doing the country a favor if you just set us up that meeting."

"You've been so nice, why wouldn't I?" the man asked,

sarcasm evident. "What the hell do you mean by the country talk?"

"Never mind that. If you want to help the war effort, just do what we say. I cannot say any more after my loud-mouthed friend already let that slip. You are to tell nobody we were here, or that anyone visited today. You do that, this all goes away, and you don't get a visit from some suits for buying from an illegal arms dealer. It's a pretty sweet deal if I do say so."

"If you're with the government, all you had to do was ask, not violate my rights and shit."

"That's the thing," Reese said.

"We're not in the government. Well, one of us technically is, but it's complicated. Think of us as deputies. We're the grunts sent to stop a very bad thing from occurring that will have long-lasting worldwide ramifications."

"You know how to spin a yarn. I'll give you that. Why should I believe anything a couple of psychos say after breaking and entering and assaulting me in my home? For all I know, you want to kill the man and take all his shit for your own. I wasn't born yesterday."

"So, we're doing this the hard way?" Luke asked. "Fine then."

"That's music to my ears," Reese said. "I've been needing to work out some stress. You'll do just fine. Tell me, what do you do for work?"

"Why?"

"Because if you work with your hands, I know not to break your fingers. I may be rough, but I'm not a savage here, buddy."

"I install flooring - vinyl, laminate, hard wood. You name it, I do it."

"Hands are off limits then, as well as legs. Got it. Let me

see here." Reese kneed the man in the groin, causing him to lean forward onto Reese's shoulder. "Just to restate. If you set the meeting, this all ends, and you get a funny story to tell at bars. You keep up the tough guy act to protect someone who's damaging this country, and you get everything coming to you."

"If physicality won't work, I might know what will," Luke said. He picked up a nearby photo of a young woman smiling next to their host's daughter and held it up. The pair were hugging each other at what looked like a carnival, judging by the Ferris wheel and bright lights in the background. "This woman is beautiful." He flipped the photo around. "Oh, would you looky here? There's an address and phone number right here for her. How convenient. You must have been sweet on her to write this down. It looks like a first date if I were to guess. Who is this? Your ex-wife, a grown-up daughter, or a photo of mother dearest when she was young? We may have to pay her a visit after you. See, we're equal opportunity and equal rights enthusiasts here."

"Wait," the man instantly said. "I'll tell you - just don't mess with my family. If Morgan's as bad as you say, I have no loyalty to that shitbag. Even if he's not, I don't care. Just don't hurt my girls, please."

"You will set us up a meeting then?" Luke placed the picture down on the table he got it from.

"I'll do it."

"Release him, buddy," Luke said.

Reese unhanded him and backed up a few steps. "At least you still have some sense in you. No point in harboring a fugitive that's helping our wartime enemy."

"When do you want the meeting?" he asked. "I can't make guarantees, but they always ask."

"This evening. The hour doesn't matter," Luke said.

"What am I looking to buy?"

"You don't talk about that crap on the phone." Reese rolled his eyes. "Is he that lax in his security that he'd talk business over the phone?"

"We talk in code. We may sound daft or outright suspicious, but nobody has cracked the code for what means what."

"That you know of anyway," Luke said. "Pick whatever you normally buy."

"Got it. I'm going to reach into my robe's pocket now. Is that alright? It's where's my phone is."

"Never mind," Reese said. He stepped forward and reached into the visible pocket of the robe's exterior and pulled out a cell phone. He handed it to their victim. "There. Now we were never here, and you don't want to know what I'll do if you tip him off. Your world turns to shit."

"Prison time springs to mind. That's aiding and abetting right there." Luke cleared his throat. "Hard time, if I recall. Was it fifteen to thirty years?"

"It's life," Reese said. "The government doesn't take kindly to saboteurs. So, no pressure or anything. It's just a normal appointment scheduling. Be smart about this," he said.

"Just please be quiet. I've never recruited anyone to be a client. I need to remember the line for that."

"I am guessing you and Mr. Morgan share an interest in bad spy movies," Luke said. "Whatever, so long as you get it done. Just be calm."

Reese watched him dial the phone. He lowered his voice to a mere whisper. "Be smart," he mouthed.

"Hello. Yes, I need to pay you a visit soon. I have a couple of guys who could use your expertise. That's right. They need hammers. They saw mine and had to have their own.

Yeah, they're on the up and up." Sweat trickled down the side of his face as he gave them a sidelong glance. "I'd bet my reputation on it."

"Hammer?" Luke mouthed the word, asking Reese.

Reese did his best impression of a spaghetti western movie scene of a gun fanning his imaginary six shooter. "You pull the hammer back, is my guess."

Luke snapped his finger with a look of realization.

"Yeah, they won't care how used it is. Alright, tonight it is. They'll be there. Have a nice day, sir." He hung up and looked at his two home invaders. "Are we done here? I did what you asked."

"Where are we meeting them?" Luke asked.

"The guy does business nearby. He doesn't do the deals there. You got a pen and paper? I'll give the place where the deals go through, and you'll receive your merchandise."

"You just worry about yourself," Reese said.

Luke grabbed a nearby notepad on a cabinet along with a pen and scribbled down the address he received. He ripped off the page and folded it up before stuffing it into his pocket. "Enjoy the new chair. Never give this person your money again, and you can consider this entire business over. We may or may not be back with more questions."

"I'd recommend you not," their host said. "My wife is at work right now, and my daughter is at school. If you come back when they're here, I'll have to defend them."

"Look at the tough man," Reese said. "You got the firepower to defend them. That much is clear. But why would a good red-blooded American threaten those trying to preserve its majesty? That is, unless he harbors sympathies with its enemies? You know I served overseas on the Korean peninsula when this all kicked off. Do you know what that means?"

"No."

"It means I love my country. I'm not your enemy, dude. You've done a service to this country you'll never get credit for, but you have proof of." He pointed toward the packaged chair nearby and backed off to stand beside Luke. "Be proud, be smart, and be quiet. That's all we ask - and to answer any more questions we might have."

"Get out please," he said. "I need to get ready before anyone comes home today. If you'd be so kind." He lifted an arm, pointing toward the front door where they'd entered a short while earlier. "I don't believe a word of this country patriotism rambling. As far as I'm concerned, you're two psychos. You get me?"

"Perfectly," Luke said. "I don't blame you, for what it's worth. We just had to throw our weight around to make sure we got results. I think we've overstayed our welcome. Let us make haste and get out of our partner's affairs. You are our partner now, you're aware. I wouldn't run to Mr. Morgan and tell him all this. You'd be an accessory then. You really don't want that."

"They send you to GITMO for that, you know. Water-boarding, torture, sensory deprivation, solo confinement, and everything is legal there," Reese said as the pair backed up toward the door. "Keep your hands in front of you. We're leaving." His hands hovered above his side. "Don't think I'm not ready to blow you away if you get sneaky though."

"Enough." Luke opened the door and stepped through. "Let's report back on what we found and leave the man alone. He's done his part."

"Whatever you say. Just remember our advice. Cut off all ties with Mr. Morgan." Reese stepped out of the house onto the porch and slammed the door shut. "Can you believe that asshole?" he asked Luke as the two of them turned and walked back to the truck they brought there.

"We may have gone a bit too hard on that guy." Luke climbed back into the truck and donned his seat belt before turning on the engine and pulling out into traffic.

Reese glanced over at Luke with a look of disbelief. "Seriously? The guy got a free chair, a funny story, and got off without serious injury. That's a win as far as he's concerned. He felt a little disrespected? So what? Suck it up."

"I see why you're not a therapist," Luke said, a shade of humor in his voice. "Take one of those phones from the bag in the back and call the number on this." He took one hand off the wheel and reached into a different pocket than before, placing the paper up on the dashboard.

Reese took it, reached into the backseat, and pulled out a phone. "Give me a second. I'll report our success to your spy babe girlfriend. That's a messy ass relationship, or soon will be, if you want my opinion."

"I notice nobody asked for that observation," Luke said.

Reese faked a laugh. "Hardy har har," he said. He dialed the number and waited. "We got the meeting set up. We're on our way back."

"Good work. I came up with a few ideas while you two were working. You'll like them." The line cut off with that declaration. Reese tossed it above the glove compartment and leaned back in his chair. "She has a plan."

"You say that like it's a bad thing."

"Is your big toe smaller than the one next to it?"

"What in the ever loving fuck are you talking about?" Luke asked. "What does my foot have to do with anything?"

"It's an old wives' tale where I grew up. If your big toe is bigger, you have the pants in the relationship. If your second toe is, your wife will be the man figure of the house. So how about it?"

"Fuck you."

"Small big toe it is then," Reese said. "Look, my point is you need to stay informed here. You being a yes man and doing everything she says - that's not going to last too long, if you want my opinion. You need to be on equal footing. That's one of the foundations of me and Angela's relationship. That, and we don't keep secrets. Which is another relationship killer that spy girlfriends are probably guilty of. Do I need to go on?"

"You'd rather I press and pry for every little detail that I don't have security clearance for? Look, she's been my best friend for years. We both have our little secrets. It just so happens that hers are necessary for her career. That's all."

"Whatever you say, man. Just keep my advice in mind. A little truth and up-front honesty goes a long way for relationships."

"I'm just going to keep driving and get us back. I'm tired of your playing relationship therapist."

4

"The meeting is set." Vickie had papers sprawled out in front of her on the motel bed. She was looking down, never taking her gaze off them. "We know where it is. We go there, and we get intel on where Ai Xiao is. There are some new gadgets that we can use to help with this outing. Mr. Hilton, you volunteered to be the one to go, didn't you?"

"Don't call me Mr. Hilton," Reese said. "It makes me feel old."

"Alright then, Skippy. You wanted to go, right?"

"I know weapon lingo better than your boyfriend here. It'd make more sense that I'd be the one to show up. You two can be nearby in case anything goes wrong. The guy's going to want to make money. I'll be fine."

"Or he's suspicious," Luke said. "I would be if I got a phone call from one of my regulars who has never recruited a new face, wanting to set up a meeting for someone new. For all we know, you could be heading into a trap."

"It's a risk we'll have to take," Reese said. "Right, boss? We didn't come all the way out here to eat pizza in a hotel."

"He's right," Vickie said. "We'll be close by, but I want you armed."

"I always am," Reese said. "Now what do you want me to do, assuming this all goes smoothly?"

"Your objective is to gain any and all intel on Ai Xiao. I doubt he'll be so forthcoming about another client, especially toward a new client; so we may have to get creative and force him to come along with us, if you get my drift."

"You're talking about kidnapping, like we did to that poor French Foreign Legion guy a while back?" Luke asked. "This guy is going to have guards posted up in there. That's a lofty ass goal."

"I never said this was going to be easy, but he is our only lead on Xiao right now. I will not let her slip through my fingers. We have a location already stocked and ready should we get Mr. Morgan outside of wherever you're meeting him."

"Odds are this guy will have guards," Reese said. "Which is assuming we even get the big man. My money's on Dutch to just send some low-ranking dealer to meet with us to offload whatever your customer ordered for us. I'm hoping we have a Plan B here."

"While you two were questioning our asset, I was doing just that. I called the local department and asked local law enforcement for help with this. I deemed it a necessary risk, even with the possibility of leaks. We're throwing everything at the wall here and seeing what sticks."

"Local PD isn't going to know shit," Reese said. He paced in front of the lone bed in the room. "How does that help us? You think they just know every Chinese girl in the town?"

"It's a source of dozens of eyes and ears," Luke said. "It's our best bet on physically finding Ai Xiao. I assume they'll call you if they find anything?"

"They'd better. I talked to a few young men who seemed like they were chomping at the bit to become more than some country cop. They'll want to make a good impression. We got some good men to help us find her. Either good or ambitious - either works so long as they find her. It's the best option I had while you two were busy. The local sheriff may be a regular horse's ass, but they'll work with us."

"Horse's ass, you say," Reese said. "I don't blame them. You get called up one day and are told to do what we tell you, otherwise you're in some shit."

"Says the man who joined the armed forces," Luke said. "I find that funny."

"Focus!" Vickie stopped the ensuing dialogue with the one word. "Now Reese will go to the meeting spot you two received. You'll see who shows up. If it's Morgan, we'll grab him and take him offsite to be questioned."

"By out-muscling multiple people with guns who don't want to be taken in?" Reese asked. "How exactly are we to enact this wondrous plan in the real world? He'll have at least six or seven men there. Even with all of us, that's not good odds for getting a target out alive. You'd have to have some kind of sci-fi gadget shit to make that work."

"Who do you think we are?" Vickie asked with a devilish grin. "We have just that, but let's not plan too far ahead." She took a nearby page that showed a top-down view of a part of the nearby town. She used her finger to point to various parts of it as she spoke. "First, we focus on the meeting in an hour or two. Luke and I will be nearby, but not in the car. I'll be on a nearby rooftop. I looked up that address and came up with a battle plan. The meeting spot is in a back lot of an abandoned store. I'll set up a position across the street looking down on it."

"Where do you want me?" Luke leaned over, trying to get a good look at the map. His shoulder brushed against Vickie's. He looked up at her. "I'd probably be better close, but I don't want to give myself away."

"You'll be here," Vickie said. She pointed to a nearby alley. "You only move here after they arrive and I confirm who's there. Before that, you'll be in the building below me."

"Speaking of which, how are you going to get up there? That looks like a store there."

"There's a ladder on the side of the building. It gives the perfect cover for you too. You'll be shopping, getting a milkshake - who cares? They won't think twice even if they do see you. You're just shopping. You're our ace in the hole here. Reese is the one I'm not too happy with. You're in the lion's den, but you did volunteer. If you want, I'll take your place."

"I said I'd do it, so I'm going to." Reese stopped with a stomp of his foot. "I may not be a professional liar and actor, but I know weapons and buying them on the black market. With Luke here, they'd know we made them. With you, they'd be suspicious. I assume we're going to have some communications going on?"

"We have the latest technology, as a matter of fact. You see people going around with those little buds in their ear? This is a step above even that. You put something similar in your ear, but it's smaller. Its signal is untraceable to modern civilian tech, and it's louder in your ear. We can adjust the volume before we go, so we don't blow out your eardrums. Unless they check your ear, they won't know you're broadcasting - even if they wave a wand over you."

"It's a gun deal," Reese said. "You're expected to be packing. If you're not, you're an idiot sucker waiting to get taken advantage of. The worst I'll deal with is some suspicions and foul language. I'm not looking to get shot antagonizing the bastards."

"After the deal goes through, we'll follow them. We'll see where they park and adjust accordingly. Luke, if they park away from the meeting, I'll need you to plant this in or on their car." She dragged the nearby box closer to the pair on the bed and reached inside. She pulled out a small square device. Its only visible source of being a technological device was the constant blue light blinking. "This will show us where they are. Now when you want to place it down, you peel off this." She tapped a thin plastic looking sheen attached to the side of it. "Then you just push it down hard for five seconds and it's as good as nailed to it. Just place it on the bottom of the car. It's easy." She placed the first device down and pulled out a different one. This one was a circle of pure white plastic, or what looked like it. "In case you need to get into the car, you use this. This will unlock the doors if it comes to it. It shouldn't, but it's something to keep in mind for the future. Remember now. White unlocks car doors. Black is the one you hide on or in the car.

"I got it," Luke said, taking the devices in his hands. "I won't let you down."

"I know you won't. You're one of the big reasons I got this job, big boy. I trained you myself, after all."

"Enough of that crap," Reese said, turning away from the couple sitting on the bed. Waves of sunlight came in from the nearby window, illuminating a veritable cloud of dust in front of him. He waved his hand, trying to get rid of the aerosolized dirt. "Let's get this place scoped out. I want us to know every inch of the place an hour before they get there."

"Agreed," Vickie said. "Let's head out."

At the deal site a few hours later...

"See anything?" Reese asked. He leaned against the car he drove in. He lifted a foot and rested the bottom of his foot against the tire. "I can't see anything from this vantage point besides this dump of a lot."

"While you're having fun, Luke is occupying himself I see," Vickie said. She had a pair of binoculars and was looking through them. She saw Luke in a nearby building. "Get into position. They should be here within the next fifteen minutes, and I won't have you out of position because you were bored."

"I got it," Luke said over the call.

She saw him leave out of the glass double doors before walking toward her. He looked back and forth before crossing the road. She lowered the lenses and watched him cross the road and enter the store below her. "Good," she said to herself. "Everything's going according to plan. Now, how is fate going to stuff a wrench into these plans? That's the first thing they teach you. Murphy's law isn't just for the memes."

"I don't like this locale," Reese said. "It's too damned stereotypical."

"We cannot argue with the intel that you yourself collected now," she said. "We're committed. Let's make this as safe as we can and push through. Now be quiet - I see a car heading toward you. It's either our boys, or it's someone getting some late-night shopping done.

"I hope it's them," Reese could be heard saying. "I'm tired of sitting here rehearsing my fucking lines. I feel more like an actor than a damned soldier."

"Be quiet," Vickie said. "We don't want them to think

they're selling a gun to a crazy man who talks to himself. That'll spook them, and we cannot afford that."

"Yes, ma'am."

"They're slowing down. Look alive everybody," she said. She looked down at the nondescript car as it approached. It pulled down a nearby alley and stopped on the other side from Reese. "I think this is our cue. Luke, hold your position. When I tell you to, head out of the store, then go down the alley to your right and do your thing. Understood?"

"On your cue," Luke said.

"Wish me luck," Reese said. When he heard the car doors slam shut, he kicked off the car and cleared his throat. He patted his sidearm unconsciously. He heard multiple footsteps approach. Many men appeared around the corner. All of them had a pistol in their hands as they entered the parking lot.

"What's this all about?" Reese asked.

"Do not draw your weapon," Vickie said. "Luke, you're up. Head to the eastern alley beside the court and get it done. Reese, buy us some time," she said. She looked over at the rifle laying on the roof beside her and back to the scene unfolding before her as the group of men approached Reese in the lot.

"I don't know how you all do deals around here, but this is a little odd, boys." Reese gave a nervous laugh and put his hands out at his side. "Take it easy. We're just here for a deal, right?"

"You're coming with us," the man in the middle said. "Follow us, and we'll get you your merchandise. We just like to scope out new clients is all."

"Forgive me for asking, but how damn stupid do you think I am?" Reese asked. "Nobody does this. I'm just here for a piece. I'm not looking for trouble out here. Just a little something to help me defend my family is all I'm here for."

"Is that why you pressed one of our clients to set up this meeting?" The man talking took a step forward, breaking the neat straight line the men formed, and came to within a few feet of Reese. "That guy is an old friend of mine you know."

Reese didn't verbally answer. He took stock of the men in front of him, noting the firearm in each of their hands. He saw their fingers wrapped around the trigger already. *That's poor trigger discipline there,* Reese thought. "Hey now, I don't know what you're talking about here, buddy."

"The thing's planted," Luke's voice said. "Moving back before they get wise."

Vickie saw Luke get out of the alley and turn the corner. He stayed out of sight of the men and pressed his back against the thin wall between the alley and parking lot.

"You want me to help here?" Luke asked.

"Negative," Vickie said. "You'd get him killed. We'd have to take down four before one shoots him. Besides, we could use this."

Christ, listen to her, Reese thought. "I don't guess I have a choice in this matter?" he asked with a nervous laugh.

"Sure, you got a choice," the ringleader of the group said. He raised the pistol in his hand to point at Reese's skull.

Reese noticed he wasn't looking down the barrel of just one gun but four. "I get it. Don't shoot." He raised his hands above his head.

"Put your damned hands down, you fool." He stepped forward and used the handle of his gun to slam into Reese's head. "Move, now! You're going for a ride to meet with the boss man you so desperately wanted."

Vickie could only look on as they led Reese out of the vacant lot and out of her sight line toward where Luke came from.

"God damn it," Luke said, his voice hushed. "What do we do now?"

"Get back to the car. Now!" Vickie said. She started picking everything up around her. "We're following him. This is our ticket to finding Morgan. We need to get him out of there. God knows what they'll do to him. Just know, Reese, we're coming for you. Don't give them any more reasons to kill you than they already have, alright? Buy for time as best you can without pissing them off."

The sound of an engine roared to life as she saw Luke sprinting across the empty street. She packed the nearby rifle into the case before she got on the ladder attached to the building and climbed down. She hopped off to ground level as Luke approached. "Let's follow him. We can't leave him out there on his own. He's not trained for this."

"I'll drive," Luke said. Without further words, he was already at the car and entered...

5

————

Reese had been blindfolded in the car earlier. He forgot how much time had passed by this point, but he was sure it couldn't have been longer than an hour or two. The air smelled of mildew. "This is how Mr. Morgan treats his want-to-be customers? It's a wonder he has any business at all."

"Shut the hell up if you know what's good for you," a male voice said.

Another altogether familiar voice spoke up after a nearby door opened. "That's one of them," he said. "There was another one with him too. He wasn't there?"

An authoritative voice answered him. "No, I'm sorry, Mr. Harrison. My men only found this one at the site you gave them. Do not worry," he said. "I'll show him as much consideration as he showed when they threatened your family. You go on home and tend to the wife and child. Make sure you tell Sharon to prepare a double helping. I love her deviled eggs."

"I will do, sir," Harrison said. "I'm happy to help."

Reese wasn't sure, but he could have sworn he heard a payoff. "You getting your thirty pieces of silver over there?"

"Ignore him," the unfamiliar voice said. "Some men do not know when to be quiet. Not like you. Now leave us, please. I have business to attend to with your home invader."

"Good luck," Mr. Harrison's voice said before the sound of a door closing left the room in relative silence.

Reese could hear nearby breathing and footsteps growing closer. He guessed he was in a basement, unfinished judging by the feeling under his bare feet.

"Do you have any idea the level of shit you're in?" the male voice asked.

"I'm tied up in a basement with a local crime lord. I get the picture," Reese said.

"You're either brave, stupid, or have a death wish," the male voice laughed. The sound of a stool scraping nearby caused Reese's head to turn. "Why did you want to find me so badly? Are you FBI or something? I sure hope not, but you're done if you are. Your corpse will be taking a nice vacation in the bottom of a nearby chemical vat and dissolving before the night is done."

"How lovely," Reese said. "No, I'm not law enforcement. You wouldn't believe me if I told you, though. I guarantee that."

"Is this the part where I ask who and what you are? I think it is."

"Why are you working with a Chinese spy that's sabotaging our country?" Reese asked.

The voice paused, taken aback. "You are not a run-of-the-mill idiot from this town. That much is clear. None of my men know who you are, which means you're from out of town. You know things you shouldn't, and you have the balls to harm one of my friends in an effort to find me?"

"Did he tell you about the chair?"

"What fucking chair?"

"We gave the dude a free chair. That shit was expensive too. He should be grateful, not doing this. I just wanted a nice chat like we're having is all. I didn't do any permanent damage, and I was careful to protect his hands and feet for his job."

"Is that right?"

Reese's vision returned to him as the blindfold was ripped away from his face. He saw Dutch Morgan standing right in front of him with three men nearby. He had a large bushy mustache and thinning graying hair perched atop his head. His men kept a close watch on every movement Reese made. His hands were tied behind him around the chair. He struggled against the bonds as his eyes looked all over, gathering every detail he could.

"Pay attention to me, you little pissant." Dutch grabbed Reese's face in his hand and forced him to look at him. "I'm what passes for power in this yokel-ass town. A man does not get to go after those close to me, regardless of the circumstances. I look out for my own."

"Where is she? Where's the Chinese girl?" Reese asked. "Surely you wouldn't mind telling a soon to be dead man? What's the harm in that?"

Dutch looked over his shoulder at the young men. "You took any devices off of him, yes?"

"We ran the wand over him three times, boss," the leader of the group said. "He didn't have anything on him that could transmit a signal. We were double sure, just like you taught us."

"Then I suppose it won't hurt, seeing as your body will

be dissolving in a vat of chemicals soon enough. Before we get to that, you're going to tell us all about your little friend you were with earlier today. If you do that, maybe we'll give you a quick death."

Reese locked eyes with the larger, older man. The cane he held in his left hand shook under the strain as he placed his weight on it. His observation was cut short by said cane coming up and slamming into the side of Reese's face.

"You answer me, boy," Morgan said. "Where's your friend? Surely he's not worth all of this?"

"Of course you'd think that." Reese spat down at the concrete floor, staining a small patch red with the blood mixing into his saliva from the blow. "Loyalty is a foreign concept in this line of work, from what I hear. You pay these men enough, and you think they're in your pocket for all time."

Dutch looked over his shoulder at his men. "The man knows how to piss me off, that's for sure."

This comment elicited some muffled laughs. Dutch broke into laughter with them before clamming up suddenly. "Who the hell are you? Why are you here?"

"You want the truth?" Reese asked. "I'm a soldier in the United States Army on a job that's way out of my expertise. You're in the way of that."

"I love the stories people come up with." Dutch shook his head with a smile. "You see the content of a man's character when he starts making up stories to try to scare you or awe you. It's also quite pathetic. Let me guess, this partner of yours was really your lover? The TV says you don't have to be in the closet anymore, my friend."

"No need to hide it," one of the men in the background said before the group joined in laughter again.

Good. Reese thought. *Keeping them laughing is better than pissing them off. Eventually, Luke and Vickie will get me out of here.* "I'm not telling you where he is, because I have the feeling you'll meet him soon enough."

"I'll give you one thing, army boy." Dutch leaned in closer to Reese. "You sure can bluff with a stone cold look on you. I respect the courage needed to look death in the face and not blink." He leaned back and spoke in a more conversational tone. "There is just one problem." He reached into his dress coat's pocket and retrieved a cigarette pack. He took one out. Without words or waiting, one of the men in the back dug out a lighter and rushed over to light it for him. "There we are," he said, puffing out a cloud of smoke. He coughed a little before continuing. "I am not here to debate philosophy with some dipshit who fucked with me and mine. Unless you talk, the rest of your very short life will be unpleasant. You can bet on that."

"It would not be in your best interest to play gangster extraordinaire this time around," Reese said. "Even an army boy has connections."

"You're going to get the boys to come ride to your rescue." Dutch pointed at the brick walls surrounding them. "I don't think they know you're here, grunt. You're on your damned own here, surrounded and disabled. That threat doesn't scare me."

"This all goes back to the loyalty argument from before. You sit here in your fancy suit, with your goons behind you all with guns, and you feel like a big man. You're real tough, but I wonder if it's the same when push comes to shove?"

"I'm getting bored with this. You either tell me where your friend is, or I let my boys get to work on you."

"I see you've not met my wife, or you'd know just how stubborn I am. You can have him work on me all night, and I ain't giving you shit."

"So be it." Dutch hefted himself off the stool and stood up. "I have business to attend to - actual business, not questioning dead men. Why did I allow myself to get caught up in this foolishness? You," he pointed toward one of the men, "you're to extract any information out of solider-boy over here. I'll be back in two hours. If he hasn't talked by then, we'll dispose of him. We have more important things to worry about than some piss ant interloper."

"You got it, boss."

"Good," Dutch said. He rolled his neck from side to side, causing a cracking sound. "Now I'm off. Have fun, boys." Dutch walked over to the stairwell and climbed before exiting and closing the door behind him.

Reese turned back to the men who were now stepping forward toward him. "You all have no idea the shit that will rain down on your organization if you do this."

"He's scared now," one said, circling around Reese's back and stopping behind his chair. He placed his hands on Reese's shoulders. "Listen to him whimper and whine."

"We ain't going to kill you quite yet," the one in front of him said. "We need to have our fun first…"

Outside just earlier…

"How are we getting in there?" Luke asked.

"I'm working on it," Vickie said. "That building only has a few entrances. It used to be an old bar. It's since closed, but it appears Mr. Morgan has repurposed it for where he takes his prisoners. My bet is Reese is in the basement, getting grilled as we speak."

"Or they're waiting on the big boss man," Luke said. He pointed out the windshield toward a nearby car arriving. "Check it out."

Vickie used the binoculars to look at the men exiting the now parked car. She recognized the one who got out of the back door. "Dutch Morgan, there you are," she said. "He wants to see what Reese has to say. That means the security for this is through the roof with him in there."

"We can't just sit out here and wait for Reese to die," Luke said. "There has to be something we can do."

"There is, sweetness, but we must pick our moment. If we rush, we get ourselves killed, and that's not going to get your partner back. Now, do you still have that device that unlocks cars?"

"Of course I do," Luke said, reaching into his pocket and pulling it out. "Why? You want me to open that car's doors too?"

"Not right now," she said, looking through the lenses of the binocular. "They have guards watching the car." She reached one open hand out toward Luke. "Give it here. I have an idea for later."

Luke plopped the device in his girlfriend's outstretched hand. "Care to share?" he asked.

"I'm going to modify it so it can undo electronic locks. If we're going in there, there's a distinct chance they have one on the door leading to Reese.

"What if it's an analogue lock?"

"They're even easier to bypass," Vickie said. "They teach us how to lock pick doors in our training," she said. "We're heading in there as soon as Morgan leaves. The security will loosen then."

"How you want to do it?" Luke asked. "Should we go in together?"

"Did you ever wonder why I have that box in the back?" Vickie turned to him with a devious smile.

Luke looked into the back seat toward the box of gadgets

and back to Vickie. "I can't say I did. I was more concerned with Reese being surrounded by arms dealers and their thugs."

"Aren't you just a big old softie for a guy who stabbed you not too long ago?"

"Male bonding is a hell of a thing that science still has not quite figured out yet, despite their best efforts. Look, I'm not leaving the guy in there. He saved my ass many times."

"As you did his and are about to do again. Focus on the here and now, not your past. I need you on your game, since we're doing this as a duo without backup."

"Can't you just call the police and have them deal with this?"

"It could alert Ai," Vickie said. "That's a Hail Mary play if there ever was one. If she's halfway decent as a spy, she'll want a mole in there. Going in alone is risky, but we don't have much choice. I could call the police, but then Ai would no doubt know that we're after her. We cannot have that. She'll be ten times harder to catch if she's alerted."

"You're the boss." Luke raised a hand to his mouth and bit off a piece of his fingernail before spitting it out.

"Don't do that. That's not attractive," Vickie said. "Now, I have been listening to Reese's device for a while. They're not hitting him yet. You don't have to chew your hand to death quite yet."

"You can do that? Can Reese hear us?"

"Not with the way I've configured it. It sounds like Mr. Morgan is having some fun right now playing Mr. Big. You should hear this. The guy is loving being the big man. It doesn't sound like they're going to hurt him while Morgan's there. They're going to wait until after. That means we have to hurry after he leaves. We're going to go in there together."

"I doubt they'll let us have him without any fuss," Luke said. "What if they want to use their shiny guns on us?"

"Then we use ours on them first. We're not just leaving him in there to fend for himself tied to a chair, or whatever they've got him tied to." Vickie pointed at the side of the building down the street. "See that alley on the side of the building? We'll head down there and head in the side. We'll go in quiet and surprise them."

"Any other wonder gadgets in that box that could make this easier?"

"You have the vest on, right?" Vickie asked.

"You know I do," Luke said. "You were the one who tied the back for me."

"You'll grab your shotgun and head in first. That thing's lethal in short range. That's assuming they even want to die for Reese, which I doubt. If you see them reaching for their weapons, then end them. Otherwise, follow my lead."

"I won't let anything happen to you. Don't worry," Luke said.

"I'll get any doors open once we're inside and watch our back. From what I can tell from the signal, they have him in the basement; so look for any doors on the ground floor. Don't move too far from me either."

"Babe," Luke looked over and rested a hand on her shoulder, "I'm not saying relax, given the situation, but focus. We're going to be fine. I'll make sure of it."

"You will, huh?" she asked. "You'd better."

"When are we heading inside?" Luke asked. "Oh, hey look," he nodded toward the bar. "There's the dude from earlier we questioned. He wanted to see his handiwork personally."

"As soon as Mr. Morgan leaves."

"What about his car? We could use that to gain access to

wherever he operates. It wouldn't take much for me to go out there, gather the tracking device from the one car, and move it to the one they came in."

"It'd be too much exposure."

"We can't lose time and not seize the opportunity. Either I do it now, or I go in while you follow them. You'd be the better candidate for that, Miss Spy," he said. "I can get Reese out. We can't let Ai Xiao blow anything else up. Any delays could be disastrous."

"We don't know how many are in there," Vickie said. "I gathered there must be at least three or four." She audibly groaned. "Fuck it," she said. "You stay here and watch a professional."

"What?"

Vickie didn't explain further, instead climbing out of the car and slamming the door shut.

"What the hell?" Luke got out and stood by the car, watching her run off toward the building in the distance. "What's her plan? She said there were guys there." He threw the door closed and chased after her...

6

"You weren't supposed to follow me you know," Vickie said. The pair drew closer to the building their friend was being held in. A large sport utility vehicle sat in the nearby parking lot with one man standing beside it and another sitting on the front of it. "Why'd you follow me?"

"You said there were guys," Luke said. "What was your plan?"

"It's changed now that you're here. They've seen us now," Vickie said. She reached over and grabbed his hand as they walked side by side. Water droplets fell from the sky as the overcast clouds above thundered. "Now play along, sweetie pie, or this will all get ugly far sooner than I wanted."

"Whatever you say." Luke put on a fake smile as best he could and walked hand in hand toward the run-down building. Its windows had boards covering where glass should be.

"You didn't bring the shotgun I see."

"Yeah, people normally walk down streets hand in hand with a shotgun, right?" Luke sarcastically asked. "This is why you tell people things and not just walk off in the middle of a conversation."

"You have your pistol?"

"I always do," he said.

"Good. Keep it handy."

"I do not like the sound of that," he said.

"Be quiet, we're getting closer." Her voice grew louder. "I thought this was it," she said. "It's been a few years since we were here. I could have sworn it was one of the best around. Oh." She pretended to see the two men for the first time. "Hello there." She waved toward them.

The men looked over, surprise written all over their faces.

"Yoo-hoo," she said. "Can I ask you a question?"

"Honey, I'm not sure we need to bother these men," Luke said.

"Oh, hush you," Vickie said. She used her open hand to lightly slap Luke's forearm with a chuckle before looking back at the men. "He's just shy is all."

The man sitting on the car hood hopped off and came to stand by his coworker. "What's this about now?" he asked.

"She wanted to ask something or other," the other of Morgan's men said.

"Yes. Didn't this building used to be a bar?" Vickie motioned toward the nearby building they were outside of. "I just know it. See, we carved our name into the wall in there when my love asked me to marry him when we were younger, and we wanted to see it again. We couldn't remember exactly where it was, but Neil's bar used to be here, yes?"

"I believe so, ma'am, but this is no longer a bar," the taller said with a shake of his head. "This property was bought by Mr. Morgan as of a few years ago."

"Oh no," Vickie said. "Can't we just go inside and see it

one more time? Just one more time? Please? It'd mean the world to us if we could see our marking of love."

"You're such a romantic." Luke wrapped his arms around her, causing her to moan and turn to face him.

"Don't you start." She moved forward and their lips met in a wet smooch. She pulled away to see both men looking away, apparently embarrassed by their little display of public affection. "We're just asking for a minute or two," she said. "Just so we can take a picture and show our kids one day, you know? Please do it for the sake of love? Surely one of you two knows how that feels?"

"Maybe we should just let them inside for a minute or two," the shorter one said. "What harm could they do? They're just a couple, cringy as they may be."

"Are you insane?" the other asked. "The boss would kill us."

"We won't tell anyone, sir," Luke said. "No one has to know we were in there," he said.

A nearby door opened to reveal Dutch approaching the group, along with a couple of guards at his sides. "Oh now," he said, "who is this?"

"Just a couple we were redirecting away from here, sir," the taller said.

"Please, sir," Vickie said. "We just want to see our memento of love and take a picture of it," Vickie said. "See, my honey bun proposed to me in that building back when it used to be a bar years ago." She snuggled into Luke's side. "We just want a photo of it, and then we'll be on our way. Please? Are you these men's boss? We don't mean to be a bother, but we simply must have a photo of it."

"I keep telling you, baby," Luke said. "We shouldn't bother folks for your photo album. Look at this gentleman. We're holding him up."

"Nonsense," Dutch said. "A photo immortalizing young love is a fine thing. I am indeed their boss, ma'am. Now, Hector, don't be heartless," Dutch said, a cocky smile on his face. "I want you," he grabbed the tall guard's shoulder and gripped hard, "to accompany them. Who are we to step in the way of true love? Just don't let them anywhere else. You understand me? I'll be waiting on you, and then we're on our way. Are we clear?"

"It's crystal clear, sir," he said.

"Good. You two can head inside. Just don't touch anything, and stay with Hector here, won't you?"

"Oh, thank you, kind sir," Vickie said. "These men were saying how kind Mr. Morgan was and they were right. We owe you."

"Keep your thanks, ma'am. You get a nice photo and commemorate your engagement. Now, if you'll excuse me, I have somewhere to be. Hector, you go in first and make sure it's ready for our temporary guests, will you? We can't have the boys making too much noise. That'd be rude."

"Of course, sir," Hector said, nodding.

"Then excuse me." Dutch moved past the group, opened the back of the car, and climbed inside.

Hector scratched the back of his head. "I'll be right back. Don't go anywhere, and we'll get you your photo as the boss says." He turned and headed for the doors his boss came out of and disappeared within.

The pair held each other in their embrace. Vickie laid her head on Luke's chest and looked up at him while wrapping her arms around him. "He's such a nice man, isn't he?"

"He sure is," Luke said. "There aren't many who'd go along with your selfish request, love."

"I'm just a romantic is all." Vickie got up on her tiptoes and delivered a feather-light kiss to Luke's cheek. "Never underestimate the power of love. Almost everyone who's not a miserable sad sack will help with it if they can."

"Sometimes you're a bit scary with your calculating," Luke said. He turned when he heard the door open to see Hector waving them over.

"Let's go get our picture, handsome." Vickie left his embrace and grabbed his hand, leading him toward the run-down building. She led him up the stairs and past Hector into the dim interior.

The bar was to their side, old and abandoned. The bottles had visible cobwebs covering them, along with a landline and cash register long forgotten.

"Now, where was it again?" Vickie led Luke around. "I think it was by the basement door. You remember? We'd both had a few drinks, and you escorted me to the bathroom before we left to walk home?"

"The bathroom is over this way then, if that helps," Hector said, extending his arm in the direction and guiding them over. He led them down a small hallway leading out of the main barroom into a small, narrow hallway.

"You're Mr. Morgan's bodyguard then?" Luke asked as they headed over. He slipped his hands inside his jacket's pockets; a slight jingling could be heard.

"Something like that," he said. "Why?"

"I was just wondering is all," Luke said.

"Hector Harris, I presume?" Vickie stopped with the men as they reached the basement.

"I don't remember telling you my name," Hector said.

"Are you sure?" Vickie asked, raising a finger to her lips. "I'm pretty sure you did. You introduced yourself just earlier." She looked up at Luke. "I'm not imagining that, am I?"

"She's right, you did," Luke said, looking Hector in the

eyes. "To be fair, her memory's scary. I'm with you there," he said.

"Look, just take your damned picture, alright? The boss may be accommodating and all to lovebirds, but that doesn't mean I have to be. It should be here somewhere, right?" He looked at the wall near the door. "I don't see it anywhere," he said.

"I don't suspect you will," Vickie tapped Luke's arm and nodded at him.

Luke broke away from Vickie. His hands flew out of his pockets, brass knuckles already on. His right fist slammed into Hector's stomach, causing him to vomit on the spot. Luke barely avoided getting spattered with the filth, stepping to the side. He straightened Hector out and pressed his forearm into his throat, pinning Hector to the wall.

Vickie leaned down and reached into Hector's belt line before removing a knife and pistol. "I don't think you need these anymore," she said to the gasping man. She tossed the weapons over her shoulder to the floor and reached one more time into Hector's pockets, this time receiving a phone. "Here we are," she said.

"You're dead," Hector could barely manage to get out with Luke's arm choking him.

Luke used his free hand to batter Hector's side with the brass knuckles. "I don't like that kind of talk, Hector old buddy," he said.

"You're going to stay here while your boss leaves to do whatever he wanted," Vickie said. "You know," she said, "you really should have a password on your phone. Who knows what creeps may get a hold of it?"

"He'll never leave without me," Hector said.

"We will see about that," Vickie said. "I can be very persuasive," she said. "All I need is a little prop to make this work." She reached down to her belt line and unsheathed the knife. She moved up beside the two men and jammed the steel into the wooden wall. She carved an L on one side and a V on the other with a heart between them. She sliced through, linking everything with a line. "You are going to smile on my command."

"You're dumber than he looks if you think so."

"Fine, we don't need you to be a part if you want to be a problem," Vickie turned to stand side by side with Hector. She used her other hand to make sure Hector's arms didn't go anywhere. "Look this way, honey," Vickie said. She stood beside her makeshift carving and, by all accounts, looked like she was simply taking an everyday selfie so far as the camera could see. Luke turned to look at the camera, keeping the man held down. Both smiled, the engraving between them fit perfectly. Hector was nowhere in the shot. "Now we'll send this to Mr. Morgan, along with a personalized message. You made some good friends tonight."

"He won't believe that." Hector coughed and wheezed.

"He said it reminded him of that picture you showed him of you and your wife. See, the thing with being personable and liked by your boss is he won't be able to tell the difference in a situation like this. He's already on his way to his next meeting. What was that, by the way?" she asked. "I'm curious."

"Fuck you."

"You know it wouldn't be too much effort to find if you have any family. Right, Mr. Harris?" Vickie asked, her voice sweet and alluring. "I would just hate to involve any of them in this, but you're being mighty unhelpful right now. The good solider act is so easy to take advantage of. All you have to do," her voice changed, now serious, "is figure out what they value most. Do you care to play the good soldier to Mr. Morgan, or do you care about you and yours?"

"You'd better kill me now," he said. "Go ahead. I don't give a fuck about my family. They abandoned me to my fate, so I say good riddance."

"I did not expect that answer," Luke said.

"Why must you gangsters always be so difficult?" she asked with a roll of her eyes. "Fine then. If we must be uncouth, then I can do that too with the best of them." She held the blade to Hector's thigh. "Feel that? It's right next to your femoral artery."

"Do it." Hector gasped for breath between sentences. "Dutch would kill me if I told you a damned thing anyway." He barely managed to take another raspy inhale. "Somebody's dying in here, and I don't fancy your odds, considering any noise will bring more men up here."

"He'd scream if I wasn't choking his dumb ass," Luke said. "You got some fight in you," he said. "Now there's nothing that can change your mind?"

Hector answered by thrusting his head forward, connecting with Luke's.

Luke kept his grip but grunted and gave a little ground.

A click to the side halted the escape attempt as Vickie readied a handgun she had tucked away. "Now don't go thinking you're smart or slick. I'll put a bullet in your head, and we'll take our chances with the men downstairs. In fact, I want you to call out to them right now."

"Why? So you can slaughter them?"

"I'm getting tired of this idiot. Can I just knock his ass out?" Luke asked.

"Go ahead. We're not getting anywhere with him anyway."

"Sorry if this kills you, but we can't waste any more time

with you." Luke delivered a punch to the side of Hector's head, rendering his body limp before falling to the ground below.

They moved his body to the side of the door. "It must be a big basement for them not to be up here already," Luke said. He pulled out the handgun at his side, making sure the safety was not on, and looked at Vickie. "We're just heading down there and hoping for the best?"

"Not quite. Let's get them up here where we have the advantage," she said. "Open the door and call for them to get up here, on behalf of Mr. Morgan's orders."

"If you think they'll believe me, sure."

"Worst case is they come up here where we have the drop on them. Don't worry too much. They're chilling down there and talking, or they'd be up here already. Just keep your piece handy and prepare to end them. It's them or Reese."

"Here goes nothing," Luke said. He gripped the door handle with his left hand and pulled it open. "Hey, they're gone. Come up here a minute. We've got a situation."

"What the fuck?" a male voice said from below.

Luke backed off and stood side by side with Vickie. They both raised the business end of their weapons toward the now opened door. Rushing footsteps approached before one man after another funneled through the door. The lead man immediately noticed the nearby unconscious Hector and saw the pair. He froze in place while the other two were distracted. "Who the hell are you?"

"That's not what's important," Vickie said. "What is important is how many people are going to walk out of this building alive. Know that if we see anyone reaching for anything, we're firing. Put your hands up above your head."

None of the three men followed the command.

"Alright then. If that's how we're playing this, fine." Vickie adjusted her aim left and squeezed the trigger, enveloping the room in a momentary flash of light before her target fell to the floor. "I'm tired of this horse shit. If you all want to die for an arms dealer, then so be it. Now put your hands up, or so help me God, you're all dead tonight."

"Let's not have any more dead bodies, eh, fellas?" Luke asked. "Now put those hands up nice and high above your head."

"Go ahead," Vickie said. "I got them."

Luke holstered his pistol and pulled out a few zip ties he had stashed away since they left the motel. "You're first, big man." He grabbed the nearest man's right arm and yanked it behind him before ensnaring him. He followed suit with the other and tied his arms behind him. "See? Wasn't this easier?" He stepped over the still alive bleeding man nearby and tied up the other.

"You know you're dead after this, right?" one of the uninjured men asked. "Hector, and for that matter Mr. Morgan, is going to rain down hell on you two idiots."

"They can try." Vickie lowered the gun as Luke tied up the last man and pushed him to the side. "I'd like to see how that goes for him once he figures out who we are. My bet is he'll run scared shitless when he realizes."

"I know I would," Luke said. "Now, is there anyone else down there besides your guest?"

Both men remained quiet with their backs to the wall.

"Sit down," Vickie said, raising the business end of her weapon toward them.

They did, however, follow the commands this go around.

"Now you are going to be good boys and stay right there. Feel free to run out into the street if you really want. All it'd do is embarrass your boss though." She looked at Luke. "After you, baby."

Luke peeked around the corner of the open doorway to see a concrete floor below with a muffled male voice emanating out from below. "I don't see anyone else," he said. "Cover me." He led the pair down the stairs, keeping his head on a swivel. He saw Reese tied to a chair in the middle of the room. The only other fixture in the room was an old toolbox sitting on a table nearby and a large locker on the other side of the room. "You get him free," he said, hopping down to the floor. "I'll go check mystery locker number one to be safe."

Vickie did as Luke said and undid the bindings around Reese's hands.

He reached up and ripped off the tape covering his mouth. A lone click nearby beat any sound that he was about to utter.

"Shit," Luke said. He heard the sound from in front of him.

The locker door opened. A man emerged from within, aiming his weapon at Luke. The only thing Luke's eyes fixated on was the black void of a gun barrel pointed at his head.

"Move one muscle, and you're dead." He approached Luke and made sure he was on the other side from Vickie and Reese, who was now out of his chair. He pushed Luke to turn around. He wrapped an arm around Luke's neck and held him close, using him as a human shield. "Now, what do we have here? Is this your buddy the boss was asking about?"

Reese stood side by side with Vickie. "If you both had listened, I was trying to warn you about precisely this," he said.

"You be quiet," the gangster said. "Now you two are going to leave, and maybe your friend here gets to walk away."

"Maybe?" Vickie asked. "That's not good enough. See, I'm figuring that you're just going to kill him if we leave."

Vickie aimed at the man's head. "You shoot him, I shoot you. It's as simple at that. If you want to live, you'll get the same treatment as the boys still alive upstairs. This is not a negotiation."

"You got balls," the gangster said. "Shame it's going to kill your partner here."

A shot rang out, and a body hit the ground.

Luke had his eyes closed and opened them as his assailant hit the floor behind him. He turned around and back to Vickie. "Jesus Christ," he said. He reached up to his right ear, where he felt the wind from the bullet. He noticed his hand felt wet. He looked at it and it was covered in blood from his previous captor.

Reese walked over to Luke. "Next time, don't let your guard down."

"Boys, be quiet," Vickie said. Her gun was nowhere to be found, but she had a phone out. "I have to clean this mess up."

"What does that mean?" Luke asked Reese.

Reese shook his head and watched as Vickie called someone. "Hell if I know. She's your spook girlfriend. You tell me."

"Yeah, we need a cleanup at my location. Local law is to be considered compromised. That's right." She hung up and shoved the device in her pants pocket before coming over and hugging Luke without warning. "Are you alright?" She placed a hand on the side of Luke's face and looked up at him. "He didn't hurt you, did he?"

"I think I'm fine. I hear ringing in my ears, but that's normal," Luke said, returning the embrace. "What do we do now? Morgan's going to hear about this soon enough, and he'll go underground."

"That's simple," Vickie said. "We'll get one of the boys from upstairs and have him take us to his boss."

"They're not going to do anything we say," Reese said.

"Maybe not at first, but we have our ways. We even have an offsite place to do it at if they're so inclined. After they see how far we're willing to go, I'm betting they're going to be mighty eager to cooperate."

"Is that what that gunshot earlier was for?" Reese asked. "It scared the shit out of me. I thought maybe one of you was the victim."

"Now let's go pick out our tour guide before backup arrives. I don't want to be here when they arrive for multiple reasons." The group made their way up the stairs and into the bar's main room again. They looked at the two men still sitting nearby.

"Which one of you wants to be helpful?" Luke asked. Neither of the two men made any indication they wanted to volunteer. "Don't everybody volunteer at once now," he said.

"I got this," Reese said. "One of you is coming with us untouched. The other is getting the same treatment as that dumb bastard." He turned and gestured toward the now dead body lying in a pool of blood under it. "Who's it going to be?" He cracked his knuckles and stared down at the two men.

"Seems the cat has their tongue," Luke said. "I know how to fix this." He got down and pulled one of them to his feet and shoved him over to Reese. "What about you? You got more loyalty than sense?"

Instead of the groveling they expected, the man instead laughed.

Reese instinctively reached for the knife on his hip, but found it missing from where they'd disarmed him earlier. He wrapped both his hands around the thug's throat. "What's so funny?"

He didn't get an answer.

"He's waiting for reinforcements," Vickie said. She was at the bar while the boys tried to get information out of the gangster. She reached down below the bar and pulled up a small device with a wire attached. "Take him and get him to the car, now. We're going to have company soon. I'll warn the cavalry, and they'll deal with them."

The two men each gripped an arm and manhandled him. They moved him toward the front door.

Vickie looked back at the lone, quiet henchman. "Guess it's your lucky day. Tell David hello for me. You'll know him when you meet him."

"Fuck you, bitch."

"Alright then," she said. She slammed the door shut behind the party.

"Who is this cavalry you called in anyway?" Luke asked.

"I can't answer that with our guest here. Suffice it to say they're not someone you want to fuck around with."

"You expect me to believe any of this horseshit?" the gangster asked. "You can't just kidnap me and take me away."

"Clearly, reality begs to differ," Luke said. "Besides, who's going to call the police? The populace you boys no doubt put on notice?"

"Fuck this noise." The man stomped on Luke's foot and reared his head back, knocking Luke's head back. He took off in a run down the street away from the group and started yelling nonsensically at the top of his lungs. Lights in the nearby buildings flipped on at the ruckus.

"Forget him. We don't need him. We can't afford to get caught up in this shit right now. The police are on their way. Let's get back to the motel, and I'll detail my Plan B for just this occasion."

"At least one of your plans went right," Reese said, watching their would-be prisoner turn a corner out of sight.

Luke looked over at Reese. "Glad you're out of that mess."

"Me too."

7

"Look what I found." Vickie snapped her fingers. "I found our ticket to finding Ai Xiao."

"Lay it on me," Luke said.

"Dutch Morgan is opening a recreational center for youth tomorrow."

"That jackass?" Reese asked. "There's no way he'd pay for something for the betterment of others."

"He would when it buys him good PR," Vickie said. "He gets to play at being Robin Hood and acting like an upstanding citizen, while undermining the very society he claims to better, at the same time making a boatload of cash. It's genius if it wasn't so glaringly obvious."

"Civilians won't know his actual business," Luke said. "They think he's some philanthropist that runs his own business - at least from what I gathered trying to look him up while Vickie was in the shower."

"It's a perfect opportunity to grab him and make him talk."

"That's hoping he knows where she is," Reese said. "What if he doesn't?"

"Then we're shit out of luck," Vickie said. "Do you have any ideas, or do you just want to shoot all of mine down? The way I figure it, he's our best lead on finding her, unless we plan to go door to door."

"Easy, superspy." Reese raised his hands up. "We're all frustrated. You need to be composed to lead."

"I'm plenty composed," she said, crossing her arms and pouting.

Luke was behind her and took the opportunity to reach his hands up to massage her shoulders. "I know, honey. Thank you for saving my life today. It was a rookie mistake I made in that cellar."

She reached up and placed a hand over one of his. "Don't ever do that to me again. I nearly had a heart attack. I just had to put him down. He was about to execute you."

"Speaking of which," Reese looked away, "thanks for getting me out. I'll make sure I pull my weight from here on out."

"Let's not be too pleased with ourselves," Vickie said. "We need a plan to grab Dutch tomorrow. Any ideas? There will probably be a large crowd at the opening, making it a dicey place to grab him if he has bodyguards - which he will, since his bodyguard will have woken up and told his boss what happened."

"What about your clean up dude?" Luke asked. "What was the name you said? David, was it?"

"He sent me an email just now. He said the two dead bodies were there, along with one dude still tied up. No mention of Hector. We have to assume he got out of there before David got there. So, Morgan's aware of us, but has no idea who we are or what we want. It means he'll be extra cautious. I don't want innocents harmed here. Give me some ideas."

"The obvious idea is to follow him to a less populated locale where there won't be kids," Luke said. "Do we have anything that could help with that?"

"I have just the thing, but it wouldn't help with the body-guards." Vickie leaned back into Luke's chest. She reached up and grabbed his hands, moving them to her waist and leaning back into him.

"For that, we have two options," Reese said, trying to ignore the pair on the bed. He sat down in the chair next to the motel room window. "Either we kill them during our kidnapping attempt or incapacitate them."

"If we can get to his car during the speech he's giving, we can make this work," Vickie said.

"They've all seen our faces," Reese said. "If he has any guards by his car, it won't work."

"I bet they won't leave a man with the car," Luke said. "These aren't superspies we're dealing with. It's a local arms dealer who's high on his own success and thinking he's bigger than he is. He's going to be worried about his own ass in a public space like that. My bet is it'll be easy pickings. What was your plan if we can get to the car?"

"There is a reason some of my colleagues call me gadget," Vickie said. She cut Luke off before the jab she knew was inevitably coming. "Also no, it's not because of that woodland animal cartoon from our childhood. Some of the other agents focus more on trying to be super spies from movies; whereas I try to do things a little smarter than trying to use guns every chance I get. I took the maximum allotted tools I was allowed. You never know when any one of them will come in handy after all."

"Out with it then, spymaster gadget," Reese said with a snicker.

"As you two may have heard, there've been people who

claim their car drove off the road and into a tree. Some of those people are just lying to evade being held culpable; but the truth is, some of them were telling the truth. It's no mystery that computers are being put in our cars, basic as some of them may be. This allows remote control. Depending on the manufacturer, this can include steering wheel function, the gas, the brakes, the radio, or even the windshield wipers, if you feel sassy."

"Yawn," Reese said. "That's been a thing for a decade or more, to my knowledge. Don't act like it's some new thing."

"It's not common knowledge," Luke said.

"For you maybe."

"Okay, Mr. Informed," Luke said.

"As I was saying," Vickie said, "we'd need to install this, and, unfortunately, I'm the only one who knows how to. It's a bit more delicate than the tracker from before, so I'd need you two to run interference, just in case."

"If I'm there, I guarantee they'll be looking at me." Reese kicked his feet up on the nearby windowsill and leaned back. The chair under him tilted back and balanced precariously as he spoke. "They'll have three dedicated guards to be near me and keep watch. Anything else will be on you, man."

"Then after they leave, we follow them and what? Have a shootout?" Luke asked. "We all know they're not coming in easy. We'll be lucky if Morgan isn't full of holes from stray bullets."

"Close, but not quite," Vickie said. "We'll stop their car. Inevitably one or two of them will get out and try to fix it. That's where Reese here comes in. He'll take them out in an ambush, and then we rush in to grab him."

"If he's armed?" Luke asked. "He's not going to go in quietly."

"Not that guy," Reese said. "He talks big, but you never know the real value of a man until you see him in a life or death situation. He could pull out a gun and start blasting, or he could panic and shut down. We have no way of knowing, so best we prepare for the worst now."

"If he wants to be difficult, then we'll do it the hard way with these." Vickie reached into the nearby box and pulled out an orb. "This releases a gas that will put anyone to sleep."

"Then why not use that before we shoot anybody?"

"Because the bodyguards will obviously not be cool with us tossing this in. We're going to have to get close enough. That'll be hard enough with one gun, never mind with three," she said.

"Can you plant them and set them off remotely?" Reese asked. "If so, you could set them while you're installing your little car controller device."

"Come to think of it, I think I can," Vickie said. "All I'd have to do is reconfigure the triggering setting and set it to manual. That's not too difficult, so long as I have tools." She scooted away from Luke and got off the bed to go digging around in her luggage. "Give me a minute and some quiet, and this will be done inside of ten minutes." She pulled out a box and moved over to the small table beside the bed. She got to work, ignoring the other two.

"I guess that settles that then," Reese said. "Why do you think the guy picked a recreational center anyway? Why not a business he could launder money through?"

"Public good will is priceless," Luke said. "Think about it," he said. "If he opens a business, the local people who gossip might put it together and talk. If he makes a place for the supposed betterment of the community, it's hard to twist that into something negative. It keeps the heat off and lessens the likelihood you'll get some vigilante nut job coming after you."

"Shit. Sounds like a waste of money to me." Reese blew a hair out from his face. "It's got to cost over a few million dollars."

"He makes that with every shipment I'd imagine," Vickie said. She was focusing intently on her delicate work, twisting the tool with an almost imperceptible clicking sound. "Especially if he's selling explosives that can level a damned building. That's pricey stuff. This is a drop in the bucket for someone with his money."

"So he wants people to like him, while he sells illegal weapons to foreign agents? What a piece of shit."

"I doubt he knows what she's up to, for what it's worth," Luke said.

"You don't think when a Chinese national came by and wanted explosives he didn't put it together?"

"They've met once and only once, according to our intelligence," Vickie said. "I doubt they went through with a big sale at the first meeting. I'm betting there's a second scheduled, but that's conjecture. My point is, he knows she's up to something nasty, but he'll accept her cash as sure as water is wet."

"He can act as prim and proper as he likes," Reese said. His chair fell forward with a thump, and he stood up. "I know the type of guy he is from how he acted and how his men treated him. He's nothing but a criminal scumbag that's trying to play the nice guy to assuage his conscience. He was happy to intimidate me and act the tough guy. He's a gangster through and through."

"Then we won't feel bad when he gets what's coming to him..."

8

A large crowd of adults with their children at their sides stood in front of an elevated platform. An enormous banner hung across the front of it that read 'Grand opening of The Morgan Recreational Center'. A group of men stood on top of it while the crowd murmured to each other. A lot of the mothers and fathers had a hold on their child's hand as they were desperately trying to rush past the stage and into the playground beyond.

"Just like I said," Reese said. "The boys up there are watching me above all." He looked up at Dutch and the small group of men at his side. The bodyguards were eyeing him up and down. One even left the group to climb down the stairs and approach closer to him. "I got one headed over."

"Just stay quiet," Vickie's voice said into his ear. "It looks like they didn't leave anyone at their car. Luke, keep a lookout while I do my work here. Reese, you let me know if any of his men head over in this direction."

"We meet again," Reese said to the approaching man. He was near the outside of the crowd, so it was easy to see him approaching. "You're conscious this time, though. You know, you're quite funny looking when you're out."

"You've got a lot of guts to be here." Hector stopped a few feet away. His voice was terse, conflicting with the excited atmosphere of the nearby kids. "You think we don't know who those two were yesterday? I swear to God, if people weren't here, I'd..." He paused and looked over to see a nearby child and her mother looking at him. The child had a look of wonder while the mother was frowning and shaking her head at him.

"You were saying?" Reese asked. "I'm just here to enjoy the opening of the new rec center. It's so nice that our community's kids have somewhere they can go without fear." He looked back at the woman. "Don't you think so, ma'am?"

"If you ask me, it's all a waste of money, but it is the first playground our little town will have since the primary school tore theirs down last year to rebuild. My Tiffany here can't wait." She looked down at where the girl was to find her cowering behind her leg on the other side of Hector and Reese.

"You scared the poor girl," Reese said, looking at Hector. "What was your name again?"

"It's Hector," he said through gritted teeth. "Your little friends yesterday caused quite a lot of trouble for us you know."

"I wouldn't know," Reese said with a smirk. "I was a little tied up dealing with some idiots who thought they were more important than they are."

"You little..." Hector's comment was cut off as a burst of static played through the speakers on either side of the stage.

"Sorry about that, folks," an older gentleman said into

the microphone. "Sorry for the delay, kids. Today we're here to celebrate a kind act of generosity from one of our own, Mr. Dutch Morgan."

The crowd erupted in applause, even the kids, except for Reese.

The older man looked over the crowd. "Mr. Morgan has very kindly had this recreational center built so our children have somewhere safe to go after school to find entertainment away from potential drugs, crime, or other some such debauchery. It's my honor to introduce the philanthropist himself - Mr. Dutch Morgan, everybody!" He extended an arm to his side and stepped away from the microphone as Dutch replaced where he had been.

Dutch readjusted the microphone and cleared his throat while the applause was still happening. Once it died down, he spoke up. "Greetings, everyone," he said. He was visibly nervous, shifting his weight as he spoke and looking left and right, never lingering his gaze on one spot for very long. "I appreciate you all showing up for the opening. For anyone curious, we will have volunteer workers here, so every child will be supervised."

Another round of applause sounded off.

"I've almost got the controller set and installed. How much longer do I have?" Vickie asked over the call she, Reese, and Luke shared.

"Depends how long his speech is," Luke said.

"He's nervous," Reese said, noticing the visible beads of sweat trickling down Dutch's face. "I'd bet not long."

"Talking to yourself, are we?" Hector scowled. He was facing his boss and standing side by side with Reese a few feet away. "I knew you were crazy or stupid."

"Keep talking. See how this all plays out, why don't you?"

"Boys, please," the woman beside them said. "Behave yourselves. Your mothers would be ashamed," she said.

"Sorry, ma'am," Hector said.

"Wuss," Reese verbally sniped at Hector.

"We cannot have children running around unsupervised after school," Dutch said. "Many parents have to work one or sometimes two jobs to make ends meet. Many do not want their kids home alone," he said. "Who can blame them? Kids can get up to the wildest things left to their own devices."

Many parents in the crowd laughed at the statement and nodded their heads.

"Parents deserve the peace of mind that their children are safe while they're at work, and that's what we're offering here - a place for your kids to be safe while you're out of the house. There's nothing more important than the safety of our children. Am I right?"

A raucous eruption of applause and indistinct agreements came from the men and women.

"You're darned right," Dutch said. "Our children are our future. Now keep in mind, there are no charges to have your child come and attend. We do not favor only the rich or middle class. Any and all children are welcome here."

"How altruistic," Reese said, sarcasm dripping off his voice.

"Don't be jealous." Hector took a step away from Reese. "I'll rejoin you later. Do be good, sir."

Reese watched Hector walk off and move around the crowd. "Hector is heading right for you two. It looks like he's going to their car. Be ready over there."

By Dutch's car...

"Everything going alright down there?" Luke asked. He was standing a few feet away from the large SUV. He was looking across the chain-link fence at the spectacle unfolding as Dutch spoke.

"I've almost got the controller set and installed. How much longer do you think I have?" she asked.

"Depends how long the speech is," Luke said.

"He's nervous, I'd bet not long," Reese said in their ears.

"This is the part that takes the longest," Vickie said. "Once this is done, it'll only take a couple of minutes to set up the kicker."

"The man knows how to play to a crowd; I'll give him that. He's the most charismatic arms dealer I've ever seen," Luke said.

"You've met two now. That's not saying much." Vickie shimmied out from under the SUV and got to her feet. She dusted herself off and reached into her purse, digging for the other instrument.

"Hector is heading right for you two," Reese said into their ears. "It looks like he's going to their car. Be ready over there."

"I see him," Luke said. "He's right - he is heading this way."

"Distract him then," Vickie said, pulling out the gadget to unlock the car. "I'm unlocking the door to set this up. I can't have him get over here. Cut him off," she said.

Luke pushed open the gate and cut off Hector about twenty feet from the fence. "Hey, buddy, remember me?" he asked. "I'm sure you do. Nobody has that bad of a memory; but then again, I've never been knocked out with a concussion before. Do you remember yesterday at all?"

"You think you're funny I see," Hector stopped a few feet in front of Luke. "We know you're that asshole's partner."

"Gee, did it take you all an entire night to put that one together?"

Hector balled his hands into fists at his sides.

"Oh, I don't think your boss up there wants a scene. You'd better hold your temper in check here, Hector buddy. A few of the parents are looking over this way. Let's not ruin this day for the children, if nothing else. That is what your boss is espousing - why he's doing this after all. We both know that's a crock of shit, though."

"Get out of my way," Hector tried to sidestep Luke, only to find the man matching his movements.

"Are we not friends anymore?" Luke asked, placing a hand on his own chest. "I don't know what I'd ever do if you didn't like me anymore, buddy. I'd be all broken up. You helped me and my missus get our memento. I thought we were pals."

"You keep this up, and I don't give a fuck about the consequences. I'll lay your ass out." Hector's eye twitched.

Luke pulled his hands out of his pockets, showing that his brass knuckles were already donned, while lifting his shirt enough to show the pistol he had on him. "Let's have at it then. I don't think you'll like the results, though. Your boss looks like he's about to wrap it up. Shouldn't you go to him and escort him off the stage? He's getting up there in age. You never know what might happen to him."

"Are you threatening us, you pissant?"

"I'm just stating a fact," Luke said. "What is he now – sixty-four years old?"

"Sixty-three," Hector said. "You are not what you seem. I won't entertain your silly goading. You're up to something. Now let me pass, or I'll shoot you right here, right now, and damn the consequences."

"I'm done and leaving. Get out of there," Vickie said. Her footsteps could be heard amid her statement over the line.

"Fine then." Luke stepped to the side. "Have at it, Ace. Don't cause yourself a stroke. High blood pressure can kill you. You and your boss should relax more." Luke let him pass and watched him stomp back toward the car that Vickie was at before. He turned back and saw Reese walking back to him.

"Sounds like everything went to plan for once," Reese said. "Hector's buddies had their eyes on me the whole time, just like we planned."

The pair turned to look back at the stage as Dutch delivered his final remarks.

"With that, I declare the Dutch Morgan Recreational Center and Playground open to the masses." He accepted the comically oversized scissors from a nearby smiling lady and cut the ceremonial tape to a chorus of cheers and excited yelling from the children.

As soon as the tape was cut, a crowd of children separated from the crowd and made a run for the playground.

"Isn't it heartwarming to see them having so much fun?" Dutch asked into the microphone on the stand. "It does an old man's heart good to see such joy. Have fun, children. You all are always welcome here." He stepped away from the microphone stand. A bodyguard stepped up and whispered in his ear. He nodded, and the group headed toward the stairs leading down onto the grass below.

"We should head back to the car," Reese said, patting Luke's shoulder and leaving.

Luke followed suit. "The real work is only beginning," Luke said.

9

"This is not the way back to that bar," Luke said while driving. "Where are they going?"

"It doesn't matter," Vickie said. "They're heading toward the edge of the town, and that's precisely where we want them. When they get close enough, I'll override their controls and guide them right where we need them, lock them in, and set off the gas. All we need to do is get Morgan out of there and take him to our questioning site. David is waiting for us there."

"Who is this David guy, anyway?" Luke asked. "A coworker or something?"

"I can't reveal too much about the guy," Vickie said. "Think of him as logistics to help us out. He's newish to the agency, like me, but he's eager to please and move up the ranks. He usually gets the shit jobs of cleaning up sites after the incident, but he's already furnished our little place to properly question Mr. Morgan. You'll have anything and everything you can imagine for getting him to talk, dear."

"Speaking of the CIA," Reese said, "who did you say shot that dead guy upstairs in that bar?"

"I did," Vickie said.

"You better pray no one hears about that," Reese said. "You're not even supposed to be operating on domestic soil."

"Tell them I did it," Luke said.

"Guess I was the one who shot the dude in the basement then. Say that I was enraged when I got out of the chair and shot the guy."

"Aren't you two sweet?" Vickie asked.

"Just don't want you getting in trouble," Luke said. "I think they're going to turn up here."

Dutch's vehicle had their turning lights blinking and their red brake lights were lighting up as they approached the intersection ahead.

"Not if I have a say in it," Vickie said with a grin. "To tell the truth, I always wanted to try this thing."

"You've never used this thing?" Reese leaned forward between the driver and passenger seat. "Tell me you're joking. Do you even know how to use this thing?"

"In theory," Vickie said. "I learned how and even used it once in training, but never had to use it in practice. Let them turn here, it's fine," she said. "Let me show you one of the features of this thing." She pressed a few buttons on the remote control in her hands and voices came from the formerly quiet radio in the car.

"Are you sure it was them?" Dutch's voice asked.

"It was clear as day, sir," Hector's voice answered. "He was shit talking and mocking us."

"I want them dead," Dutch's voice said. "Nobody kills my boys and gets away scot-free. Have their family's been taken care of yet?"

"The arrangements are being made."

"Take me to their houses now. They deserve to know how their sons died. Two crazed killers busted into his workplace and ended them after everybody left for the night."

"That's the story he's going with?" Reese asked.

"Nobody kills my men and gets away with it. You all are my family, and I protect my own, son. Now take me to Lee's place directly after this meeting. I owe his daddy an explanation for why his son never came home last night."

"Yes, sir."

"Why did they target us?" Dutch asked. "We never bothered them before. I can't believe I actually believed that bullshit excuse they gave. They seemed so genuine. I just wanted them to be happy and get a nice memory, but I guess I'm a little soft. It's my fault they're dead. If only I hadn't been a fool, they'd still be alive. I'm sorry, boys."

"It's not your fault, boss," Hector said. "They're liars, murderers, and cowards. All three of them are scum of the earth as far as I'm concerned. The woman seemed to be the brains of the three from what I've put together. Her and that wannabe tough guy are an item, I think; or maybe it was all an act."

"I've got the boys looking into them. Before night's end we'll know who they are, where they are, and why they're doing this," Dutch said. "It just makes no sense. We've stayed off the radar from the public. For all they know, I'm just a businessman."

"They're more than they seem," Hector said. "Which is precisely what worries me, sir," he said. "They may be feds."

"Nonsense," Dutch said. "We've left no evidence for them to track us here. My bet's on vigilantes who are just following up based on rumors they've heard. It'd also make sense, considering two of our brothers are dead. Feds don't lie to get in, kill multiple people, and try to sneak off with another. This is either an upcoming young buck in the game, a vigilante, or someone we've fucked over in the past. Do any of you remember them?"

Assorted male voices answered negatively.

"We can use that maybe," Reese said, snapping his fingers. "Think about it. They think we might be arms dealers."

"Invasion of his property to save one of our own does sound like gang behavior," Luke said.

"We're the scariest gang you don't want to mess with," Vickie said. "Be quiet. I want to hear."

"Hunt them all down," Dutch said, fury in his voice. "I want to question them and see just who we're dealing with. Besides," he said, "killing them now would be hasty. Even just one would do. The girl would probably crack first. The other guy looked tough, but who knows until you try? I'll leave the preparation for that to you, Hector. Pick your best and get it done."

"Right away, sir," Hector said.

The low sound of a dial tone filled the now silence from the car's radio.

"He's calling in our hunters," Reese said. "We need to do this before he gives the order, or we'll have more shit on our plate. And we haven't even made headway on Ai Xiao yet."

"I'm taking control of their vehicle now, but let me lock their doors first."

Reese turned to look at the vehicle ahead of them. It veered a little to the left, drawing a honk from an oncoming car that passed by before it got fully back into the proper lane.

"You aren't very good at video games I take it?" Reese asked.

"The worst," Luke said.

"This chatter is not helping my concentration. Shut up," she said.

The car turned onto a nearby road leading out of town. The heads visible through the back window showed the occupants were clearly distressed at the situation. That, and the voices coming through the car's radio again, namely Dutch's.

"Where are you taking us, you simpleton?" Dutch asked. "We're heading back to our warehouse, not out this way, you lout. Turn us around, now."

"I'm trying, sir," a panicked young man's voice said. "The steering wheel is locked in place and so is the gas. I don't understand what's happening. There's nothing underneath any of the pedals - I've looked. It makes no sense."

"Then pull the parking brake, you imbecile!" Dutch's angry voice yelled.

"You can try if you like," Vickie's voice was one of a predator toying with its prey. "I don't think it'll move either. You're at my mercy now, boys."

Reese turned away from Vickie and whispered to Luke in the driver's seat. "Has she always been like this?"

"When she first gets a power, she'll abuse the fuck out of it; but she's relatively harmless, I assure you."

"I do not," Vickie said. "This is a perfectly justified time to use this."

"Not to be happy at fucking with people's heads this much though," Reese said. He looked out the front window. "Whatever, it looks like it's working."

"Get this vehicle under control right now. We're going to be late, and they are not one to be kept waiting."

"What is this now?" Luke asked. "It sounds like a customer is who they're meeting, or a prospective one anyway. I doubt the big man does sales personally, based on what I've heard from him."

Hector's voice came next. "With all due respect, sir, our men have the first half of the shipment there. They will make the sale if we're sidetracked because of rampant stupidity, or whatever this is."

"I have a name to uphold, old friend," Dutch said. The sound of what sounded like a slap and a yelp of pain followed. "I didn't get to where I am by being an asshole to every customer and blowing them off. Not when they're paying as much as they are for such a niche product that we've been holding onto for close to five years now. We need the space it's stored in, and you know it. I will not have them canceling the second half because of our rudeness. In her culture, it's disrespectful to be met with lower-level employees."

"I am sorry, sir. I did not know. I simply wanted to assure you."

"Instead of playing therapist, figure out how to stop this car right now. My plans will not be derailed because we didn't take this trash heap to a mechanic sooner. Am I understood? I spent too much time building this business to have it trashed by pissing off a huge buyer that's our way into even more lucrative deals. Figure it out."

"Someone's pissed," Reese said. "It sounds like they're splitting the explosive shipment into two. One's already being sold today, and the other is our best bet to intercept her."

"That just means we're on the right track," Luke said. "He'll know where the meeting is to take place and when." The car was exiting the town now and heading into stretches of open roads, trees, and occasional houses.

"Where are we stopping them? If we do it on the highway, people may see as they drive by."

"I have the perfect place in mind," Vickie said. "There's one of those big welcome to signs. Do you remember the one? It had trees near it and some bushes. We should be away from prying eyes when we open the door and drag him into the trunk. We've got zip ties in the trunk and a gag. We'll be there in a few minutes. Get yourselves ready. Also, remember not to breathe in any of the gas, or we'll have to drag your dumbass out too. That stuff's powerful. I'd know."

"Did you breathe it in during training or something?" Reese asked. "I remember in the army they made us take our mask off and breathe in tear gas, and boy was that something. Everybody, myself included, had liquid snot running out of our noses, our eyes were watering, and everything burned once we took that mask off."

"Delightful," Vickie said, clearly not happy. "I see that the CIA took something from the army. They wanted us to know just how powerful the sedative we were using was and feel the aftereffects, so we wouldn't use it willie-nilly on people."

"We are still going in the opposite direction, you fools," Dutch's voice interrupted them. "Must I do everything? Get out of the way." Shuffling and grunts filled the audio space. "Son of a bitch," he said. "It really is stuck."

"You see how much he trusts his subordinates," Reese said.

"Don't worry, fellas," Vickie said. "You'll stop and get some beauty sleep soon enough. It sounds like they could use it with such high blood pressure. We're coming up on the sign. Both of you get ready. Park us behind the sign with the trunk hidden if you would. Reese, help him, since it'll be covered in brush, and he'll need another set of eyes."

"I'm on it," Reese said. "Aren't you glad I'm your wing-man? Can you imagine what would happen if I wasn't? We'd have to fix a ding on a company car. The horror!"

"Wise ass," Vickie said. "Alright, initiating the turn. Prepare for some yelling from the stooges up there."

The brake lights on the car ahead lit up as they approached the welcome sign.

"We're slowing down," Dutch said.

"Good work, boss," another male voice said. "I knew you could do it."

"Shut up, you kiss ass. I didn't do anything," Dutch said.

The car turned off the highway and onto the grass before disappearing through a thick bush behind the sign, out of sight.

"Now it's my turn." Luke got off the main highway and slowed down. He did as Vickie instructed.

"Slow it up," Reese was now on his knees looking out the back window as Luke backed the vehicle up out of sight of any passing motorists. "Turn the wheel left a little and keep it steady. We're close. Oh, tell me something. Is this glass reinforced at all?"

"Why?" Vickie asked.

"Because it looks like they're quite angry. I wouldn't be surprised if they try shooting us soon."

"I released the gas already," Vickie said. "They'll be sleeping like babies within the minute. Just get your heads down. The worst they'll manage is breaking some glass."

Gunshots rang out as everyone got their heads down. Sounds of glass shattering met their ears, but it wasn't their windows.

"Wait here," Vickie said. "Even if someone calls in the shots, we'll be gone before they show up. If not, I can talk our way out of it with my credentials."

"You hope," Reese said.

"In my experiences, I doubt they'll believe the CIA story, sweetheart," Luke said. "Do you remember how many desperate men tried that same story when we used to go out collecting for your father?"

"It tends to work better when we have evidence of it. He won't want to go to a black site for the rest of his life. He'll talk if he thinks it'll save his skin. I'll leave the questioning methods to you."

The car came to a stop. The front windshields had brush and lots of branches in front of it. The view out the back window was clearer, showing a darker area covered by the nearby sign and Dutch's car firmly behind cover, away from prying eyes.

"Get to it, boys," Vickie said. "I'll undo the locks when you're in position. Hold your breaths and ignore the eye irritation. So long as you don't get a good breath of it, you're fine. If you feel like a nervous nelly, you can use the gas masks in the trunk."

"You always look out for me, don't you?" Luke opened the driver's door as Reese got out of the back on the same side.

The trunk popped open and revealed two gas masks inside. Each man grabbed one and put it on, making sure to securely fasten it. Reese double checked his gear and walked over to Luke before doing the same.

"What are you doing?" Luke watched as Reese gently tugged on various parts of the mask.

"Just making sure this is put on correctly, for safety's sake. I don't want you passing out when we're lifting the dude and doubling my workload is all."

"Oh, I see."

Reese ceased his motions before leading the pair back to

Dutch's motionless car. He tried to open the front driver's side door, only to find it locked. He raised his hand and pointed to the door with an annoyed expression. He heard a noise, indicating the door had been unlocked before trying again and flinging it open. "Check in the back too. He might have moved back."

Luke threw open the back door and leaned down to look inside. The inside of the cabin was filled with what looked like white smoke. It soon came out and floated up into the air. The blast of gas caused both men's lenses on their mask to fog up.

Reese reached up and wiped the glass over his eyes to try to restore his vision. "Damn things never change. I hate these."

"I can't see shit. Is this normal?" Luke asked. He groped around in the still obscured inner cabin. He gripped what he thought was a shoulder and tugged it toward him. A body fell toward him. "There's Hector," he said.

"He's up here," Reese said. Dutch's head dangled out of the side of the vehicle. His arm was hanging down toward the dirt below. "Help me get him out of here. Someone's going to see all this smoke shit."

Luke moved the few feet and helped Reese hoist him up. Both men had an arm of Dutch's over their shoulder and hauled him the few feet over to the car. They placed him down on the ground, face down. "Hand me the restraints," Luke said, kneeling and pointing at the trunk above.

Reese grabbed the white plastic devices and tossed them to Luke. "Here. Make sure his hands are behind him and get his ankles. The old fart's not flexible enough to get out of that."

Luke got to work. "This brings back memories," he said. "The amount of people that I had to tie up and persuade to pawn their belongings is more than you think. Mind you, I didn't hurt them, just scared them a little unless they tried to hurt me."

"I was a special case then?" Reese helped Luke lift Dutch up again and stuffed him into the trunk.

Luke slammed the trunk shut. "You held me at gunpoint when we first met. I wasn't in a cheerful mood with you."

"I have that effect on people."

Luke got back in the driver's seat and waited for Reese to enter before pulling out, waiting until a break in traffic allowed the ingress back onto the highway.

"He's secured back there," Luke said, leaning his head so he could see the traffic. "How long does that stuff keep them out?"

"Long enough for David's men to get here and take the other reprobates in."

"They're going to prison?" Reese asked.

"Not really," Vickie said. "We're not law enforcement - you know that. We're not even supposed to be operating here, as you love to point out. They'll show up a while after we get there. We'll hold them there until this whole thing is over."

"I don't know." Reese looked back at the white smoke still rising behind the sign. "That stuff is dissipating pretty fast."

"It'll be fine," Vickie said with a dismissive wave of her hand.

Luke managed to perform an illegal turn, crossing two lanes of traffic and heading back into the city limits. "Now guide me to where we're taking our eminence."

10

Dutch was knocked out. His arms were tied behind him, and he had a blindfold over his face. His head was drooping down. His chin almost rested on his chest in the dark room.

Reese tested the restraints for any weakness. He backed off and gave a last look at Dutch before opening the nearby door and exiting. "It's quite a bit of stuff you put in here, David, was it?"

"That's my name, David Heron," a thin man with glasses said. He had a noticeable overbite. "I assume this is all for a good reason? We don't care about arms dealers, Ms. Jones. Now I was told to get this place up to snuff for this questioning. We can listen in here while he's questioned."

"He's leading us to Ai Xiao. He knows where their delivery of the second half of the explosives is and when it will be. You couldn't be bothered to place a camera so we could watch? Talk about being lazy. No wonder Karen bitches at you so often," she said.

"Second half?" David asked. His nasally voice turned

loud. "You're saying that woman has explosives primed and ready?"

"Possibly," Vickie said. "It depends on how old Morgan in there does his explosives deals. I'd assume he'd give her a primer and a trigger in the first shipment. I don't know. This is our only lead. That's why we need the info in a rush. That's why I told you to make sure this place is stocked to the brim. Now my associate here," she reached over and laid a palm on Luke's toned clothed stomach and rested it there, "he'll be the one doing the questioning. Trust me, he's good at what he does. Well, that and getting information, but what can you expect? I trained him."

"So long as he gets us the intel we need to foil any more destruction on U.S. soil, I don't give a brick shithouse door who he is." He turned to Luke. "Are you familiar with how questioning works?"

"Not your CIA method of it, but I've been a debt collector for years. I know how to get answers."

"That works for me then, Mr. Enforcer," David said. "Feel free to use any tool in there or just use plain old mental manipulation. We need dirt on where Ai Xiao is quickly. For all we know, she's setting up the first bomb as we speak. I added something a little out of the ordinary in there in the room's corner if you want to play on his public image. I assume one of you can draw worth a damn. It's a tattoo machine. I tested it, and it works fine."

"You think that'll convince him?" Vickie asked. "Go with your normal routine. He'll break."

"I know how to use one," Reese said. "Some of the boys do tattoos for others using less than legal setups. A real one would work just fine. Just don't ask me to give a good one. I can barely draw worth a damn."

"I assume I have permission to lie?" Luke asked.

"Who do you think we are?" Vickie giggled. "We're CIA. Of course. You can lie all you like if you think it'll help."

"I'm going in with you," Reese said. "I might have an idea that'll help."

"Who are you?" David asked. "Are you the army grunt I heard so much about? The story made its way around the agency that a collector and an army man helped the young Gadget here."

"The man, the myth, the legend," Reese said.

"We'll stay out here," Vickie said. "Unless it looks like you need help, I'd rather gather everything we'll need for our capture."

"That works for me," Luke said. He moved to the door and rested his hand on the handle before turning back to Reese. "Let's get this done." He threw open the door and let Reese close it behind him. "Are you awake yet, lazybones?" Luke wandered over and stopped a few feet in front of the chair. "Hey," he said, slapping Dutch's cheek. "Wake up."

"Huh?" Dutch managed to get out. "Where am I?"

"An undisclosed location," Luke said. "I'm sure that's what you tell your prisoners, isn't it? It's a hole in the ground you're not getting out of until you tell us precisely what we want," he said.

"If I don't?" Dutch asked.

Reese cracked his knuckles. "Then you get to experience what true pain and terror are."

Dutch turned his head, trying to ascertain any information his limited senses could afford him. "We're in a basement. I can tell by the smell," he said. "You two have become quite the pain in my ass. Why not set me loose and let me pay you six figures each?"

"This isn't about money," Luke said.

"It's always about money," Dutch said. "Who are you

with? The mafia, the cartel, or maybe you're with someone else?"

"Someone else fits better," Reese said.

"Are you going to remove the blindfold?" Dutch asked. "I already know who you are. It wasn't that long since you were in this very seat. What was your name again? I apologize. I tend to forget nobodies."

"You're going to tell us where your deal location with Ai Xiao is going to be. We know the first half of the shipment reached her today. Where is the second sale going down?" Luke reached down and grabbed Dutch by the neck. "Make this easy for once."

"I didn't get to where I am by giving up my clientele, you inbred idiot," Dutch spit on the floor in front of Luke's shoes and angled his head up. "You'll not get more than two hundred thousand. Now release me before my boys storm this place like you did with mine."

"You'd better hope they don't," Luke said. He reached into his coat pocket and pulled out his brass knuckles. "Do you hear this?" He shifted the armaments in his hands, causing them to clink. "These are brass knuckles, and I'm going to get some practice I've been missing. Business has been a little slow, and you're going to be my entertainment for the night."

"That would phase me if I hadn't done this very same thing a hundred times before. Just ask your friend, whoever you are. Is this the part where you promise me that I'll take less pain if I talk?"

"The tough guy act is brave, I'll grant you that." Luke swung, connecting with Dutch's stomach. He backed up as Dutch instinctively leaned forward and let loose a downpour of vile vomit onto the floor below, along with a strained noise.

"You're a strong bastard, ain't you?" Dutch asked. "I'm guessing you're the muscle in your little operation? Are you new to the scene in this town? You're trying to make your group famous with this stunt, aren't you?"

"Aren't you full of questions?" Luke asked. He took aim, this time aiming much lower. He put as much force as he could and slammed his fist down onto Dutch's knee from above.

"Not the legs, you simpleton," Dutch said after a cry of pain.

"Next time I'm swinging from the side and aim to put you in physical therapy for a few months."

"I did need some time to relax," Dutch laughed derisively. "Give it all you've got, you ape," he said. "Come on. Hit me as many times as you want. I am not telling you where my deals are."

Luke carried through with his threat and knelt down. He readied a hook and punched Dutch's right knee as hard as he could muster. A loud cracking noise echoed in the concrete room. "You'll get your little vacation. Now listen to me. This is only going to get worse, and I'm not just talking about physical torture."

"You think you can break me mentally, you intellectual midget?" Dutch asked.

"I've got something to loosen your tongue." Reese circled around the seat and removed the blindfold. "Now, which of these would you prefer? You can see the table over there. Pick your poison."

"This place is a dump," Dutch said. He blinked his eyes rapidly, trying to adjust them from the prior darkness. "You must be starting anew with this level of base."

"You don't want to pick?" Reese wandered over to the table. "That's fine," he said. "I don't mind picking. Now you like playing up the silver tongue to the people of this community, so we need something fitting." Reese walked along the table, his hand trailing over various tools and instruments before stopping. "Here we are." He picked up numerous long pieces of wire.

"Going to be hard to talk if you're going to choke me."

"Who said anything about choking you?" Reese asked. "Are you familiar with what happens when you sit on your arm, and you get that numb pins and needles feeling?"

"Oh no," Dutch's voice was laden with sarcasm. "Not the pins and needles. Truly you are a dastardly villain. Keep wasting time. It's in my favor for you to do so."

Reese stopped center in front of Dutch and pulled the wire taut between his hands with a snap. "Are you also familiar with the sensation of blood being deprived so long that it rots?"

"An arm or a leg will shed off ten pounds. My woman's been begging me to lose some weight. Go right ahead," Dutch said.

"I'm not talking your hands," Reese said. "On the bright side, this will act as a tourniquet. I never keep up with medical talk. Are tourniquets in now or out? They keep changing their minds." He shrugged. "Not that it matters. Once the blood flow is cut off for long enough, we'll have to chop it off or risk you dying. We can't have that. You're our guest." He stopped talking and tied each wire around each limb Dutch had and tied them as tight as he could. "In a few minutes they'll go numb," he said, tying off the first on the arm nearest. He tossed a length to Luke. "Inside of an hour, we'll have to amputate."

"You're sick animals," Dutch struggled against his binds.

"Not all of them."

"Think of this as a time limit, Mr. Morgan," Luke said,

securing the first to Dutch's upper right thigh. "It's to help incentivize your speaking. You obviously have no qualms about speaking your mind. We're just helping you make the right decision. Now you're a man who likes to run his little arms emporium yourself, it seems to me. I wonder how hard that'll be with no limbs."

"Gentlemen, let's not be cruel and unusual here. Surely you have some standards like normal human beings."

"So, killing's okay, but amputation is a bridge too far?" Luke asked. "You have a strange sense of scale, old man. Now," he wandered off to the table, leaving Dutch with Reese. "Let's utilize something I bet neither you nor your boys thought of. You strike me as a man who loves people to think well of him."

"Doesn't everyone?" Dutch asked. "Tyrants claim fear is better than respect, but they're fools. Money forms loyalty, not fear. The carrot motivates better than the stick by my summation. You should learn from that."

"I like the stick pretty well, though," Luke said. He picked up a box-looking device with wires coming out of it along with a rotary tattoo gun. "Tell me, Mr. Morgan, do you have any tattoos? Surely a man of your standing in the criminal underground has one or two. You can tell us."

"What is your point?"

"I wonder how the public would like if you got a tattoo on your forehead that said arms dealer. I doubt they'd want to send their kids to your little recreational center for fear of one of your business associates being nearby. You know how middle-aged housewives are. They latch onto any bit of gossip and turn it into a monster. I'd say a tattoo like that would cause some waves."

"You wouldn't," Dutch said. His eyes were wide. He

watched Luke hand over the device to Reese, who put on a pair of latex gloves and turned it on with an electric whir.

"Do you want arms capitalized?" Reese asked. "I would, since that's your profession after all. Which color do you prefer? I'm thinking red on account of all the blood your business has spilled. Maybe I could add some blood teardrops to tie the entire ensemble together? What do you think?"

"That's a nice touch. A limbless man with that tattoo would certainly cause a splash at the next public meeting he attends. He'd be the talk of the town. Maybe they could put a highchair in behind the podium for him so he could reach the microphone."

"You two are inhuman," Dutch said, his voice finally showing the slightest shudder.

"I told you before, Mr. Morgan," Luke said. "You are going to tell us where this deal is, one way or the other. It's up to you how far this goes. If you talk now, none of this happens. You keep stalling though, and you're getting a fresh tattoo as soon as my friend here changes the cartridges to red ink."

"Pardon," Reese said. "It's been a little while since I've held something like this."

"Do you feel that tingling sensation yet?" Luke leaned down and put his hands on his knees, bringing himself down to Dutch's eye level. "The longer you wait, the more unpleasant the feeling of taking those off will be too. Think about that. Well, come to think of it, an hour isn't really all that long, is it?"

"It sure isn't," Reese said.

"To think a man might cut off all his limbs to spite his face. Is that the saying I'm looking for, buddy?" Luke looked behind him at Reese, still fiddling with the device.

"Most people give up the noble act quickly. We'll see if Mr. Morgan here is as true to his boys as he acts like. Tell me," Reese came up beside Luke and looked down at him, "do you think your men are dedicated enough to wipe your ass for you? Do you think they'll feed you? Sure, you might hire a caregiver, but that's a lot of money."

"You all don't have the balls. When this town finds out I've been kidnapped and mutilated by the likes of you, they'll hunt you down."

"I think I should draw a makeshift Chinese flag next to the arms dealer print." Reese reached forward and traced along Dutch's forehead. "I'm thinking Arms here." His finger trailed along above Dutch's right eye and traced over. "Then over here I'll put Dealer. Above it," his finger brushed aside some hair, "I'll put the flag here. We'll, of course, have to shave your head for all this. You look like you can regrow that. We're all about safety first here. We can't have hair irritating the fresh wound."

"If you touch me with that needle, I swear to God above me and my boys will have your head and everyone's you've ever cared about, you little twerp." Dutch bucked against his restraints.

"I think we found ourselves what he cares about," Luke said. "Funny, because the no limbs thing would be much worse for his public figure than a little tattoo. Or was it publicly being outed as supporting a foreign combatant and being culpable for every life she ends? That's the kind of thing that gets men to talk when the FBI rounds them up, and they all start turning on each other."

"His silence indicates he's made his choice," Reese activated the device. A quiet whirring noise filled the cold room. Shuffling, grunting and straining could be heard as Luke moved to the side, allowing Reese full access to their prisoner.

"Have at it," Luke said. "How about it, old man?" Luke asked, looking back at Dutch. "This is the last chance before the world will know who you are and who your allegiances are to."

"Once I start, there is no stopping. This horse's ass here would never let me live it down if I only wrote Arms on your forehead, as hilarious as that would be, come to think of it." He stifled a laugh at the thought of only the one word on Dutch's head. "I may just move the words a little farther apart and place the flag on his cheek here. That's more visible. He could grow his hair out to hide it otherwise."

"Good thinking," Luke said.

Reese leaned in and placed his left latex clad hand on Dutch's head, keeping it from moving. His right hand had the inking implement and brought it closer.

"Alright already!" Dutch said. "Don't touch me with that, and I'll tell you the damned meeting spot. It's not like you'll be able to interrupt it anyway. With me gone, they'll have upgraded security for that meeting. You'll only waste your lives going there anyway."

"Talk about cutting it close." Reese barely managed to back away just before the needle reached Dutch's forehead. "Go get a piece of paper and write down what this shitbag says while I keep an eye on him."

"Sure thing," Luke said. He jogged over to the door and exited.

"I told you the tattoo idea would work." David had a smug look on his face while Vickie's was more one of anger.

"I told you so's are not attractive, David. Keep that in mind for your girlfriend you're trying to woo."

"We need something to write down the location and

time." Luke held out a hand. "Good idea, David. I know she wouldn't ever say it, so I figured someone should."

Vickie slapped Luke on the shoulder hard with a glare while David handed him a notepad and pen. "You're supposed to back me up, you idiot."

"I tell the truth, sweetie," Luke said. "Now if you'll excuse me." He ducked back inside the room and over to the pair. "I see you two are having fun," he said, sidling to a stop a few feet away to the side of Dutch.

Reese tossed the tattoo gun onto the concrete below. "I was hoping to get some practice in. What do you say I just tattoo the back of his hands? He can still wear gloves at least."

"That depends on if Mr. Morgan wants to hold up his word," Luke said. He held the notepad in his left hand and prepared to write. "Where and when is the deal, Mr. Morgan?"

Dutch didn't immediately answer, instead just glaring at the pair of men.

Reese got to a knee and picked up the device before turning it on again. "It seems he's changed his mind. That works well enough for me."

"You keep that thing away from me." Dutch leaned back and away. "Are you familiar with the old, abandoned car factory outside town?"

"You're joking," Reese said. "That's a setup if I've ever heard one."

"We prefer not to sell explosives inside the city limits," Dutch said. "We prefer some privacy, as does our clientele. It's going down tomorrow night at nine pm. It should be outside in the parking lot."

"You know if you're lying we'll be back, and there will be no talking out of that branding, right?" Luke looked up from the notepad and finished writing down the information. "In fact, I wager you'd be shitting far more bricks than you ever did tonight."

"You asked for the location and time, and I gave it to you. We're in a hurry to offload some niche cargo is all, and our newest customer just so happens to want it."

"Ai Xiao you mean," Luke said. He tore off the paper and folded it up before stuffing it into his pants pocket. He reached down and undid the bands restricting Dutch's blood flow to his arms and legs.

"You know her name?" Dutch asked. "How? We've never mentioned her to anyone."

"We have our ways." Luke tapped the side of his head. "Like I said, we're not who you think we are. You really don't want to fuck with us."

"Unless you relish getting thrown into a black site and never getting to experience fresh air and sunlight ever again."

"What?"

"It's not for me to say, old man." Reese turned his back to the prisoner and walked toward the door with Luke. "Have fun there. Thanks for the information."

The two men left the room and closed the door behind them.

"Nice work," Vickie said, "even if you did take this nerd's advice." She jabbed a thumb toward David. "We now know where she'll be, and when she'll be there. We can secure her there."

"That's assuming she shows up," David said. "If she has enough explosives to carry out her plan, and she senses anything's off, she won't show. It'd simply be a matter of moving to another town and finding another arms dealer. Scum like Morgan are a dime a dozen, unfortunately."

"It's the best chance we have," Vickie said. "We'd both better hope that doesn't happen. We're the new kids on the block. Let's prove to management that we can do better than the old guard."

"You're talking office politics?" Luke asked.

"Something like that," David said. "There are operations going on all over the country doing the same thing. The CCP has been diligent in sending their operatives over here under the guise of college students over the past two decades."

"You want to tell them any more confidential information?" Vickie asked. "This is why you're with me and not someone more senior."

"I thought they were agents," David said. "Who are you two, then?"

"I think you call us assets or something," Reese said. "We were roped into this role a while ago, and we're on the encore tour - not by our own volition, mind you, but there was an implied threat."

"No, there wasn't," Vickie said.

Luke and Reese gave her a long, hard glare.

"Okay, maybe there was a tiny, implied threat."

11

——————

The dark room had a lone occupant lying in the only bed. It was a lithe form, tossing and turning. She eventually sat up and scooted over to the edge of the bed. The only illumination in the room was the digital clock on the table beside the bed. A feminine sigh came from her as she looked over at the desk in the corner of the room and got up. She walked over to it and sat down in the computer chair. She looked at the already open window, then read it.

"You have done well thus far, Ai Xiao," it read. "It is a pity your partner was apprehended, but you've done as we've said. Check your phone, and you will see what we agreed upon. Finish the job, or our deal is broken," it said. She read the rest out loud. "I trust you received the funds from our mutual contact and the goods from Mr. Morgan. Make sure to use them in compliance with what we said. Do not delay - that is an order." Shaking her head, she got back up with a squeak of the chair.

She walked over to the night table in the dark room, picked her phone up, and turned it on. She went to the recently received messages and saw a picture of her family.

Her grandfather was smiling, carrying her cousin in his arms as they all smiled at the camera. Her parents were beside them in the shot. The little boy was waving his small hand. A brief text could be seen under the image. "Please come back soon, dear. We miss you," it read. "The government is taking care of us like they promised. Make us proud."

"Why me of all people?" Tossing the phone on the bed beside her, she reached over and groped around in the darkness, reaching for the lamp's control. Finally finding it, she turned it on and looked down at the top and shorts she wore. "I'm too nervous to sleep. A walk would do me just fine and settle my nerves."

She got up, moved to the large dresser adorned with a mirror, and looked at herself. Grabbing a nearby hair tie, she put her long black hair into a ponytail behind her head. She leaned forward and inspected her beautiful face in the mirror, then reached down and grabbed a nearby makeup kit before opening it and applying some. "It never hurts to look good," she said. "That's what the higher-ups told me - keep my head down, look normal, and get the job done. That's all that matters to them."

She placed the kit down and turned to look at the night table in the light. She saw the handgun they'd given her, which she'd barely managed to smuggle in; but they told her a favor was called in. They were correct. No one searched her and thank God for that.

She walked over and picked up the gun and holster, which she put on around her waist, checking to make sure it properly secured the weapon before she left the room and went down the hallway. She walked down some nearby stairs and came to a large open room she'd been using for a living room of sorts.

She looked out the nearby window at the night sky. The road outside was empty, showcasing the lit indoors of the many houses around her. "If they don't keep their promise, I don't know what I'll do. All this for a college degree. Why didn't I listen to my mother?" she asked. She closed the blinds and turned to the television. She grabbed a nearby remote control on the coffee table and switched it on.

The local news came on, lighting up the previously dark screen. "Thank you for tuning in to the eleven o'clock news here on Channel 43. We have breaking updates from the war front," a male news anchor announced. A small square appeared over his shoulder. It showed a bird's eye view of a distant land. Smoke rose from fires lit far below. Cracks could be heard, and the occasional explosion accompanied a large cloud of dirt erupting from the artillery.

"American forces attempted to invade the city of Shenyang earlier today. You see footage here showing the attempt. Officials called the attempt 'necessary to the war effort' when asked about it. Rumors of reaching Beijing by year's end are tenuous at best, if you ask me, since our foes have shown extraordinary resilience in open warfare. Here joining us now is a special guest. Welcome, Mr. Valentine. It's good to have you."

The frame showing the war front disappeared, replaced by a man in a military uniform in what appeared to be a studio. "Hello, Patrick. It's good to be here tonight."

"Mr. Valentine," the news anchor twirled a pen in his right hand as he spoke and occasionally tapped it on the desk, "we've all heard of the grand plan to invade China's capital within the year. I realize you can't speak about everything candidly live on air, but is there anything you'd like to add? Do you believe we'll reach that deadline? This administration seems full of confidence."

She turned off the television. "They're going to get impatient. The Americans are making too much progress," she said. She grabbed a coat from the nearby rack and donned it, putting on the gloves that were in the pockets, and threw open the front door. The crisp, cool night air hit her in the face as she stuffed her hands into her jacket pockets.

They're fools, she thought. *I know they had to have sent a party goon to take that photo. I can't believe they've forced my parents to move into our house. It's probably to make taking these photos easier. Haitao is a saint for putting up with all that,* she thought. *I'd have lost my mind years ago putting up with all of them in those conditions.*

The thought of her boyfriend having to deal with her parents filled her head. Memories flooded in, and she found herself smiling before reality crept back into her fantasies of being home again. She got into her car that was parked in the driveway and backed out onto the road. "I may as well set them now - no point in waiting. The cover of darkness should help."

Memories of the arms deal from earlier that day came to the forefront of her mind. She remembered placing the goods in the trunk of her car. The fools hadn't given her a detonator, but the regime would not accept that as an excuse. She'd been taught how to make such devices just for this type of occasion. "Christ above, I'm sorry," she said.

She sped through the sparse streets, coming closer to the first half of the task she'd been given. The command didn't spare any detail. They knew what they wanted - food production stopped to the advancing American forces. They wouldn't take failure as an option, and she knew it. "I've done a lot of morally gray shit, but bombing," she gripped the steering wheel tight, "that's another level. But what choice do I have?" She bit her bottom lip as she continued driving in the small town.

She exited the city limits relatively quickly. She was familiar with this stretch of road by now, as she'd been doing exactly this for a few nights already. Insomnia and her own conscience had seen to that. She slowed down her car and looked to her right. A small house could be seen at the end of a dirt road. A silo, barn, and a fenced area were all visible. "This is the place," she said. She turned off her car lights, popped the trunk, and shut off the engine.

She removed a portion of the explosives from the trunk and slammed it shut. She placed the bag on the trunk with a purpose before pulling out a mask from her jacket pocket. Putting it on, she gathered her supplies again. She got down low and continued her way toward the rural house.

She replayed the mission briefing in her mind. *Your mission is to destroy the local food processing plant and as many corn silos as possible with the explosives you purchase. Collateral damage is irrelevant. Get it done.*

She could see a light perched above the nearby barn's doors, shining down on the path to the large silo nearby. Choosing to take the path behind the barn, she was able to stay out of the light and circle around. She could see in the country house that someone was still awake and walking around, judging by the lights still on. Occasionally she saw a dark figure pass by the window, and she found herself holding her breath.

She got out of sight behind the barn and took off into a run toward the nearby corn silo. She reached her goal and peeked around the building, making sure nobody had caught wind of her. *Not that I'd know what to do if someone saw or heard me,* she thought. A mental image of her pulling out her pistol and shooting a farmer in suspenders played in her head.

She stopped just shy of the tall structure. Kneeling down, she placed the bag on the ground. She took out a suitable portion and wired it just the way they taught her all those years ago, before she left her country. "Did that wire go here or over on the side?" She hesitated, looking down at her handiwork. The plastic explosives were almost ready to go. There was only one last thing. "Which way did it go again?" She closed her eyes and swallowed. She used a hand to wipe away some sweat.

Her hands shook, and she could feel a panic attack coming soon if she wasn't careful. "It will not explode if you get this part wrong," she said. "Remember what your instructor told you. It'll only fail to detonate. Not that that's much better for me." She suddenly got a mental image of what she had been taught. "There." She connected the detonator to the device and pulled out her phone. "Now for a little proprietary software connection, and you'll be set." She navigated to the newfound app she'd been sent.

A menu came up, prompting her to input the current date and time. She input the information, and then another prompt came up. This time it asked for a desired target time. She put the time she'd been ordered to. "There we are," she said. She grabbed the bag of explosives and leaned forward to inspect that her handiwork was affixed correctly and out of sight, and that the timer was working before getting to her feet and heading off to her next objective with what she had left...

Later that night...

She pulled into the nearby parking lot and parked in

one of the many open spaces. Three cars were already there. She took off the gloves and mask and tossed them in the passenger seat. "God forgive me," she whispered to herself. She looked over at the cars. "That's the pastor's car, but whose are the others?" She got out of the car and paused before shaking her head. "It's not my business," she said, trudging with her head down toward the church's double doors.

She got to the door and barely managed to get out of the way as a panicked looking man busted out of it. "Run, lady. He's got a gun!" The man didn't say anything more. He ran past Ai, quickly got into his car, and left in a hurry.

Ai looked back at the door but was not deterred. She entered the brightly lit interior, shutting the door behind her. She saw no one, only the various paintings and depictions of Jesus Christ hung on the walls. "Hello?" she called out. "Is anyone there?"

She was met with nothing but silence. She looked at the stained depiction of Christ looking up and praying. "Pastor?" She walked between the lines of pews, trying to listen for any signs of others.

As she approached the front, she heard hushed voices. She couldn't make out what they were saying, but the soft thud she heard afterwards spiked her heart rate.

Her hand hovered over her handgun's holster as she inched closer to the room where she thought the noise was coming from until the voice became clearer.

"You be quiet, old man," a young man's muffled voice could be heard. "As soon as this idiot leaves, you're either telling me where it is, or I'll make sure you go see your so-called God a lot sooner than you expected."

She had her ear pressed on the door, but the voice was barely audible. She took her weapon out and made sure the safety wasn't on. She knocked on the door and dashed behind the first row of nearby pews.

Nobody answered the knock for what seemed like forever to her, but eventually the door opened.

The voice was clear as day and sounded angry now. "Get the fuck out of here!" the young man yelled.

She reached into her pocket and tossed the first thing she found, a simple quarter, over toward the other side of the large hall.

"Huh?"

She stood up, weapon aiming in his direction. "Put it down," she said in perfect English. "Do it now, or I fire," she said.

The young man realized what was happening now. He didn't try to raise the gun in his hand toward her, apparently smart enough to know when he was at a disadvantage, or simply not suicidal. "Whoa, easy now, Chun King," he said.

"I'm going to ignore that for your sake," she said, moving around the seating. "You are leaving. Right now!"

"Am I now?" The young man's hair was dyed green. He looked no older than eighteen, if even that. "This has nothing to do with you."

Ai looked through the open door to see the priest laid out on the floor. She could see blood coming from his nose, and he looked roughed up. She glanced back at the young punk. "I will not repeat myself. You have ten seconds, so start moving."

"If you're in here, you don't believe in killing others," he said. He sidestepped, moving closer to the entrance, despite his words. "

"Five seconds left." Her words were cold. "I'd run if I were you."

The young man kept his movement toward the doors,

his pace noticeably quickened with the last threat. "You're lucky my boys aren't here with me, or you'd be dead, bitch," he said.

"Two seconds," she said. She kept the business end of her weapon pointed at him and never blinked.

"I'll get you for this!" He busted down the door with his shoulder and started into a sprint.

She followed after him and stopped in the open doorway. Standing to the side, Ai peeked around the corner. One of the few cars was speeding off, along with the sound of burning rubber. She placed the gun back into her hip holster, shut the front doors, and ran through the church hall and over to the open room she saw before.

Ai rushed over to the man, now trying to get up. "Take it easy," she said. She helped him get to his feet. "You need to get those disinfected."

The priest caught his breath and moved to a nearby chair in the small room. "I'm okay," he said. He looked up. His white beard and hair reminded her of her grandfathers. "You saved me," he said.

"What was that brat doing in here?" She gave him his space and backed off.

"He was trying to take the collection money, I assume. Every once in a while someone tries it - whether it be a down on their luck homeless person, a kid, or whoever. I'd never been here when it happened in person though. Not until tonight. I was just heading into the back to grab a book for one of my congregation before I left for the night. He stayed after services because he was going through a tough time. I almost forgot about it until I went to leave." The priest stood up and led Ai back to the main hall. "Come with me," he said.

"Are you sure you're alright?" Ai asked. She followed the

preacher over to the nearest pew and the pair sat down. "That looks pretty bad," she said. "Shall I escort you to the hospital?"

"This?" the preacher asked. He touched the budding bruise above his eye with a hiss of pain. "This is just a bruise. I think he might have broken my nose." He exhaled a long breath. "I worry about that kid. To be at a point in life to do that, he's hurting deep inside."

"He's lucky to not be bleeding deep inside since he had that gun. Did he point it at you?"

"He did before he bashed me with it." The preacher reached a hand up to the side of his head with a look of anguish. "He got me pretty good."

"It's a miracle I got here when I did," she said.

"God does indeed answer prayers. Tonight has cemented that in my mind."

"That's an odd way of deciphering tonight's events."

"Think about it." He tapped the side of his head. "There I was, staring down the barrel of a young man's gun. I prayed to God almighty to save me, and then you turn up. This is not a coincidence, trust me on that. This was preordained. Now speaking of which," he shifted in his seat, "why are you here, Ms.? I'm sorry. I'm terrible with names, especially after a few fresh knocks to the head."

"Lyn Song," she said. "It's no problem. I'm new to town and won't be staying for long. I wanted to thank you for making me feel welcome these past two Sundays. My parents converted years back and always imparted to me to take part in services."

"They are good parents," he said. "They put you on the track to salvation. I've seen you here the past few weeks. You can call me Filipe or Phil, as the locals here say, if you prefer.

Now why were you here tonight, Ms. Song? You missed services, if that was your intention."

She stared ahead up at the area where the choir sang every Sunday morning and some nights throughout the week. "I'm going through a tough time in my life right now. I guess I wanted to see if I could catch you while you were still here."

"Just in time it seems," he said. "God had a plan when he had you walk in when you did. I'm sure of it."

"Someone sure has a plan," she said. "I guess saying I hate my job undersells it, but I can't say too much. To say my employers are sticklers for confidentiality is an understatement. They're telling me to do things I don't agree with and threatening me if I don't - that I'll lose everything."

"They cannot force you to do anything, Ms. Song. Here in the U.S. we have labor laws."

"I wish it was that easy." She looked down at the floor. "I don't know what to do. My family is depending on me with this job."

"You're sending them money?" he asked. "You're a good daughter."

She didn't answer his question, staying quiet.

"Would you like my advice, Ms. Song?"

"Go ahead."

"Tonight, you should go home and pray about it. Do what you feel is right. I'm not saying abandon them or ignore their wishes, but at the end of the day it's your choice. If you'd be happy doing another job, then explain to your parents. I'm sure they will understand. They only want their daughter to be happy and secure. Every parent wants that for their child."

"Maybe you're right," she said. "I'm sorry to have taken up even more of your time. You need medical attention, and here I am complaining to you after you've already had such a terrible night."

"On the contrary." The preacher got up and looked down at her with a warm smile. "Being able to chat with the woman who saved me is quite invigorating. It reminds me that God's love is absolute, and He has a plan. Just trust in Him. It'll get you through life, and you'll know you're doing the right thing. Does that help?"

"A little," she said.

"Good, because I'm not on my A game tonight, as I'm sure you see." He tried to straighten his clothes a bit and wiped a bit of blood away.

"I have one more meeting in this town before I leave the day after tomorrow. This will probably be the last time we meet," she said, joining him on her feet. "I'll escort you back to your car and even your house if you'd like. I'd hate for that little punk to get to you in the parking lot or back at your house. He's young and dumb enough to do it for hurting his pride."

"Pride is a dangerous thing." The preacher and she walked side by side down the rows of pews on either side. He rested his hand on the back of each pew as he passed them by. "I'd like to think that young man will look back at tonight in shame and ask forgiveness."

"Not everyone wants forgiveness."

"Those are the truly pitiable," he said, his voice turning sorrowful. "All this love is just waiting for them to reach out and make an effort, but they're too afraid, or don't feel they're worthy. Everyone is worthy." He pushed the front door open and exited the building with Ai. He locked behind them. "Let's get home for the night. Just know, Ms. Song, even if you're leaving this week, you are always welcome in my congregation. I will tell everyone what you did tonight. You didn't harm him. God worked through you, and no one aside from me was hurt. That's something to celebrate."

"I'm not so sure your wife will agree with that."

"It wouldn't be the first time we've disagreed, and it won't be the last."

"I forgot to ask earlier," Ai stopped in the middle of the parking lot, "did the hoodlum get the money from the offering?"

"He did," the preacher said, strolling along. "I figured what was a little money when it came to living?"

"Here," she reached into her pants pocket and pulled up a clip of money. "Take this."

"You don't have to replace it, Ms. Song. You've already done so much for me and this entire church community tonight."

"Something inside me tells me to give you this." She slapped the bills into his hand and gripped it in a hand-shake all in one motion. "Call it God telling me to do this if you like."

"You are mighty generous," he said, wide eyed.

"Let's get you home, Filipe..."

12

"Wake up, sunshine." Luke slapped Reese's leg.

"What the fuck?" Reese sat up with squinty eyes. "Dude, why are you in my room?"

"A better question is, how are you not up? Your drill instructor is disappointed, I'm sure. Who is he so I can go ask him after all this?"

"That guy can eat my ass." Reese sat up and rubbed his eyes, yawning. "The deal is not until tonight. I thought I'd catch up on some sleep. Contrary to popular belief, soldiers don't get rested very often. I thought I'd seize the opportunity."

"The boss lady demands your attendance," Luke said, leaning against the wall.

"The same boss lady who's dragging us both around by the balls?" Reese asked.

"I get the sentiment, but we both know this job's worth doing."

"That doesn't change the fact that she's acting different from the last time I worked with you two. You can't tell me you haven't noticed. She's cagey, keeping things to herself more and more. She sends us out like we're her personal soldiers."

"We are her personal soldiers," Luke said, "for all intents and purposes. It's a job I'm familiar with, keeping her safe. I've been doing it for years before this. It's not new to me."

"Well, all I'm saying is you need to keep an eye on her. Do you want your girlfriend keeping secrets? This is how you get that if you're not careful."

"I'll keep that in mind," Luke said. "Now get ready. I'm heading back before she bitches at me. Hurry if you can. I got breakfast waiting from a nearby fast-food joint. Hopefully you like biscuits and gravy."

"Sounds delicious."

Luke opened the door and headed back to the room he and Vickie had shared the previous night. "He's on his way." He shut the door behind him.

"Just in time," Vickie said. She got up and walked over to Luke, showing him the laptop screen. "I found something that could be a lead. The deal's not until tonight, but why waste a whole day?"

"Why show me social media pages?" Luke walked over to the abandoned brown bag and pulled out the large, sealed container before opening it. "Aren't you going to eat?"

"After I'm done," she said. "Information is power." She clicked on a profile page depicting a church. "According to the pastor's wife, there was a break-in last night."

Luke opened the utensil pack and discarded the plastic. "I don't think our saboteur is busting up churches."

"Maybe try listening the whole time before jumping in." Vickie rolled her eyes. "It says here that her husband is claiming a Lyn Song intervened late last night. The thief beat her husband up pretty good before she got there, but no one died."

The door opened to a grumpy Reese. "What was so important that I had to get up at seven in the morning?"

"She thinks our spy may have played hero last night at the local church."

"Why would you even think that?" Reese asked. He took the brown bag Luke offered him and took out a container that was similar to Luke's. "People planting bombs don't save people." He didn't even bother opening the small package containing plastic utensils, grabbing the gravy covered bread with his hands instead. "Doubly so for a spy in wartime. She's causing chaos, mark my words."

"It's a lead, and something strange happening in a small town like this is rarely a coincidence. It won't do us any harm to go over there and ask the man about last night and this Lyn Song. We can say we're private investigators. We'll let him know we're after a dangerous criminal. He'll talk since he wants to help. It costs us nothing but time and effort, and we have plenty of time before tonight's meeting."

"Lyn Song is an odd name for a place like this, granted." Reese took a bite from the biscuit, leaving gravy around his mouth. He talked with a full mouth to boot. "What are the odds of something like this happening when we're here?"

"Odd things follow us around I've found," Luke said. "Please don't talk with your mouth full."

"I echo that sentiment," Vickie said. "Apparently, the savior, Ms. Song, donated nearly as much to cover the offering as the thief stole." Vickie scrolled down the comments, sifting through them.

"You think our bomber's found God?" Reese asked. "I doubt it. If you ask me, she probably went there to secure funds for the second deal tonight. That's why she was there. The Chinese aren't exactly big on religion."

"She went to steal money and then ended up donating instead?" Luke asked. "That makes zero sense."

"More sense than the alternatives," Reese said.

"How about setting aside our preconceived notions. Eat your breakfast and go to check. From everything that I'm seeing about this pastor, his name is Filipe Soto. He's third generation. His family came from Mexico years back. They're hardworking and look like they're honest. His dad's been working managing a nearby shop."

"Is that relevant?" Reese asked.

"Look, just head over there around eight and ask the man about his savior and his thief. For all we know, the thief was Ms. Xiao, and this Song was a good Samaritan."

"I haven't eaten fast food breakfast in years," Reese took another bite. "It tastes about as I remember - greasy." He handed the brown paper bag to Vickie. "Here's your sandwich."

Later that morning...

"You do the talking," Reese said to Luke as the men got out of the car.

"Don't get along with men of the cloth?" Luke asked. "Fine by me. We need a soft touch with this one, and that's not in your toolbox."

"I'm a weapon, not an orator," Reese said, kicking a rock further down the sidewalk before the pair turned and approached the front door of the single level house. He hopped up the few steps and turned to wait for Luke. "I admit, I am curious."

"Then let's find out." Luke approached the door and pressed the button to its side. "Just don't scare the old man."

"As if I would. My mother raised me right. You don't mess with preachers. It's not right."

The front door opened, and Filipe stood with a smile behind a screen door. "Good morning," he said.

"Good morning, sir," Luke started. "We're sorry to bother you at such an early hour on this fine morning, but we heard you may have been involved in an incident last night at your church?"

"Who are you two young men?" Filipe opened the screen door and stepped out. He moved over to a nearby rocking chair and sat down. "Come, have a seat," he said. He gestured toward two nearby rocking chairs to his side.

The two men took the offer and got comfortable on the front porch. "We're private investigators looking for a very dangerous criminal." Luke cleared his throat. "We believe you may have interacted with her last night. We're just here to get your testimony about what happened."

"Someone in the congregation put you up to this, I'm assuming?" Filipe asked. "My wife has told me that everyone on our social media page is buzzing about it."

"They just want to be sure you're safe," Luke said. "We're here to make sure you stay that way."

"Alright." Filipe rocked back and forth, drawing a slight squeak with every movement. "I was staying late last night after services. A few of us always stay after the appointed time to talk and engage in fellowship. You understand? It went on for quite a while last night." He looked over at Luke and met his eyes. "We must have been there a few hours afterwards. See, one member of my congregation is having a rough go of it and needed to talk."

"It's understandable," Luke said. "Please continue, sir."

"It got down to just the two of us eventually, and I remember promising to get him a book to read that I thought would help him. I told him to hold on for a quick moment while I went to the back room to fetch it."

"What's all this noise?" An elderly lady came to the nearby door. "Oh, we have company?" The front door opened to reveal an older lady with a smile. "Hello there," she said.

"Hello, ma'am," Luke said. "We're private investigators here tracking a violent criminal that's very dangerous. Our clients told us that your husband here had an incident last night."

"Boy, did he ever," she said. "You should have seen him last night. He was bleeding all over the place, and you can see the black eye on him. I told him we should call the police, but at least someone's on the case. I hope you find whoever did this to him."

"As I was saying," Filipe said, "when I went to the back-room, I heard someone yelling out front. I picked up the book and made for the door, only to find myself pushed back as I approached the door. I fell to the floor and looked up."

"Who is it you saw?" Reese leaned forward.

"I saw a young boy no older than sixteen. He had dyed his hair green." Filipe's tone was glum. "He was there for our collection's money. We donate most of that to charity and local homeless shelters, you know."

"You gave it to him?" Reese asked.

"I did. The kid seemed angry enough. He was not shy about pointing that gun around, I'll tell you."

"It's a good thing you did," Luke said. "What happened then?"

"We put the money in a locker that a few of us have the key to," Filipe said. "He wasn't satisfied with how quickly I did what he told me to. He struck me with the handle of his weapon a few times. I finally got the lock open, and he struck me again, knocking me to the carpet below. I remember rolling into a ball, trying to defend myself and praying to God."

"So, he grabbed the cash and then what happened?" Luke asked. "I'm sorry, but even minor details can have lasting effects on this case. Please be as accurate as you can. What did the kid look like?"

"He had green hair, was pale, and had some band shirt on. I don't recall the name. He had a nose ring. Does that help?"

Luke pulled out a notepad and scribbled down the details. "Yes, it does. Can you go on?"

"I heard the kid muttering to himself about something or another. Suddenly, we both heard the front doors slamming shut in the main hall. The kid walked over to me and started threatening me to not make any noise. The next thing I know, we heard a knock on the door, so the kid goes over to investigate."

"Wait until you hear this part," his wife said.

"He opens the door and looks around. I crawled over to see out the door and saw a young woman standing there pointing a gun at him. The kid knew she had him beat. She gave him ten seconds to leave, but she gave him more like fifteen or twenty. I don't think she wanted to kill him."

"What did she look like, Mr. Soto?" Reese asked. "Did she give you a name?"

"She was a foreigner. What country she is from, I cannot say. She said her name was Lyn Song."

"Give us a geographical guess. We just need to know what kind of nationality," Luke said.

"I'd guess Korean," Filipe said. "Song is a relatively

normal name in Korean culture if my memory serves me, but I was never a scholar."

"Korean you say?" Luke asked. "Tell me, did you get a good look at this Ms. Song?"

"Is this relevant?" Felipe's wife asked. "What about the hoodlum?"

"Karen, please," Filipe said. "Let our guests do their jobs. It's no doubt harder than we both know. They know their field better than us."

"I'm just saying it's common sense." Karen looked over at Reese. "Don't you think so?"

"You may have a point, ma'am," Reese said.

"We will get to the troublemaker in due time, Mrs. Soto," Luke said. "Did you get a good look at her, sir?"

"I did," Felipe said. "We talked for maybe ten minutes afterward. She's such a kind young woman. She's in a bad situation."

"Bad situation?" Reese asked.

"It's not my place to say, sir. It had something to do with her family. She never elaborated more than that. Apparently, it has something to do with her job that she hates. She seemed sad, or maybe distant."

"Is there anything else?" Luke asked.

"She said she'd be leaving town soon. I think she said tomorrow."

Reese and Luke's eyes widened, both turning to look at the other.

"What? Is that important?" Filipe asked.

"Possibly," Luke said. "Tell me." He dug into his pocket and pulled out a photo of Ai Xiao Vickie had printed off for them. "Did the young woman look like this?" He handed the photo over to the old man.

"Yeah, this is her. Do you two know her?" Filipe asked.

"I can't believe it." Reese stood up. "Are you sure this is her?"

"I'm sure. Why? What's so special about her?"

"We think she's who we're after."

"There's no way," Filipe said. "She saved me last night. She's a good woman. You're after the wrong person here."

"Have either of you two called the police about last night's beating from the young man?" Luke asked.

"No. I keep telling him he needs to, though," Karen said.

"Call them if you like and tell them about the kid if it'll make you feel better. We need to head out and follow up on this." Luke got up along with Reese. "Have a good day, you two." The two men walked down the steps and back toward their car.

"I'm telling you two gentlemen she is not dangerous," Filipe yelled after them. "You're wasting your time."

"Thank you for your help," Luke waved as he entered the car and rolled up the windows.

"I cannot believe this shit," Reese said. He climbed into the car and looked over at Luke. He fastened his seat belt. "Why would she do that? She had to have gone there to steal it herself."

"Maybe she has faith," Luke said, starting the engine. He looked past Reese and waved at the older couple still on their front porch. "Why is that so unbelievable?"

"In that regime?" Reese asked as the car pulled out onto the road. "I doubt it. Not in that country."

"In a country with over a billion people, I'd say it's not out of the realm of possibility."

"Then why would she be doing this shit? That's a commandment or something, right? Don't kill or something, I think it was."

"Remember what the old man said. She was doing this job for her family. That's what she told him."

"It's just a sob story she told the old man to keep him nice and content," Reese said. "Think like a spy. You don't want the old man calling someone, so you distract him with a bullshit made-up story. It's textbook misdirection."

"Strictly speaking, you're probably right, but I'd like to believe she didn't go to rob a church of its offering money."

"Don't get what you want confused with what's real," Reese said. "That's liable to get us both killed."

13

———

"Why did you ask them to come along, anyway?" David asked Vickie. Both agents were in different seats, working on their respective devices. "We could have done this job ourselves and not furthered the clown show that is your reputation at the agency."

"My clown show rep got your ass this job," Vickie said, giving a sidelong glare at David out of the corner of her eye. "No one wanted to work with you after your last incident, if you'll recall. Don't look a gift horse in the mouth."

"You said you wouldn't bring that up again."

"It's not my fault you couldn't control your temper. You ruined that man's life on a hunch."

"It turns out that hunch was correct," David said.

"He killed himself because of you, David!" she yelled in the tiny motel room. "You made it so the man couldn't go outside for fear of being killed by someone."

"It was just a tattoo." David looked away, his voice losing its bluster.

"That was not just a tattoo," Vickie said. "I don't even want to get into why the fuck you're so into those things. I'm surprised they even let you join with how much ink you're carrying around."

"It's a new era, a new generation. We have new ways of doing things. No one cares about ink anymore."

"They tend to when that ink says that they're traitors to the nation. You're God damned lucky you even have a job. It's only because we're in wartime that it's getting over-looked to such a degree. They let me take you, so they didn't have to deal with you - the caveat being I have to. The only reason I didn't yank that machine out of that room was because I knew they wouldn't be dumb enough to use it."

"We should be out there - not cooped up in this shithole of a motel," he said.

"You'd be driving. My ride's out inquiring about our latest lead." Vickie wiped a bead of sweat away from her forehead. "You'd think they'd at least have air conditioning."

"Fuck this." David plopped his laptop on the floor by his feet and marched for the door. "I'm getting out of here."

"Hold your horses," Vickie said. She watched him stop in his tracks. "I'm all for getting out of this dump. We need to stay productive on her trail."

"So? We can at least go out and look. We could get lucky and spot her on the sidewalk."

"Your plan is to pull over and shoot her real quick or something?" Vickie asked. "Don't be hasty. I have some things I need to look up. I've been trying to find this new name we heard about - Lyn Song. There are no social media accounts with that name."

"She could be renting a house, apartment, or even staying in a motel like this one," David said. "It's not a huge town, but we can't go searching every one."

"No, but we can run searches, you numbskull, but not on

this abysmal connection. We need something faster and more reliable."

"I doubt there are any websites we can force to allow us access to their records."

"We don't need their permission. We can peek into the big realtor websites' databases and find out if any Lyn Song leased, rented, or otherwise is staying near here. If worse comes to worst, we set off a ping on friendly forces' radars. We call it in, and we're good. You know how it is with intelligence gathering. They turn a blind eye to it so long as we get results."

"I guess they didn't teach us cybersecurity for giggles," he said. He walked back over and got his laptop. "Let's go and get a steady connection. Bring your software."

"Forgot to bring yours?" Vickie asked. "You're lucky I don't tell how unprepared you are," she said, rifling through the box. She pulled out a usb drive and pocketed it.

"I know just the place," David said. He pushed open the motel door and walked toward his blue sports car not too far away. "It serves a great coffee. Its Wi-Fi is top-notch."

"For the record, the inevitable question is a resounding no, and it never will be yes," Vickie said. She climbed into the passenger seat.

He turned the engine on and moved toward the edge of the parking lot. "I wasn't going to ask."

"Yes, you were. You've done it before, and my answer is still the same. I already have a boyfriend," Vickie said.

"I already know," David said. "I'm just saying you two live in different worlds. He's going to tire of all the secrets. It's a tale as old as intelligence agencies since time immemorial."

"Not happening, bottom line," she said. "Now, where is this place?"

"It's not far at all. It's in the middle of this place." He turned the wheel after the light above them turned green.

"It had better not be. We need to be back there and hear what the boys found out."

"What could a bookie offer you, anyway?"

"This is not a productive line of questioning for you, let me assure you. Suffice it to say, I know he'll get what we need done. Your feelings about him are immaterial. Make your peace with it. He got the info we needed for tonight. What have you done for this?"

"I cleaned up after you on two different occasions, Miss High and Mighty Jones," he said mockingly. "Dead bodies are tough to keep hush hush in a small town like this. You're lucky to not have seen any of those on the evening news."

"How difficult that must have been," Vickie said. "Did they fight back?"

"No thanks to you, not to mention that I had to lift that guy up by myself at your little kidnapping site."

"Guy? You mean guys? There were three. There was Dutch Morgan, some bodyguard named Hector, and one other."

"This guy isn't talkative, but there was only one there when I arrived," he said.

"The dude's probably running shitless," Vickie said. "We'll deal with him later if he tries anything."

They pulled into a nearby coffee place's parking lot.

"Go inside and get me a black coffee, large," she said.

"Right. I was going to ask if you'd like to accompany me?"

"No, I would not," she replied.

"Fine then," he said, throwing the door open. "Be that way, why don't you? Don't break a nail in here from all that work."

She heard the door slam at her side and lifted a lone finger on her left hand. She got back to work. "Let's hope I remember how this goes. Remember, worst case I get yelled at by some white-collar bureaucrat before I scare them shit-less with my own threats. You got this," she said.

She occasionally looked up, searching for any sign of David. On one such occasion, she saw him standing just inside. "That's just the use for his expertise. Wait in a damned line, you self-aggrandizing hothead," she said under her breath.

She returned to her work for a time until the opening of the door shocked her, causing her to stiffen. She looked up to see a cup hoisted in her direction.

"Here," David said.

"You have fun in there?"

"As a matter of fact, I did," he said. "In fact, you're going to want to kiss me when I tell you what happened."

"Nothing on this Earth will make me want to do that."

"I think I saw her in there," he said.

Vickie stopped what she was doing and looked up at him. "In there?" she asked. "Are you sure?"

"It looked like the girl we have a picture of. She's just chilling in there, drinking what looked like tea and eating a sandwich. I think it was a vegetarian variant. I'm not one much for those. I like the BLT."

"Shut the hell up, you moron. We have a chance to end this now. We can't wait for Luke and Reese. I want you to go in there and get her."

"What? You want me to just walk up to her and tell her she's under arrest in the middle of a public place with no badge to flash? Are you insane?" he asked.

"Just go act like you're flirting with her. I'm not asking you to go in and tackle the lady to the ground or some shit.

Go in there and work your magic. When you two leave, I'll be right outside waiting to back you up. The hard part will be getting her to not want to call for help when you approach."

"You are a nasty woman," David said. "Did anyone ever tell you that?"

"Go prove me wrong, big man. You have your gun and taser on you, right? Use one of them if it gets dicey. Preferably, we'd get her alive, but dead is fine too."

"You'll put in a good word to the higher ups if I do?"

"I'll put complaints in my official report if you keep stalling."

He swiped back her coffee. "Give it. I need this for my story." He kept his coffee and turned around. "Fine then. Prepare to be amazed."

"At least let me keep my coffee, you ass." Vickie pouted as she watched him walk back toward the café's double glass doors.

Inside the café...

Ai Xiao took a sip from her black tea and took a bite of her sandwich. She heard the bell ringing, indicating another customer had entered the establishment. She turned and saw a man who had just been in here previously. *He's got two coffees - why is he back in here?* she thought. She saw him look around until eventually finding her. *Oh, don't even tell me,* she thought. She saw him walk over towards her with a bright smile. *Of course he is. This is the part where my mother would tell me to give him a chance, isn't it?*

"Hello there," David said, having reached her table.

"Hi," she said, looking up at him. "Can I help you?" she asked.

"I sure hope so," David said. "My date kind of abandoned me. I'm stuck here with this extra coffee. Would you like it?"

"Me?" she asked. She recalled her training preparing her for this. *They said I shouldn't arouse suspicion. Helping this guy wouldn't be out of the ordinary. He doesn't look like he's a threat. The man's almost as thin as I am. It's not like I have anywhere to be until tonight. What harm could it do? He's a little cute, I guess.* "Uh, sure," she said. "Take a seat if you'd like."

"Thank you." He took the seat across from her and slid the unopened black coffee over toward her half of the table. "I'm sorry, I haven't introduced myself. I'm David," he said.

"I am Lyn Song," she said. "It's nice to meet you. You said you had a breakfast date?"

"Yeah, and she dipped out on me. I thought I'd order her favorite drink as a surprise, but that's gone to pot now."

"Gone to pot?" she asked, her voice full of confusion. "I'm sorry. I'm not familiar with that phrase."

"It means it's all for nothing, since she's not here."

"Ah, I see." She took another bite of the rapidly dwindling sandwich. A thin slice of tomato fell onto the wrapper below. "I'm sorry to hear that. I'm sure she had a good reason."

"I don't pretend to know women, Ms. Song. I've found it's a fool's game. That's what my father told me."

"He might well be right," she said, before finishing her meal. She picked up a nearby napkin and used it on her hands before folding it and wiping her mouth thoroughly. "What is this drink, if you don't mind my asking?"

"Black coffee," David answered, taking a sip of his own beverage. "She's not an imaginative girl. She's very vanilla."

"Honestly, I'm surprised you came over to talk to me," she said. She opened the cup and took a drink.

"I can imagine why a lot of guys don't come over."

"Really?"

"Sure. Most guys are afraid of rejection when it comes to a beautiful woman," he said. "I've never subscribed to that belief system. I say just go for it. What's the worst that can happen? They say no?"

"I wasn't going to say that. I was going to say due to how I look. Do you know what I mean?"

"For your heritage?" David asked with a wave of his hand. "No. You can't help where your parents lived before you were born. Right? Nobody should be treated differently based on how they look, in my book."

"You'd be surprised how many people in this day and age still do this abhorrent practice," she took another swig of the dark liquid, "especially with this war going on."

"I try to ignore the outright ignorant," David said. "I would advise you to do the same. It won't lead you anywhere you want to go. Why bother arguing with a fool when it brings nothing but annoyance and wastes time? Come to think of it, if you did, then you'd get up and leave this table right this minute. Don't take that advice then. I'm quite enjoying this talk."

"You talk so ill of yourself." She upended the paper cup and chugged the rest of its contents. "You shouldn't do that. No woman will want a man who belittles himself. They want a nice catch."

"You're giving me relationship advice too? I guess I need it, but damn. I guess that means you're not interested?"

"Not so much. I've got too much going on in my life, David," she said.

"That's the story of my life." David let loose a large breath and saw her picking up her purse. "You're leaving?"

"It's about time for me to go. I hope your day turns around, David. Keep at it. You'll find someone. Trust me."

"Huh? Oh, alright then," David sounded disappointed. His next words sounded distant. "Have a good day, Ms. Song."

"You too, David." She got up from their table and looked out the windows into the parking lot. She saw a woman sitting in a car, staring at her through a pair of binoculars. *Is he a distraction?* she thought.

"Did you forget something, Ms. Song?" David asked. She looked back to see him still seated, taking a drink from his hot coffee.

"I temporarily forgot where my car was. I parked out back." She turned and headed toward the other set of doors. She looked over her shoulder and saw David getting up and walking her way. She reached one hand into her purse and gripped a solid object. She wiggled her hand, causing the keys within to jingle as she walked. *Who the hell are they? It doesn't matter. I'll lose them and double back to my place.* She walked through the standard door in the back and came face to face with the fence out back of the café.

She pulled out the extendable baton from her purse and lowered herself, preparing to strike. She didn't have to wait long as the door opened within a few seconds. Springing into action, she swung with all her might toward her follower's knees.

David barely had time to close the door behind him before the blow sent him to the ground. He cried out in pain.

She got to a knee, placing one of hers onto his back, stifling any more noise. "I don't know why you're following me, but leave me alone for your own good. I am sorry for injuring you." She resized her weapon and placed it back in her purse, then got up, allowing David to breathe freely again. She sprinted around the corner, coming back into the parking lot. Looking over, she saw she was still being watched.

She inserted the key into her plain rental vehicle and tossed her purse into the passenger's seat. She immediately started the engine and got moving, looking behind her as she approached the road intersection. She saw David limping around the corner. He was leaning on the restaurant's wall to even steady himself. She returned her attention to driving and heard an engine behind her start up.

She pulled out into traffic amid a horn blaring. "Sorry, I'm not sorry." She sped through traffic, going well above the speed limit in the small town. Glancing into her rearview mirror, she noticed her chaser was closer than she thought. She weaved through traffic on the four-lane straight road.

She paid no heed to her follower, focusing on her own driving. "There's no way I'm outrunning her in this heap. I'll have to get fancy." She glanced down at her car's clock and smirked. "I know just the place. I knew all that boring research would pay off. The local train should arrive soon on this track." She turned the car onto a road heading out of town. She could see some railroad tracks crossing in front of her. There were no cars ahead of her. The nearby sign was flashing. Its roadblock was lowering as she approached. "No choice here."

She looked over to her left and saw a familiar train approaching. The sound of its whistle got louder as it approached its next stop. She did not slow down. It was do or die now, as far as she was concerned. She could hear her own heartbeat in her ears and could feel the adrenaline rushing through her veins. She felt powerful as she looked over at the encroaching locomotive. Her car busted through the lowering wood blockade and barreled over the tracks, narrowly avoiding breaking both sides of the safety device.

She stopped on the other side of the tracks and looked over her shoulder. Her follower had slowed to a stop on the other side of the track until the train behind her blocked her view. She slammed on the gas again and made as much distance as the feeble contraption could muster.

14

————

"What happened to you?" Reese asked, taking a handful of chips out of the bag he had in his hands before throwing them in his mouth. Loud crunching accompanied the motion.

"I don't want to talk about it," David said. He had a brace over his knee from earlier in the day. He gritted his teeth and looked down at the recent damage.

"Is it broken?" Reese asked. He tried to lean closer but leaned back when he saw David swatting at him. "Easy there."

"He got beat up by Ai Xiao," Vickie said. She had a sour look on her face, and she was curt. "I gave him a chance, and look what happened."

"You two saw her?" Luke asked, wide eyed. "When was this?"

"While you two were questioning Filipe," David said.

"How did it happen?" Reese asked.

"You aren't going to let this go, are you?" David asked.

"Never," Vickie said. "You may as well say it. We won't

get any peace otherwise, and we need to finalize our plans for tonight. Do it now so we can focus."

"Jesus! Fine," David said. He clenched his teeth as his inadvertent movement caused a jolt of pain. "She sent me in to get her out of a nearby café. We had a pleasant enough conversation, and then she bolted. I think she saw you." He gave a pointed glare toward Vickie. "Something spooked her after she got up and she bolted toward the back exit. Naturally, I followed her so she wouldn't get away."

"I see that worked well," Reese said.

"She was waiting just outside the door with a damned baton or something. She smacked me good in the kneecap and then put her knee on my back. She warned me not to follow her and ran off. Next thing I know I was hobbling around the corner, trying to get in sight of her, but saw her pulling out into traffic. Imagine my surprise when I see my boss driving off in chase, leaving me to fend for myself with a jacked-up knee cap."

"Oh, cry me a river," Vickie said. "You're perfectly fine. It's not like it was a fatal injury. I knew you'd be fine."

"You fucking just left me there to chase after our mark by yourself," David fired back.

"I came back and drove you to the hospital." Vickie stood up and walked away. "To hear you tell it, I just left you there for all time. I was the one who got you to the emergency room."

"Only after you lost her." David held a hand over the injury and nursed it. "The doctors said I should have never been putting any weight on it after the so-called accident."

"That sounds like a you-problem," Vickie said. "I never told you to go walking around like an idiot afterward. I assumed you'd use your phone and call an ambulance.

That'd have been rational, but no. You need me to clean up after you."

"You're supposed to look after personnel." David was clearly tired of this conversation, judging by his tone. "I assumed you'd do just that instead of going off to play cowboy."

"I figured two shots were better than one."

"Okay, kids," Reese interrupted the pair. "Do you want to hear how our morning went?"

"For once, it seems ours was the peaceful one," Luke said with a chuckle. "Now that's rare. We talked to Filipe as you directed. It turns out he identified his rescuer as Ai Xiao."

"Not the troublemaker?" Vickie asked.

"That makes sense," David said. "She didn't strike me as a terrible person."

"Just one that buys explosives and does God knows what with them, right?" Reese asked. "Never forget some of humanity's worst killers had dynamite charisma and good looks. Don't fall for it, Mr. Secret Agent Man."

"I'm not some simp, soldier boy."

"That remains to be seen," Reese said. "The old fool seemed convinced she was some kind of hero. She had him mesmerized and fooled hook, line, and sinker. She's manipulative."

"He was adamant," Luke said. "He claimed she did everything she could to not kill the young hoodlum that beat the shit out of him. Whether that's true or not, I don't know. Apparently, she gave him hundreds upon hundreds of bucks to replace the money that was lost. What did she look like? A little picture rarely does justice to a person."

"What do you think she looked like?" David asked, still annoyed. "She was five foot two or so, had black hair, and looked like she took care of her makeup. It wasn't too thick, but accentuated her natural beauty. She was obviously Asian. To the untrained eye, she could pass for Korean, Japanese, or Chinese. She claimed she suffers quite a bit of belligerence because of her looks."

"I'm sure she spun you quite the yarn. They're taught to play the victim and gain sympathy points," Reese said. "You said she carried a baton?"

"I became close with it, yes."

"Odd choice of weapon," Reese said. He laid down on an open part of the floor and stared up at the ceiling above with his arms behind his head. "That's not exactly lethal - it just cripples."

"There is the theory she's found God." Luke couldn't help but laugh as he aired the theory. "Maybe she doesn't want to kill. Soto also said she told him about her parents and how she hated her job. Maybe her family's being threatened by the regime back home?"

"It's irrelevant anyway," Vickie said. "If she's going to plant the explosives she's buying, then I don't care if she feels extra sorry afterwards or not."

"True enough," Luke said. "Now I assume David's out of the game for tonight's party?"

"I better be," David said. "I did my part earlier today."

"You accomplished nothing, just like me. How is that doing your part?" Vickie asked. "Regardless, you're correct. We'll be shorthanded tonight. That's why we're not crashing the arms deal. We're going to do this smarter. You and Reese will handle the tailing. While he was off playing Don Juan in the café earlier, I set my software to search the big-name realtor websites for any houses rented by a Lyn Song in the last two weeks. We got lucky." She handed a copy of a nearby stack of papers to both Reese and Luke.

"What are you going to do?" Luke asked.

"David and I are going to set up a camera to make sure we know when and if she leaves. Once she gets home, we're going to enter it and apprehend her there. It's risky on her turf, but it's the only choice I see. We have an ex-bounty hunter and a soldier who's one of the toughest men in the world. I want Reese taking point once we're inside."

"Just my luck," Reese bit his lip. "I get to go around in the dark where traps could be. Fuck me," he said.

"You're the only one who's seen their traps up close and personal. You're our best chance at this," Vickie said.

"I'll do it. I just won't like it," Reese said. "Don't get me wrong. I've got the skills, and I'll get it done. I'll just bitch about it before and after."

"I would too, to be honest," David said. "I don't envy you."

"I've been studying the ground plans. Check that pile there." She reached over and pointed to another stack of papers on the bed. "I marked who would go in which entrance. L for Luke, R for Reese, and V for me."

"I've got the front? It works for me," Reese said.

"I can take the north side, sure."

"Then I'll take the back. Make sure we synchronize before anyone heads inside," Vickie said. "I want all of us in there if anything pops off. Is that clear?"

"Not like I want to be caught by myself in there," Reese said.

"Everyone, bring all your weapons," Reese said. "Luke, I want you to have that shotgun we picked out for you. I'll use a rifle like your girlfriend there since I'm most comfortable with it. Remember, we shoot to kill, not incapacitate. A moment of hesitation is enough to get us all killed on the battlefield. Nobody better puss out and leave us hanging."

"When have you ever known me to run?" Luke asked.

"It is one of your dumber, but more respectable, qualities..."

15

_____

"This place is still sketchy. I don't care what anyone says," Reese said, sitting on the front of the car. He looked through the pair of binoculars at the parking lot of the nearby abandoned factory. "Morgan said they were doing the deal outside, yeah?"

"That's what he said," Luke said. "I have no reason to doubt him. They want this deal to go off quicky and without a hitch. Going inside a shady property just creeps everyone out and wastes time. To a casual onlooker, it'll just look like a meeting. Not that there would be any casual onlookers out in this middle of nowhere."

"Looks like our first guests are showing up," Reese said. He followed a train of cars as it approached the large, abandoned building's parking lot. "That's Morgan's men, if I had to bet."

Luke kicked his legs out on the front of the car. The tree lines obscured much of the factory, but it did its job of concealing them. "I can only see the number of cars, but that's a safe bet, since Ai would only have one."

"Unless she has more partners we don't know about,"

Reese said. "That's always a possibility." He watched the men file out. They were wearing the same sort of suit that Dutch had been. "It's Dutch's boys though. It's the same dress code and everything."

"She's probably already here." Luke kept watch to their sides. He occasionally looked over his shoulder, making sure no one was behind them. "She wouldn't want to give them the advantage."

"Or she'll be fashionably late," Reese said. His free hand reached inside the bag in his lap, only to return empty. He tossed it on the grass below, littering it with the junk food container.

"They're getting out now. It looks like they're waiting. She'll show up soon."

"I wonder if Vickie and David have the cameras set up over there."

"Knowing that guy, they'll screw that up too," Reese said. "They could have grabbed her today, and he gets his kneecap busted up. Now we're sitting here in the early evening."

"I'd imagine they're going to send you back to the front lines after this assignment. I wouldn't want it to end yet if I were you."

"Unless your girl can convince my higher ups to make this permanent, I'm destined to head back there until this war is over." Reese lowered the binoculars and rubbed his eyes. "I'm getting a headache."

"Hand them over," Luke said, extending an open palm. He took the tool and looked through them toward the deal site. "My prediction is she'll pay, they'll deliver, and we'll tail her. This shit will be done by tonight. Would you like to make this job permanent? This whole CIA thing?"

"Better to be aimed at by one enemy than a dozen or more at a time. Yeah, I'd rather have this."

"I'll see what she can manage. I give no promises, alright?" Luke said. He was still looking through the binoculars when he blindly reached his free hand toward Reese. He felt it get grabbed.

"Deal," Reese said.

"One day I'd like to get back to just collecting," Luke said. "It's not like I have a choice in this either. They have dirt on both of us, and we both know they'll get their money's worth."

"Such a cynic," Reese said. "You know, I'm wondering why she didn't just kill David earlier today."

"She doesn't seem to enjoy killing, or she wants to keep things as quiet as can be. I wouldn't want to be on the police's radar if I was planning something this heinous."

"Maybe," Reese said. "I think she's careful. A gunshot would have caused a panic and a slew of 911 calls. She's calculating if that's the case. If she was Zhang's partner, I'd believe it. That guy was as nasty as the day is long. Hopefully, among all that tech shit, Vickie brought some antivenoms. If Ai's anything like him, we'll see it coming into play."

"As far as I'm concerned," Luke said, "if you're willing to plant explosives and kill innocents, nothing is out of play. I won't underestimate her, no matter how unassuming she looks or acts. Actions define us."

"We know she's got some on her," Reese said. "That's her actions."

"I think I see her," Luke said, his voice now full of nothing but business. "She has a briefcase. That's the money, I bet."

Reese's face went blank, and his attention snapped back to their front. The pair grew quiet. "I see her." He kept his voice low. Both men got off the front of their car and got low to the ground, leaving the car doors open behind them. They took their place behind nearby trees and peeked around at the nearby parking lot.

She approached the men and said something they couldn't hear. They exchanged more words they couldn't hear from where they stood until one of the men reached inside their car. He pulled out a backpack and moved toward her. He pointed at the briefcase in her hands.

She said something else. This time, the men around her tensed up. Their hands hovered over their hips.

"Something's wrong," Luke said.

Reese grabbed the binoculars and looked through them. "Motherfucker, she's hardcore. She's wearing the same explosives they sold her. She made it into a vest."

"You think she's robbing them?" Luke asked.

"She's a crazy bitch. I don't know, dude. Maybe the regime didn't give her as much as Morgan wanted."

She opened her jacket. She had a small handheld device clutched in her left hand, squeezing it. She spoke as a bright red light blinked every so often from her custom clothing. Even from this distance, you could make out wires and a small display. She walked up to the men, still frozen on the spot, and grabbed the backpack. She left the briefcase and backed away, never turning away from them.

"Get in the car," Reese said. He reached over and tapped Luke on the shoulder. "She's getting out of here now."

"Got it..."

Just earlier...

Ai Xiao came to a stop. She was around the back of the factory, where she'd agreed to meet Morgan's men. She looked over into the passenger seat of the small car at the briefcase. *There's not enough in there,* she thought. Memories of the previous night flooded her mind. She saw herself giving away a sizable chunk of her allocated funds to the priest in a spur-of-the-moment decision. "Why?" she asked herself. "Why did I give it away on some whim?" She gritted her teeth and stifled the cascade of tears threatening to fall from the sheer panic she felt racing through her chest.

It felt tight. She was stiff all over, and her heart was racing as she looked in the back seat at the vest she'd spent all day stitching together. She reached back and grabbed it. As she put it on, she was careful to grab the connected device. "God forgive me for what I am about to do," she said. She checked her hip holster and confirmed her pistol was still there. *Not that it will do me much good. That's why I'm wearing this sacrilege thing.*

I'm going to die tonight. Ai looked down at her trembling hands. She grabbed the wheel, trying to steady them, while clenching her teeth unconsciously. *They're already here. We have a few minutes. Calm yourself down. Playing it cool will sell this better. If they see you petrified, then they'll either assume the explosives are fake, or that I won't push it - neither of which I want. It's not like the vest has a ton of explosives - just enough to blow up. The rest went into the silos. That doesn't make me feel better.*

"Sitting out here all night won't do anything. Let's get this over with." She grabbed the briefcase and got out. She made sure the flashing light on her vest was hidden by donning a large coat over it. *Can't go spoiling the surprise,* she thought. She walked with purpose. She turned the corner and held a straight face.

Four men stood outside of their nearby car. The only source of light in the abandoned lot was a streetlamp flickering above every so often. "Hello, boys," she said, her voice full of confidence. She swaggered ahead. "Having a good evening?" She had her left hand tucked behind her, squeezing the device all the while for dear life.

"So long as you got the money, we're going to have a fine night, Ms. Xiao," the one nearest their car said. He pulled out a backpack and walked over toward her. He pointed at her briefcase with a wide smile. "You know the drill," he said. "Open it and show us the money, and you get these."

"I have a better idea," Ai said. "How about you hand me that backpack full of explosives, or we all go boom?"

The men snapped to attention and tensed up. "What?" the nearest asked.

"Dumbass," she said with a derisive laugh. "Oh, now you see it?"

The nearest man backed up, holding up a hand as if to fend something off. "Let's not be hasty here, ma'am."

"Drop the backpack now, and back away." She watched him lower the bag to the ground before scurrying off, almost tripping as he backpedaled.

He slammed back first into the car's side, a mortified look on his face.

"Good boy," she said. She calmly walked forward. She revealed her left hand holding the dead man's switch and opened her jacket, revealing the explosive vest underneath. It was adorned with what explosives she had left. Red wires and a red flashing light were on her chest. "If anyone gets any bright ideas," she said mid stride, "I'll stop squeezing this, and we all go boom. It's called a dead man's switch, gentlemen. Don't do anything cute. Now you can keep this." She came to a stop beside the backpack. She lowered the briefcase to the ground and picked up the backpack with her free hand.

Backing up, she told them, "That's all I have, and all you shall get from me. I'm sorry for the manner this went down, but it had to be this way," she said.

"You're dead when the boss hears about this," one of the men said.

"You'd be within your rights after this little stunt," she said. She was nearly back to her original position in the parking lot. "Now you all get to go home to your little families tonight. You should be grateful for that, at least. Now you all are going to sit here until I am out of sight, like good little boys."

"What's stopping us from following you?" the talkative one asked.

"A shockwave and flying metal debris that could impale you if you're unlucky." She turned the corner and turned around to run toward her car. She tossed the backpack in the open back window and flung the driver's door open. She hopped inside and used her free hand to press a button on the side of the dead man's switch. The flashing light on the vest disappeared. She took off the God forsaken suicide vest and tossed it in the back before turning the engine on and burning rubber.

As the smell of burning rubber faded, her back window exploded in a rain of glass shards. She bent down, trying to get out of the way when she looked up at the rear-view mirror. "You dumb assholes," she muttered. She could see the group of four men had followed her and were opening fire on her retreating car. "Calling me on my bluff, huh? All's fair in love and war." She turned a corner and kept going, successfully getting out of the impromptu firing line. She breathed a sigh of relief and looked over her shoulder once more out of habit. "Dumb bastards," she grumbled to herself. "You got most of the money. Consider yourselves lucky. It's just a few hundred short. On a deal worth tens of thousands, that's chicken feed."

She glanced up at the mirror occasionally, to assure herself she really did get away. She noticed one car a ways back from her. "That's not their car," she said. "Still, better safe than sorry. I'm getting an odd feel from it." She drove through the small town without further incident and found herself back home before she knew it. Grabbing the back-pack she'd taken, she jogged inside.

She closed the door behind her and pulled out the phone from her back pants pocket. "Almost out of power." She connected it via a charging cable and placed it on a nearby table. "I'll need this fully charged on my departure."

I'd just gotten comfortable in this town, and I already am forced to leave, she thought. She walked through the nearby kitchen and out the back door. *Better safe than sorry.* She hopped down the steps into the open backyard and grabbed the nearby bicycle, leaning against the chain-link fence connecting her and her temporary neighbor's yard. She put on the backpack with great care and hopped on the bicycle. Entering the nearby road behind her house, she was off to the races toward her next and final target...

16

Luke pulled up behind David's car at the agreed upon meeting point near Ai's house. "She said as soon as we got here, we're going in. Let's go and not be late," he said, taking the key out of the ignition.

"That's music to my ears," Reese said. "Let's get this shit done and over with."

The two men got out of the car and walked up to David's car. Luke knocked on the window until it rolled down, revealing Vickie. "Same positions as before? We're ready. Are you?"

"Anything to get away from this guy. All he does is bitch and moan about earlier today." She threw the door open once Luke was far enough away. She got on her tiptoes, gave him a quick peck on the lips, and rubbed his chest. "Let's get this bitch, just like how I taught you."

"I got the front," Reese said. "You two go in at the same time and take her flank."

"That's the plan," Luke said. "She won't go down without a fight, so everyone has their vest on, yes?"

"Always," Reese said. "I've seen too many guys get lazy and forget, only to get shot."

"Of course I do," Vickie said. "Now get your weapons. They're in the back." She knocked on the nearby door to accentuate her next words. "Pop the trunk."

In response, the trunk unlocked and floated upward, revealing a shotgun and two rifles ready for the taking.

"Remember," Reese said, taking one of his babies out of the trunk, "with a flick of this, it goes from fully auto to single shot. Use it well, I'd recommend single shot for safety's sake. I'd rather not hit a civie through a wall accidentally."

"Agreed." Vickie made sure it was set to single fire mode and checked its already installed shells. She confirmed it was locked and loaded before handing the shotgun to Luke. "Here, big boy," she said while handing it over. "Do your preliminary checks, and then we're heading inside immediately."

He went through the motions that Vickie had taught him a few nights ago at the shooting range. He reached forward into the trunk to the open box of shells beside where the shotgun had sat just a few moments ago. He shoveled as many as he could fit into his pants pocket. "You never know how much you'll need. Better safe than sorry."

"Amen, brother." Reese followed Luke's lead and grabbed another two prefilled magazines they'd worked on previously, stowing them away on his person. "Let's lock and load." He unloaded the magazine at the bottom of the rifle before reinserting it and readying it for battle with a satisfying click. "Is the priority dead or alive?"

"Alive if she gives us the chance, dead otherwise. Preferably, we'd try to get her to tell us where she's planted her surprise packs so we can disarm them and prevent that tragedy. It's hard to get intel from a corpse in my experience."

"Got it, but I'm not dying if she feels like putting up a fight," Reese said. "Now remember in there, no firing unless you see what you're aiming at. We're not together. The last thing we need is for Luke to fire off that beast of a gun and clip me with friendly fire because he couldn't see."

"I understand. Don't squeeze the trigger unless I want something to die. It's Basic Firearms Safety 101."

"Alright then, boys and girls, let's go bag us a spy," Reese said.

"Everyone, make sure your comms are working," Vickie said. She raised a finger to her ear. "Check."

"Mine's working," Reese and Luke said.

"On my mark when we get there," Reese said. "Let me know when you both are in position. I'll go in first and grab her attention."

"Let's go."

The group broke up and headed toward the house a few streets over. Luke and Vickie went together, with Reese breaking off. The two talked as they jogged.

"If anyone sees us, they're calling the police. You realize that?" Luke asked with a chuckle.

"Let them," Vickie said. "We'll be finished long before they reach here. It's at least a ten-minute response out here." The pair continued in silence.

"This is my cue. Good luck, love," Vickie said before she peeled off and went her own way.

"You be careful," Luke said.

"Always am," she said over her shoulder.

Luke saw where he was supposed to be and got there as soon as he could. "I'm in position," he said.

"Hold," Vickie said. "I'm almost there."

"I'm ready - holding," Reese's voice was low.

Almost a full minute passed before Vickie spoke up again. "I'm in position. On your mark," she said over the call.

"Three, two, one, go." An enormous crash was heard, along with Reese yelling. "Put your hands up, or I shoot to kill."

Luke tried to open the door, only to find it locked. He backed up a few feet and ran full tilt at the door. He slammed his shoulder into it. It opened under his assault with a loud crash. He lifted the business end of the shotgun up as soon as he was inside. "Put your damned hands up or I fire!" He paused and surveyed the room he found himself in. "I don't see her over here," he said.

"She's not in this part of the house either," Vickie said. "What about the front?"

"All I see here is her phone," Reese said. "Damn it to hell."

"Check the house, and don't let your guard down. We're going to clear this room by room," Vickie said.

Luke did as she ordered. "This room's clear," he said. He moved to the next. He kept the shotgun pointed ahead of him and turned while entering a new room, attempting to remove any potential blind spots.

"There's nothing in the foyer," Reese said. "I'm going upstairs while you two check the downstairs. If you hear gunfire, you know she's up there."

"The living room is clear," Vickie said.

"The kitchen's clear," Luke said as he entered the tiled room. He flipped on the lights and confirmed his findings. He kept moving into what looked like a computer room. "Computer room's clear too. I think she ducked out."

"She's not upstairs either," Reese said. Loud stomping could be heard rushing down the stairs. He appeared in the nearby living room. Vickie made her way there, and the group met up again.

"What do we do now?" Luke asked. "She could be out there planting those bombs as we speak. I think we should stay here," Luke said.

"I disagree," Reese said. "We can't lollygag around while she's out there. She might never come back here."

"She'll be back," Luke said, walking over to a nearby table. He picked up the phone that lay there. Its screen had not yet faded to black. He pressed the photo button, bringing up the album. "This is why. Look at this."

Reese and Vickie came up on either side of him.

"It's her family, and the charge is low. She'll be back for this," Luke said.

"It's surprising they even let her carry photos of her family," Vickie said. "That's in the top ten rules of spying right there."

"Are we really going to bet on her ass coming back here for some family memories?"

"Why not do both?" Vickie asked. "David, you hear me?"

"I sure do," his bored voice came through.

"Call the local PD. Invoke my name, and tell the chief to send his men to the local processing plant. We have reason to believe she may be planting the bombs there as we speak. Have them conduct a sweep of the premises. If you can convince them to send in the bomb squad, do that."

"The company is going to moan about this," David said. "They will not want some local PD stopping their operations."

"Just do it," Vickie said. "We're staying here for when she comes back. This way, we're covered on both sides. Get it done if you want that good peer review."

"Alright already, sheesh," David said.

"Alright people," Vickie said. "There are three doors on the ground level and there are three of us. The math seems pretty simple. However, seeing as I'm not a combat expert, Mr. Hilton, what would you suggest?"

"We should have someone upstairs," he said. "I saw a balcony upstairs with a door leading in. That's a way in, and she may have a way up there. I don't want her to get our flank. I'll stay upstairs. You two should stay down here. We'll keep this place locked down with that."

"I've got the front door, you've got the back," Vickie said. "Remember, boys, we want her alive. She can't tell us where the bombs are if we fill her full of lead."

"Works for me," Luke said.

"Reese?" Vickie asked. "I want to hear it from you."

"Don't kill her," he almost spat the words out. "I got it already."

17

Ai finished at the last bomb location and inspected her handiwork. She climbed down from the ladder that she'd found inside the building. *That will work. It's all set. Now to just wait,* she thought. She had affixed it to underneath a catwalk in the corner of the processing plant. Getting in wasn't as hard as she pictured it would be. She used the blind spots the guard posts afforded her and snuck in with hardly a peep.

She'd set the charges exactly where her handlers told her to. One set on each corner of the factory, with one in the middle. *That'll bring this place to the ground along with every worker in here when it happens,* she thought. Her stomach rolled over at the thought of the death her handiwork would bring to untold amounts of innocents. She zipped up the backpack and slung it over her shoulder. Getting to her feet, she dropped a hand to her stomach.

"Now to get out with no one noticing anything," she whispered to herself. *Easier said than done.* Reaching down to her belt line, she took out the baton she'd strapped there. She extended it and got it ready for action, staying low to the ground as she moved behind stacks of crates. As she dashed between the rows of crates, she heard voices nearby.

"Thank God for overtime," one female voice said. "Hey, Bo, come over here for a minute, will you?"

Rapid footsteps greeted the woman's voice and came to a sudden stop behind her. She laid a hand on the nearby shipping container.

"Yes?" a male voice answered. "What is it?"

"I need you to move these by tomorrow morning. We need to get ready for the next shipment. We can't have this backing up."

"Begging your pardon, miss," Bo said. "Where am I going to put it? This is the loading area. We're already beyond our capacity."

"These are non-perishable packaged food packs in airtight shipping containers. Put them outside. Besides, it would make it easier when we have the new influx of drivers if we can load and unload out there. We are one of the biggest suppliers of soybeans and corn. We're going to get these supplies where they need to go. Now stop bellyaching and get moving."

"Yes, ma'am," the man said. The footsteps faded away.

She peeked around the corner and saw a woman holding a clipboard. She was scribbling something on it. She took the opportunity and moved through the open area between crates.

"Bo, was that you?" the female voice asked.

Ai did not verbally answer. She merely waited in her new cover. She reached up and touched the Halloween mask she had bought a few weeks back. *I Should have gotten a mask that had better air flow. This Presidential mask makes it hard to breathe.*

"I asked you a question."

Ai gripped the weapon in her hands. *Don't come over here, lady. Please,* she thought. *I can't afford this tonight.*

The footsteps stopped just around the corner. "I could have sworn I heard something." Shuffling could be heard. A shadow approached, signaling the woman was not stopping.

Here we go, Ai thought. She watched as the woman walked forward into view. She was looking the other way. She swung the baton, aiming for the back of the woman's neck. She connected with her blow but missed her target. It hit the woman in the back of the skull, and the woman's eyes rolled up in her head.

Ai lunged forward and grabbed the woman before she could fall to the ground. She lowered her to the floor and dragged her around the corner out of view. She broke off into a run toward the nearest door and slammed into it with her shoulder, then closed it behind her. Coming out under the light, which was affixed to the side of the building, she turned and ran toward the relative safety of the darkness nearby. Just as she reached the dark side of the building, she heard an engine starting in the lot.

She dared not move except to turn and look at the newfound noise.

A large truck was at the security checkpoint. The security guard on duty raised the impediment and waved the driver to enter. Its engine roared to life and jolted forward toward her.

She took off running away toward the back of the building. She could hear it slowing down behind her. Looking over her shoulder, she could see the lights nearing her shadow on the blacktop. She heard it honking behind her. *I'm spotted. Shit!* She turned to watch where she was running and saw the smaller fence in the back she'd jumped over. She didn't bother slowing down, instead jumping once she was a few feet away. She didn't clear the obstruction. Her left foot got caught and caused her to fall face first down into the grass on the other side.

"Holy shit!" a male voice called out. "Are you alright?"

She could hear footsteps approaching her even in her daze, as everything felt woozy. She staggered to her feet and took off anew. She ducked into the nearest alley and kept running. The scene she had just lived replayed in her mind. *It's sloppy, but all they know is someone was on the property. That's all,* she thought.

She heard the distant voice of a man. "There was someone over here, but he ran off after tripping on the fence. He went that way."

She couldn't stop running. She knew her bike was close. It would only be a little further before she could get back to her house and spend her last night in this rural country town. She turned another corner and kept the pace up. Her lungs were burning now with every breath she took. She pushed through the pain until she recognized the alley where she'd left her bicycle. *This is the last time I take a damned bike. I'm already beat,* she thought.

She finally reached her destination and climbed aboard, removing her mask and throwing it in the backpack over her shoulder. She pedaled, moving forward out of the alleyway and back onto the road. The roads were not busy at this time of night, only one or two occasionally passing by in either direction. She pedaled and breathed a deep breath. She looked over her shoulder one last time and shook her head.

She looked up at the upcoming traffic light in the small town. Sirens sounded in the distance as she sat underneath the red lights pouring down from above. *What? There's no way they called the police that quickly. Relax, just play it cool.*

You're just a girl out on a ride if they ask anything, she told herself. The light turned green, and she turned right. She could hear the sirens grow louder behind her. She looked over her shoulder for a moment and saw the red and blue lights heading in the direction she just left. *Something is not right about tonight,* she thought.

First, I felt like maybe someone was following me after I got the goods. Now the police are called? Fuck it, she thought. *I'll just leave tonight and not bother sleeping until I'm well out of the city.*

Later, back at her house...

She opened the gate leading to her backyard and rolled the bicycle over to where she first grabbed it. She leaned it against the fence and walked slowly toward the building. She looked at the side door and saw something was amiss. *I locked this,* she thought. *Now it's unlocked? Something's off here. Damn it. I need my phone at least before I get out of this town.*

She walked around the house but stopped before reaching the front. She saw an unfamiliar car parked across the street, just sitting there under a nearby streetlight. She moved back to the backyard and directed her gaze downward. She saw the basement window she'd left unlocked. *If anyone's inside, they're watching the doors. I'll just sneak inside, grab the phone, and get out before they realize I'm here.*

She lowered herself to a knee and carefully placed her palm on the small window, pulling with moderate strength only for the window to jerk out of place but otherwise remain impassable. She tried opening it again, this time with more force. It creaked open slowly but surely. She squeezed her feet and legs inside the narrow entrance and got onto her belly on the grass. She wiggled her way through the small opening with her slight frame and landed on her feet in the basement. She reached up and closed the window.

She looked around the near pitch-black room and waited. *I can't see shit. I should let my eyes adjust. I never really stopped and thought about how creepy this place is with all the lights out.*

She desperately tried to remember the layout of the basement. Come to think of it, she only came down here when she was crafting the vest she used. Spending so little time down here over the last two weeks left her guessing. She reached a hand out in front of her as she walked forward carefully. She stopped when she felt something at hip level. It felt solid. *That's the worktable,* she thought.

Utilizing the landmark, she turned herself to where she thought the steps leading upstairs were and walked even slower. She used her foot to feel out where the first step was with every pace. Eventually, her foot touched something, and she felt it out. *The steps, finally,* she thought. She pulled out her baton and extended it to fight with any would be intruders.

She climbed each step slowly, making sure to limit any sound she generated. She looked up and saw a faint light trailing into the room. *The basement door's still open. At least I've got that going for me tonight. It's the only reason I've been able to navigate this mess.*

She reached the top of the stairs and could see out into the kitchen. She was slow and calculating with every movement. She peeked around the door and saw a man seated on the tiled floor, leaning against the nearby wall, facing the back door. He seemed to be having difficulties either staying focused or awake, one of the two. He had one hand on his head, as if nursing a headache. She gripped the baton in her right hand before turning to look the other way. No one else was in the kitchen, from what she could tell. This left her with two choices. *Either I take the guy out or try to sneak by. I know which is the safer option,* she thought.

She stepped up into the kitchen, weapon clutched in her hand. She tiptoed over to the man in the darkness. She raised her right hand up and behind her, preparing to swing the non-lethal instrument. *Sorry, buddy,* she thought. *You shouldn't be in my place.*

She swung down and met her target on the immobile man. The sound of steel meeting brass erupted, and her baton bounced backward.

"I'm awake," he said. "Son of a bitch." He scrambled to his feet and backed off from her, holding his hand.

She gave him no respite and followed, preparing another strike, this time aiming at his head again.

Luke lifted his non injured hand and had steel meet with brass again, this time sparks flew along with a flash of light. He grunted in pain and rushed forward. He lifted her off the ground and slammed her into the nearest wall.

She delivered elbow after elbow into his shoulder, eventually causing him to drop her. When he did, she lifted a knee and hit him in the groin.

Luke backed off and fell over.

"Nice to see they teach you to fight above the belt over there," Vickie was now in the nearby doorway. "You're coming with us tonight."

"The hell I am," Ai said.

"Careful with her," Luke barely managed to get out.

"I got it, darling. Just watch me work," Vickie said. She reached behind her and produced a small device. She pressed a button on it and a low buzzing was heard. An arc of electricity danced between the two prongs of it. "Reese!

Get down here now!" Vickie was forced to dodge blow after blow before her sentence had even finished.

"Get out of my house," Ai said, between swings of her weapon.

Vickie lunged forward with her weapon and connected with Ai's chest. Before she could press the button, she felt a hand on her shoulder. She pressed the button anyway and shared the electricity coursing through both women's bodies. Both fell to their knees after she managed to end the shock.

The fight was far from over as Ai fell to her back and delivered a powerful kick to Vickie's jaw before rolling backward and bouncing to her feet.

Vickie got up and twirled the taser in her grip. She tilted her head to the side, eliciting a crack. She had a devious smile adorning her pretty face. "Alright, let's quit the foreplay."

Ai didn't respond except to swing her melee weapon from the side, aiming at Vickie's head.

She leaned back and felt the swoosh of air. "Grab hold of me again, sweetie pie. I dare you." She jabbed the shocking device toward her again.

Ai jumped back this time, intent on keeping her distance from the agent. She had forgotten Luke was back there, however.

He pushed her forward toward Vickie, knocking her off balance.

She had two options: fall to the floor, or somehow keep her balance. She was intent on option number two. Instead of trying to fight gravity, knowing it to be a fool's errand, she chose another method. She went with the momentum. She planted her free palm on the floor and cartwheeled toward Vickie. She utilized her leg's momentum to strike Vickie in one swift motion with a kick to her head, knocking her to the tiled floor below.

"How graceful." Reese stood in the nearby doorway to replace Vickie, who was now on the ground. "Try your little ballerina tricks on me all you want, little girl. That shit won't work."

"Who the fuck are all of you?" Ai looked behind her and saw Luke struggling to his feet. She backed up and swung the baton, striking him in the face, knocking him back to the ground. She moved a few feet away and saw Reese stepping forward toward her. "Get out of my house! I'll call the police, I swear." She dropped a hand and placed it over her ribs. She panted between words from the recent exertion and tried to remain upright.

"Please do," Reese said. "I'm sure they'd love to hear from the girl who was planting bombs all over the town tonight. Cut the bullshit," he said once he'd passed Vickie and put her behind him in the room. "Tell me, Ms. Xiao, have you ever fought in the war?"

"You know my name?" Ai's eyes were wide, first in awe, then in panic. "Who are you?"

"We're with people who know what your mission is," Reese said. "We know you're trying to sabotage our food production, so my brothers and sisters in arms starve while they fight your people overseas."

"You're a solider." She put it together, trying to catch her breath. "So, you hate me?"

"I hate you because you're trying to kill innocent Americans while fighting dirty. Now come here," Reese approached again.

Ai backed up into another room, trying desperately to maintain her distance. She swung the baton, trying to keep him at bay. He dodged it effortlessly before continuing the approach, slowly and steadily. His pace wasn't much faster than walking, but it felt intimidating to her somehow. She hadn't felt this knot in her stomach in a fight in a long time - since she was trained, as a matter of fact. She knew the feeling well. *I could be outmatched,* she thought. *Fuck it, it's do or die now.*

She tried for another strike. Reese caught her hand and gripped it.

"You're fast, but you're tired," Reese said. Her right hand was in Reese's grip. He was pushing her backward. She wasn't strong enough to counter the brute strength he showed. She was left with only one choice. She jolted her knee up and into Reese's groin.

He let out a strained noise but held his grip steadfast. He gave a final push, and she felt her back colliding with the wall. He got close enough so that that was not an opportunity she'd have again. "Are you two alright?" he asked without looking away from her.

"My hands might need looking at, but I'm fine," Luke used the nearby countertop to pull himself to his feet with a grunt. He hurried over to Vickie. "She's out," he said.

"I'm calling an ambulance," David could be heard over the line. "I guess I'll be the one to field all the pain in the ass bureaucracy. We'll probably get some police, too. They always send them with the paramedics."

"Come subdue her," Reese said. "I've got my hands full making sure she doesn't slither out of this."

Luke looked behind him back at Reese before turning back to Vickie. "I've got it," he said. He reached inside his jacket pocket and retrieved a pair of zip ties. He gripped her wrists and put them on before tightening them. He did the same to her feet. "She's not going anywhere now."

"We have a problem, guys," David said over the line.

"What now?" Reese asked. He slid Ai's feet out from under her, causing her to slide to the ground.

"There are people here, a lot of them, and they don't look too friendly. I think they work with Morgan, judging by how they're dressed," he said.

"Perfect timing," Luke said.

"Damn it." Reese turned and got low to the ground. He stepped over Vickie and got to a crawl once he was inside the living room. He crawled to the window and got up, grabbing the blinds and moving them to the side a little. "That's a lot of them," he said. "This could be bad." He raised a hand and gestured toward himself.

Luke took the sign and left Ai in the kitchen with Vickie. He took up a position on the other side of the window and looked for himself.

"You're telling me," David's voice said. "I'm out here with no weapons."

"What is happening?" Ai asked. She pushed herself along the ground like a caterpillar, trying to move toward the two men. "What is out there?"

"Who do you think?" Reese asked. "It's the armed and dangerous criminals you pissed off royally earlier with your suicidal stunt. Nice touch with the suicide vest. That takes balls."

"We just need to waste time," Luke said.

"What?" Reese asked.

"Emergency services will be here soon. I guarantee they won't want to stick around then. If we're lucky, they'll get rid of them for us."

"Then all of us go down to the station, and we waste four to six hours," Reese said.

"Better than being at the mortician's for four to six days before our burials."

"Untie me," Ai said. She tried to move closer to the men. She reached the carpet of the front room and tilted her neck up to look at her two captors. "I'll help you fight them. I swear on my family."

"Yeah right, lady," Reese said. He took another peek through the blinds. "Like I'm going to believe you after all this. You must think we're stupid. You'd shoot us and make a break for it. I wasn't born yesterday."

The conversation was interrupted by the sound of a phone ringing coming from a nearby table. The previously dark screen of Ai's phone showed a white screen with two icons, one green, and one red.

"I got this one," Luke said. He moved over and grabbed the phone before hitting the green button that looked like a phone. "I assume you're the angry men outside," he said. He kept his voice calm.

"What the hell?" Hector could be heard on the call. "Where the fuck is Ai Xiao?"

Luke looked down at the nearby small Chinese woman. "She's here. You want to talk to her?"

"Wait a second," Hector said before he paused.

"Here it comes," Luke said with a roll of his eyes.

"I know that voice." The Eureka moment Hector had was evident by his voice. "You're one of those two jerkoffs that was causing us trouble. Where's the boss?"

"Wouldn't you like to know? Now, do you want to talk to Ms. Xiao or not? I assume you want to tell her how angry you are at the little show she gave your men earlier. Pro tip for next time - don't divide explosive shipments into two parts, you idiots," he said.

"You inconsequential little shit," Hector's voice was cloaked in rage.

"Here, he wants to talk to you." Luke walked over the

short distance and lowered himself. He shoved the phone to her ear.

"It's me," she said. "You need to leave these people out of this. It's me you want."

"You're not getting out of this so easily," Reese said.

Luke raised one finger to Reese, interrupting his interjection.

"You think you can negotiate with me after the stunt you pulled earlier? You're a dead woman. You and any of your kin. I knew the boss shouldn't trust a Chinese girl. He just wouldn't listen."

"You don't want to mess with these men. I think they are federal law enforcement. If you kill them, you will be in prison for the rest of your life."

"Your concern is duly noted," Hector said. "Now put the other guy back on."

She motioned to Luke using a quick jerk of her head.

He lifted the phone and got back on the line. "You should take her advice, you know. She's the only one of you that knows who we are."

"Bullshit," Hector said. "You're not feds. You guys killed two of us."

"You're right," Luke said. His voice got serious, with a distinct edge to it. "We're not feds. We're something much worse. Your boss knows who we are, and he was a good little boy and squealed to us. Why do you think you all fell asleep, you idiot? He sold you out to get a nice sweet little deal for himself. Yet here you are playing the loyal fool, willing to go to war for a boss that sold you down the river to save his own skin."

"Any last words?" Hector asked.

"Yeah," Luke said. "How well do you boys like law

enforcement? They'll be here inside of a few minutes. We called them before you showed up."

"You're bluffing."

"Am I now?" Luke asked. "You want my honest advice? Get away from here now for you and your men's sake. If not, you're going to be getting three hots and a cot on the taxpayers' dime soon. That's if the local PD takes you in and doesn't fire when they see the weapons you're packing out there."

The line went dead with the final veiled threat.

"You call that stalling for time?" Reese hissed.

"It got him talking. What did you want me to do? Grovel and beg? His men would have charged in right then and there, thinking we were weak."

"Whatever," Reese said. "Get your shotgun and get over here. It looks like they're preparing for something out there. I want us to set up a crossfire. You're at that window over there."

"Untie me," Ai struggled against her bonds. "I beg of you. I will help you fend them off. I don't want to die any more than you do. It'd be foolish to run with bullets flying around."

"Not on your life, literally speaking." Reese stayed out of sight of the window and ran toward the stairs. He climbed up and grabbed the rifle leaning against the wall at the top of the stairs. He rushed back down to see Luke with his weapon where he assigned him earlier.

"I'll die like this," Ai moved as best she could on the floor. "Surely you'd rather keep me alive. At least put me somewhere out of the way if you won't let me help."

"Jesus, you bitch a lot," Reese said.

"You shouldn't use his name in vain." She found herself automatically chastising the irritated soldier.

"Says the terrorist planting bombs around town. Shut the hell up and wiggle your way back in the kitchen if you're so concerned."

"Maybe she could actually help," Luke said. He reached up and slid the window to the side with a low sliding sound. "What do we have to lose? If we die, we can't bring her in to question anyway."

"Listen to your smarter friend, please. I won't betray you. I swear on my family's lives. Three guns will be better than just two."

"Where am I?" Vickie asked from the nearby kitchen. She got to a sitting position and held her head. "Oh, my head feels like it's split open. What happened? Why are we contemplating freeing her when we just got her under control?" She stayed low and crawled over toward Luke to peek out the window. "So that's why. They're going around the side of the house. Free her," she said.

"You're God damn joking," Reese said. "She'll kill us all."

"She'll die with us if we don't."

"Swear to God above you won't betray us, Ms. Holier Than Thou," Luke said.

"I swear to the good Lord above. I just want to stay alive. I won't run or kill any of you," she said.

Vickie dug out a knife from her belt line and cut the zip ties. "Good enough for me. These are going back on later, to be clear. Now you're coming with me. We're defending the back of the house while the boys take care of the front."

The boys watched the girls head toward the back of the house.

"This was not my idea," Reese said. "I blame you and her if she kills us or escapes."

"I'd rather get an 'I told you so' than be dead," Luke said.

"Let's just focus on surviving before we start assigning blame. Hector's out there, and he's pissed."

"Because of you," Reese said.

"That's neither here nor there."

Their bickering was interrupted by a loud crack and the sound of glass shattering and falling at Luke's feet. He didn't waste time. He angled his boom stick out the window and squeezed the trigger in response.

There was no more talking. Every moment now was a struggle to stay alive. Both men stayed away from the window, only returning fire when no more lead projectiles were flying at them. Their aim had to count. They weren't getting many opportunities.

"Christ alive," David said over the call. "This is a war zone out here!"

"Keep your God damned head down," Reese screamed toward Luke across the room. He was on one knee, lowering his head even closer to the ground.

Amid the large influx of gunshots, more noise came from the back of the house. Luke could see Vickie in the small room in the back, while Reese could see Ai from his position.

She was posted up in the kitchen. She'd overturned the table and was taking cover behind it. She fired out the nearby window every so often.

Screaming filled the air when gunshots didn't overtake them. No one could really tell where they were coming from. Truthfully, they were probably coming from every direction as all four of them unleashed lead onto the men outside from their cover.

Reese crawled over to Luke's position and reached out to touch his arm, getting his attention. He pointed up the nearby stairs. He leaned in close and still had to yell to be heard over this racket. "I want you upstairs, now. You'll have a better vantage point, and their vans will be less useful as cover. You'll be able to cover all three of us from up there. There are windows on every side."

"Got it," Luke said. He stayed as low as he could and followed the order from the more experienced combatant. He reached the stairs and got to his feet before running up them without hesitation.

Reese bit his lip and looked up at the window. Bits of glass were still clinging onto their original position. The remainders had webbed and shattered long ago under the onslaught of lead being flung into them. Bits of those clear pieces littered the floor nearby, cutting his leg.

In between the volleys of projectiles being flung, they could hear voices either calling that they're reloading or calling for cover.

"They're getting close over here on this side!" Ai called out.

"David, tell Luke that he's needed on the south side - right now! This is imperative. We cannot get overrun in here, or we're all dead."

"Cover the south side, Luke!" David yelled into all their ears.

"I see it," he said. The sound of slugs firing off from upstairs accompanied nearby screams, some petrified out of fear, others in pain.

"Thanks," Ai called out.

"North side looks iffy."

"Get to the north side," David called out, acting as an intermediary. "Keep moving up there. Keep them guessing. The authorities should be here within a few minutes."

Reese reached down to his belt line and plucked a green grenade off his belt. "Here I thought I'd never find a use for you, beauty," he said. He backed off from the window and stood up, allowing a free range of motion. He primed the explosive and chucked it as close as he could manage to the barricade of vehicles outside that their attackers were using as cover. "Watch out, out there."

"What?" David asked, a moment before a thunderous explosion caused the earth to shake underneath them. Everything went silent, except for the ringing in everyone's ears from the constant racket. Reese tried to see what his tactic had accomplished, but all he could see was a cloud of dust obscuring his vision. He knew better than to stand in front of the window for long, however, as he got down again.

His curiosity was sated as the efficacy of his explosives soon made itself known. A stretch of human intestines came flying through the window, landing with a splat near his boots. "That answers that," he mumbled.

"They're trying to get in the back door, near the kitchen," Luke said. "I'm fending them off, but I can't keep them off the other sides at the same time."

"Hold the back door. Ai's busy with the sides," Reese said. "We cannot allow her to be flanked. Then we're all dead."

"Roger that," Luke said.

Reese fired a few more shots blindly out the window without exposing himself, but angling his arm up above.

The constant blaring of gunfire slowed to a halt. Voices could be heard outside along with a familiar sound - sirens.

"The cavalry's almost here, and they're going to be on edge," David said. "Don't do anything stupid, and let them take you in. They're not going to be taking any shit."

"They'll be scared coming onto this shit show," Reese said. "Let's not give them a reason to be trigger-happy."

Ai fired another shot out the window, causing a clear as day male scream.

"Let them retreat," Reese said. "They're running." He stood up and peeked through the tattered blinds.

"I understand," Ai said.

"They're retreating from the backyard too," Luke said.

"Same on the north side," Vickie said. She walked into the kitchen. "Everybody put your weapons away, and put your hands up when they enter the house. Do not make any sudden moves, and get on your bellies before they enter. We want them as calm as they can get given the circumstances. That goes double for our troublemaker here." She gripped Ai's shoulder tight. "Are you going to honor your word?"

"I helped you, didn't I?" She placed her gun back in her hip holster. "I honor my word."

"Everybody get ready to kiss carpet," Reese said. He turned away from the human remains and did as he said. He tossed his rifle to the side and got down on his stomach, along with everyone else downstairs.

Luke bounded down the stairs and saw what was happening, quickly following suit near Reese.

The siren was just outside, and the sound of an engine shutting off was heard. "Oh my Lord!" an obviously older officer called out after a door slammed shut outside. "We need backup out here. Right now."

"Settle in. This could be a while," David said. "They only sent one car out here, and he's not suicidal enough to head in there by himself after seeing the aftermath of your fight."

18

"Frankly, I'm surprised we're all in one cell," Luke said. He spread his legs apart as he leaned back on the bench of the communal cell. "I thought they separated male and female prisoners in county."

"They normally do," Vickie said. "I'm going to make an example of this police chief when I get my fucking phone call. He'll be lucky to still have a job, impeding us like this."

"We were just involved in a shooting in his nobody town," Luke said. "To be fair, we both know how many people claim to be high-ranking officials when they're desperate. The fact they allowed us to stay together amazes me, if nothing else."

"Truly amazing," Reese's sarcastic voice said. "It's not like we're trying to save the citizens of this town from bombs or anything. He's truly helping the populace by holding us here."

"Quit your bellyaching," Vickie said. "Now, when they give me my phone call, I'll get us out of here. They won't want to fuck with the higher ups."

"They'd better get us out of here if we want to disarm

those bombs in time. Speaking of which," Reese turned to Ai on the far side of the group on the bench. "When are they set to go off, mad bomber?"

"I cannot tell you except that it's soon," Ai said. Her voice was dejected. She was looking off into infinity as she spoke.

"Why even do this?" Luke asked. "What do you gain?"

"I doubt you care for my reasons," Ai said. She stared at the monotone gray floor. "Suffice it to say, I don't want to do this. I'm being forced to."

"Now that part I believe," Reese scoffed. "Your government isn't keen on taking no for an answer.

"You do not know the half of it," she said.

"You know many people will die if they go off. Right?" Luke leaned forward and looked at Ai. "Is it worth whatever they're holding over your head? I mean, you're not even in their country anymore. Why do their bidding when you're here?"

"The situation is more complicated than you know," Ai said. She planted her elbows on her knees and cradled her head in both hands. "It's not so simple as I'm doing their bidding because they'll kill me."

"Who cares why she did what she did?" Reese asked. "We should ask about where the bombs are."

"On the ride over, they said they hadn't found anything at the factory," Vickie said. "You must have hidden them well."

"Is the woman alright?" Ai asked.

"Woman?"

"I guess you don't know."

"Like you give a damn about a woman at that factory," Reese said. "Why worry when you'll just kill all of them tomorrow evening? Your act doesn't fool me."

"You've already made up your mind. I'd be a fool to argue with you."

"I can't believe we're sitting here on our ass when we should be doing our unique version of questioning this bitch," Reese said with a gentle elbow in Luke's side. "She'd talk within an hour I bet."

Luke didn't immediately answer, choosing instead to study Ai. "I don't know. She's an enigma. It might take longer."

"All the more reason whoever's in charge of this pissant town's police should be fired. He's endangering national security. This dumb bastard could endanger the entire war effort." He got up and walked over to the bars and wrapped his hands around two of them. "You hear that, you fool? You're going to cost us the war with this pissing contest of jurisdiction, or whatever you're doing."

"If you don't shut that racket up, you'll be sitting in there even longer," an older gentleman said.

"We deserve our phone call at least. That's all we want," Reese said.

"You'll get it soon enough. Now be quiet. You'll rile up the others."

"Sit back down," Vickie said.

Reese released the bars and balled his hands into fists. He turned and punched the air in a shadowboxing display. "Yes, boss woman," he said after a flurry of punches. He dropped to the floor and started doing push-ups.

"How can you be full of energy?" Luke asked. "After the night we've had, I'm tired."

"That was a drop in the bucket," Reese said. "Her countrymen don't give a crap if you're tired or not on the battlefield. You find energy where there was none, or you die. It's as simple as that for a grunt."

"Just do that and burn off some energy then," Vickie said. She leaned on Luke at her side. "I'll get this whole mess settled when I get my phone call, and we'll be out of here within an hour.

"You hope so, little lady," the same male voice that scolded Reese said from in front of their cell. He was a middle-aged man, and he had a smirk on his face. "One of you gets their call. Who's going first?"

Vickie stood up and stepped around Reese. "I am," she said.

"I don't have all night." He unlocked the door and swung it open. He waved her over. "Hurry it up," he said. He pointed down the hallway. "Stand right there."

Vickie followed the commands and tapped her foot while she waited for the man to close the cell door.

He led her down the hall and turned the corner to an empty hallway with doors on either side. "Is it true what they say?" he asked. "That you're with some higher-up on the federal level?"

"Someone's been talking, I see," Vickie said. "I guess they never heard of subtlety."

"It's true?"

"I'm not at liberty to speak about anything on this case. Just know this whole thing is inconvenient and dangerous. Tell your boss to believe every word my coworker is telling him, because it's true. You go do that."

"It's to the left here," he said while pointing ahead. A sign on the passing wall showed a picture of a phone with an arrow pointing toward the nearing turn.

They made the turn. There was a line of phones nearby. Each station had a divider to give some sense of privacy.

"You're on the far-left phone. Read the instructions carefully, Miss."

"Right." Vickie followed the instructions on the paper pinned beside the phone. She dialed the number and got ready.

"What is the nature of your call?" a male voice answered her.

"Business, logistics to be specific. I need assistance. My name is Vickie Jones."

"Please hold for one moment while I forward this call to the relevant client. Have a nice day." She heard music replace the voice.

"I sure hope they hurry," the guard said. "You only get five minutes, and you aren't saying much."

The music cut off abruptly. A different, much angrier male voice answered. "What the hell happened now? Why are you calling me at this damned hour? It better be good."

"I caught the suspect," she said. "There is just one hitch. During the apprehension, we were subdued by local authorities, and I just got my phone call."

"Where the fuck is Heron at? He's your partner, for Christ's sake."

"Injured, and he should be talking to them already; but we've been here for almost an hour now, and we're still locked up, sir."

"It's going to be a right pain in the ass to get the penal system to delete this call from their database. You know that?" He sighed. "Fine. I didn't realize you two would need so much babysitting."

"Thank you, sir," she said.

"Alright," the guard clapped his hands, "your time is up."

"I have to go - lockdown time." Vickie hung up and walked back toward the guard. "I'm ready, officer."

"Then come on," he said, leading them back toward the

communal cell. "I also take it you're with that guy that's pissing off the boss?"

"More than likely," Vickie said. "He annoys anyone around him."

"Rumor is he was trying to swing some big clearance, and people thought he was joking."

"What did you think?"

"I reserve judgement until I hear more than rumors, Ms. Jones."

"You heard that, huh? What happened to a private phone call?"

"Who said it was private?"

"Good point," she said.

They neared the cell, only to find the group already enthralled in a conversation.

"You should calm down and gather your energy." Luke was leaning against the wall with his eyes closed.

Reese paced back and forth in the confined space. "You waste time your way, and let me do mine."

"Alright then," Luke said.

"Back away from the door. Anyone else want a phone call, or is the one phone call to a higher power enough?" the guard asked as he unlocked it and swung the door open. He waited for Vickie to enter before closing it and locking it again with a loud click and sliding of metal.

"Are we good?" Reese asked.

"We're set," she said.

"Then I don't need one," he said, continuing to walk as she moved around him and over to Luke on the bench lining the room.

"Are you sure you're alright?" Luke wrapped an arm around her once she sat down. He took a closer look at Vickie. "You're bruised." He cringed, looking at the wound.

"You need medical attention," he said. "Can that be arranged, officer? Please?"

"I'll see what I can manage," he said. "Now, if you'll excuse me, I have work to do."

"You should stay awake," Luke said. "I think you might have a concussion. Though I am baffled how you got it on the top of your head."

"Acrobatic combat, or whatever passes for it," Reese said.

"I am perfectly fine." She pulled away from Luke. "Focus more on convincing our guest here to spill where and when those charges are set to go off. Use this time productively instead of complaining like children who got a detention."

"I insist you at least get it looked at by a doctor," Luke said. "We'll take care of this. Trust me. Let me do my job."

"Fine, you big crybaby. I'll get it looked at, but you'd better answer when I call."

"I will."

Rapid footsteps turned everyone's heads. "Whoever you called has got some pull, lady," the same guard from before rushed back to the cell. "You are all free to go, but you are going to be escorted to your location by two of my best and finest. Your boss said you needed all the help you could get, whatever that means."

"Let's just get moving," Vickie said.

Everyone stood up and followed her lead, except for Ai Xiao.

"That means now, princess," Vickie said. "Up and at it. If you're a big enough girl to do what you did, at least have the dignity to face the consequences," she said. She turned up her nose and walked out of the cell. She and Luke left first.

Reese walked over and grabbed Ai by the forearm. He gave a yank, pulling her up out of her seat, and placed her down on her feet. "Get up and walk. Now!"

She got to her feet and walked. She felt Reese's hand on her shoulder, guiding her. Her eyes never left the tiled floor below.

"Don't think the sad puppy dog eyes are going to work," Reese said, "not after what you've done."

"I don't deserve such a thing as forgiveness, that I know deep in my heart," she said. "I deserve death..."

19

Ai Xiao was tied to the chair in the dark room with her hands tied behind her. Luke and Reese were both in the dim room. The illusion of freedom from earlier had not lasted as long as she'd have liked. They'd forced her out of the police station and into a van she'd never seen before. In there she was handcuffed, blindfolded, and escorted to wherever this was. The guards that were sent from the jail had left, and she knew she was in for it then.

Luke took the blindfold off her. "Let's go over this again and see if we can't figure out where you planted those bombs."

"No matter how many times you ask me this, I cannot answer it," Ai said.

"I don't believe that excuse, Ms. Xiao," Luke said. "I've listened to what you've said. You don't strike me as the kind of woman who'd set explosives and leave them to explode, killing hundreds of innocent men and women. For goodness' sake, you chastised my partner for taking the Lord's name in vain. Something here does not add up."

"She could just be running out the clock," Reese said. "I

say we get physical and convince her to talk that way, like we normally would."

"Let's break this down further before we devolve into savages," Luke said.

"We can't waste time," Reese said. "Do it my way."

"After this line of questioning, we will if she doesn't budge. How about that?"

"Fine."

"Now, Ms. Xiao, answer me this." Luke pulled up a seat and lowered himself onto it, bringing him down to her eye level. He locked eyes with her and asked his question. "We talked to a Mr. Filipe Soto earlier this morning. Surely you remember him? He's a lovely pastor at the local church. He had a lot to say about a Ms. Lyn Song. We all know that's you. Do you remember Mr. Soto?"

"Of course I do," she said. "He was getting mugged by some kid when I got there. What about it?"

"We both know you didn't have to give him as much money as you did that night," Luke said. "As a matter of fact, I'm betting that's why you had to pull that stunt with Morgan's men. Am I correct in my hypothesis?"

She paused before answering. "Yes. It was a stupid mistake of mine to give that money away. It caused far more problems than anything else."

"Why did you do it?" Luke asked.

"Does this matter?" Reese asked. "Those bombs could go off in twenty minutes, and we're sitting here playing psychologist to a deranged terrorist playing nice."

"I don't know myself, if I'm being honest," Ai said.

"Okay. Let me ask a different question then - see if we can approach this differently. Why were you at the church in the first place?"

"You won't believe me even if I tell you, so why not? As

your angry friend here probably knows, China is not the freest nation in the world. Religious freedom is not at the top of their priority list. My family has been in the underground society that worships the one true God for close to four generations now. The official law says religious freedom is protected, but the reality paints a very different picture. It wasn't unusual that we'd receive news growing up that one of our own had disappeared mysteriously overnight."

"You're a practicing Christian then?" Luke asked.

"Sometimes I don't know anymore." She looked away from Luke. "At a very young age, my family and I were relocated. Someone had squealed on us, and they relocated my entire family to a new place to live. They claimed it was to defend us from any persecution, but most of the adults knew exactly what it was. When they saw my grades in school being as high as they were, they took me from my parents and trained me."

"I'm putting this together now," Luke said.

"They've held my entire family over my head my whole life. The threat was never direct, but I can read between the lines. They were saying, 'You'll do what we say, or your whole family will be killed.' I believe that threat more than anything."

"You're just trying to make us feel sorry for you," Reese said. "I'm not buying it."

"That is your choice to do so," Ai said.

"They're holding your family hostage," Luke said. "They trained you from a young age and then sent you over here?"

"As a college student, yes," she said. "They didn't activate me into service, as you know it, until after the war broke out officially, and there were boots on the ground for both sides."

"You worked with Zhang?"

"I know of the man, but I wouldn't ever call us friends. He had a penchant for the dramatic, as I recall."

Luke reached up and placed a hand over an old wound site that Zhang had given him with his blade. "That's the man I remember. He was also prideful, and it was his downfall. How long did you work with him?"

"Not long. The man was intolerable. It was his way or the highway. I stayed away from him as much as I was able. The last I heard, he was trying to earn some money in some small town and disappeared."

"He disappeared alright." Reese broke into a loud laugh. "He disappeared into a holding cell for the rest of his life, without any sunlight." His voice upped in volume as he marched over and planted both hands on the arms of her chair. He stared down at her with unflinching eyes. "Which is precisely what's going to happen to you if you don't tell us where the fucking bombs are so we can save innocent lives here, lady!"

Luke placed a hand on Reese's arm. "We're getting to that, I'm sure."

"You two know what happened to Zhang?" she asked.

"Know?" Reese asked. "Lady, we were the ones who caught him. Hell, you're talking to the man who fought him with brass knuckles."

"He used a long blade," Ai said. "Which of you used brass knuckles?"

"This man here." Reese placed a hand on Luke's shoulders. "You should know your situation. You can make this better for yourself or do what your partner would have."

"Getting back on track," Luke said, "we have your phone."

"You've seen the messages?"

"We saw pictures of your family," Luke said. "We couldn't access the document folder. Now, if you won't tell us where the bombs are, at least tell us how to enter that folder."

"The password is Salvation. Don't laugh."

"Far be it from me," Luke said, reaching into his pocket. "Going to need your unlocking password as well."

"Six zero one."

"Looks like God - interesting password." Luke input the numbers into the device, and it unlocked in his hands. "Good, that looks like the truth. Now let me enter the other and see what's inside."

"You think this is worthwhile?"

"Just trust me," Luke said. "Here we are," he said. "Oh, this is really classy. They weren't even subtle with it."

"No, they were not," Ai agreed with Luke. "I do what I have to for my family. What would either of you two do?"

Luke reached over and handed Reese the phone. "Check this out."

Reese snatched the device and looked at the screen. "Holding your family hostage, eh?"

"They will kill them if those bombs don't go off," she said. "Of that, I have no doubt in my heart."

"Please, Ms. Xiao," Luke leaned forward, "think of what your family would say."

"You do not know my family. Do not act as if you do," she said.

"I know if they're as devout as you claim, they wouldn't want you to trade hundreds of lives for their own."

"Yeah, like that one Bible saying," Reese said. "The needs of the many outweigh the needs of the few."

Luke and Ai both looked up at him with a blank stare.

"That's not a Bible saying, buddy. That's something else

entirely, though the meaning of it holds true here, none-theless." He returned his gaze to the restrained woman. "Do they know what you're doing to secure their safety?"

"No." Her voice was brittle now, nearly ready to break.

"If you told them, what do you think they would say?" Luke asked.

"They'd be ashamed of their daughter," she said. "You think I don't know that? I'm doing everything I can for them. It's all for them. I don't give a damn about this war or any of these political games they play with people's lives."

"Good, we're making progress," Luke said. "Now, where did you get the money for the deals with Dutch Morgan's goons? Is that from the home front as well?"

"No," she said. "That's one of your countrymen."

"Who?"

"His name is Eric Griswald," she said.

"You're shitting me," Reese said. He walked off and shook his head. "Griswald is involved in this?"

"Is this some big shot in your country?" she asked.

"Like you don't know," Reese said. "He's a prominent philanthropist that's acted the patriot this entire war. He's funding you and your ilk? Why? I don't believe it."

"My government, for all their faults, knows how to inspire loyalty through money. Just as they say, 'The love of money is the root of all evil'. They know how to exploit greed to their advantage. To my understanding, they've promised him contracts and given him an advance to prove their good will to the tune of a few hundred million.

"This is huge if it's true," Reese said. He returned to the pair and leaned against a nearby wall. He lifted his foot and pressed it against the wall while he crossed his arms in front of him.

"I appreciate your being forthright," Luke said. "So, we

have a traitor sending operatives like you cash as a favor to your country."

"There are probably others, but he's my contact when I need money. We work through an intermediary, and they get me the money that way."

"You said earlier that you think your parents would be ashamed of you. Do you know what would make them proud?"

"Please don't say what I think you're about to."

"If you stood up to evil and did what was right, they'd be proud of their daughter."

"Right before the bullets killed them. You're probably right."

"You think they'd want to know their lives had been bought and paid for with innocent workers' lives? I know they wouldn't," Luke said. "Please, do the right thing here, Ms. Xiao. I don't want to hurt you or have my friend do so. Let's all do the right and just thing here. You know deep down what you're doing is wrong. I know you do. I believe you know right from wrong. Please don't prove me wrong."

"You are asking me to let my family die," she said. That sentence finally did it. The tears she'd been holding back finally were unleashed. "I can't just tell you, or their deaths would be on me."

"It'd be better than having hundreds of innocents dying because of you, surely?" Luke asked. He reached out and gently laid a hand on her forearm. "Please, what would your family want? Look deep into yourself, and tell me what they'd want if they saw you right now."

She sat there quietly, letting the tears trail down her cheeks. She sniffled occasionally before speaking up. "They'd want me to tell you."

"I am sorry to put you in this position, but maybe you

should honor that wish. It's either that, or a lot of kids get made orphans because of you. You and I don't want that. Nobody here wants innocents hurt. Just tell us where the bombs are, and we can disarm them, saving countless lives."

"Assuming we're not too late playing therapist over here," Reese said.

"My friend thinks I'm a fool to even talk to you. Please prove him wrong," Luke said. "Shut his ass up so we don't have to listen to him."

He didn't get a laugh as he wanted as she turned quiet.

"I'm not asking just because it's my job. I hate seeing unnecessary death, and I have a feeling you do too," Luke said. "Have you ever killed anyone in this job yet?"

"No," she said between sniffles. "I made sure to never kill anyone. I might have broken a bone or two, but I never killed anyone."

"You're about to break that vow if you don't tell us. Think of it this way. You either kill hundreds of people, or they kill your family. Right? Why make yourself a killer to appease a group that doesn't give a shit about you or your family? Why lower yourself to their level? It frankly doesn't make much sense. Do what's right. You know deep inside what God's telling you to do."

"I do," she said with a nod of her head.

"Then do what you know to be right. This is a critical point in your life. You can either look back and be ashamed, or you can be proud of what you do here tonight. What's your choice?"

Reese looked at Luke and then over to Ai with a raised eyebrow, keeping his silence for now.

Ai gathered herself as best she could without the use of her hands and spoke. Her voice was stern and full of steel this time. "The bombs are at the processing plant, as you suspected. I hid them as best I could. One is inside an air duct on the second floor on the east side. One is under the catwalk on the west side on the first floor. The next is on the north side. I hid it behind a row of snack machines. The last is on the south side. It's not too far from the exit there. I put it in a janitor's closet. It's buried behind a bunch of cleaning supplies."

"Did we get all that?" Luke looked over his shoulder.

"I'll go check." Reese kicked off the wall and headed for the nearest door.

Luke returned his attention to Ai. "When are these set to go off? Are they soon? Please, you have to tell us."

"Tomorrow morning."

"I need specifics," Luke said. He was practically begging at this point. "Do we have time to call the bomb squad?"

"What time is it?"

Luke looked down at the watch on his left wrist. "It is now ten minutes after midnight."

"You have less than two hours. They go off at two a.m. Please," she looked him straight in the eyes, "you must let me out of this chair. I will help disarm them. I swear."

Reese threw the door open and entered again. "That's not happening, Eve. Now calm down,"

"Eve?" Luke asked.

"It's the only Bible female name I know. Alright? So, sue me."

"Quiet please," Luke rolled his eyes. "You know how to defuse these things?"

"I am the one who built them," she said. "Yes, I know how to dismantle them. I will do so if you only give me the opportunity. You'll never find them along with the second set without my help."

"Second set?" Reese's tone made his displeasure obvious. "For fuck's sake, lady." He stomped the ground. "You expect us to let an admitted terrorist out because you've seen the light? Screw off with that Saturday morning cartoon shit. You're lying through your teeth. You plan on utilizing us as a way to get your hands free, and when the moment is right, you'll bolt off into the night."

"That is always a possibility," Luke said with a tilt of his head. "You've played ball so far, but it's not my call to make." He looked over at Reese. "Go ask our friend what he wants us to do here."

"Who is this?"

"Nobody you need to know about," Reese said. He muttered to himself as he left the room.

"Excuse me, I'll leave you to your thoughts. For what my word is worth, I believe you did the right thing by telling us. I am so sorry for your situation." With those words, he got up and made for the door.

He could hear sobs now coming from Ai behind him. He felt a tightness in his throat, listening to the young woman now weeping openly behind him. He quickly exited the room and closed it behind him.

"What do you mean, you don't know?" Reese asked. "You're not seriously considering taking her up on that so-called offer, are you?"

David had his feet kicked up on a nearby table and leaned back in the chair. He reached up and took off the headset before placing it near the laptop. "Get back in there and get us the second batch's location. Right now."

"On it," Luke opened the door and yelled. "Where's the second set?"

"Different silos of corn outside the city limits!" her elevated voice said between gasps for breath.

Luke closed the door and looked at the two men in the small room. "So?"

"If there are two sets, we need to include the local bomb squad," David said. He lowered his feet to the hard concrete floor with care. "They won't be able to get everything, though. Not in this town. We'll have to head point on the other set. Now don't panic," he tried to reassure them.

"Don't panic?" Luke asked. "We're not bomb experts." He gestured to him and Reese. "I beat people or coerce them. It's way out of my league."

"Then use her," David said. "We still have the numbers advantage."

"She's lethal and unpredictable," Reese said.

The argument was interrupted by a ringtone from Luke's pocket. He pulled it out. "It's Vickie." He answered it.

"Put me on speaker," were her first words.

Luke did as she said. "You're on," he said.

"Where are we at?" Vickie asked.

"She gave us the place and time of the explosives, but this small place's disposal can only get to the food processing plant," David said.

Luke spoke up. "Some think we should use our newest acquisition to honor her vow of disarming the bombs."

"It's ludicrous," Reese said.

"She would know how to dismantle them," David said. "She made them, by her own admission."

"We should let her atone," Luke said. "Judging by every-thing I heard, she's quite the devout follower."

"It's an act," Reese said. "She just wants loose, and then we're holding the bag for letting her escape."

"The alternative is letting the silos blow," Vickie said. "Innocent farmers may be harmed. We will do everything in our power to prevent that. If that means using her, it's fair game. Take the phone in there. I want to talk to her and explain this whole thing."

"You're joking." Reese brought a hand up and rubbed his forehead. He lagged behind the group and finally caught up.

"Ms. Xiao," Vickie said. "Ow, be careful."

"Sorry, Ms. Jones," a male voice said. "It's quite the nasty injury you have here."

"Is that guy clear to hear any of this?" Reese asked.

"He's fine," Vickie said. "He knows who we work for, but little else. He knows what happens if he tells anyone, including his wife. That'd be endangering national security, and that's a serious charge. I made that very clear before I called."

"If my men there set you loose, you swear to help them dismantle the explosive that you yourself planted?"

"I will undo this evil I have sown, yes," Ai said. "I submit myself to whatever law enforcement agency you deem fit."

"Know that if you try to escape, their orders are to shoot to kill. Neither of us wants that. Do you understand the terms?"

"I do."

"Good," Vickie said. "First off, where is the first silo you're heading to?"

"It is to the north of town," Ai said.

"I can track this signal. I'll be there. Do not dismantle it until I get there. Is that understood? I can learn and speed this up. I won't be late. I'll run out of here half treated if I have to."

"That won't be necessary," the nurse's voice said. "I'm almost done."

"Now get busy, and keep this phone on. Every second we spend here chattering, the closer they are to going off." The call ended with that.

Luke closed the phone and put it away. "You heard her. Let's get her out of this."

"If you try anything," Reese pulled out his knife, holding it in front of her face for a moment, "then you die."

"That's not necessary," Luke said. He freed her hands out from behind the chair. He watched Reese bend down before cutting off the ones restraining her legs to the chair.

She waited for him to get up and back off before getting to her feet. She rubbed her wrists. "Let's move."

"You stay in front of me," Reese said.

"I am disarmed, sir," she said. She moved toward the door they had come in. "I intend none of you any harm."

"It's this way," Luke caught up with her and guided her through the building.

"I sure hope you're genuine, lady," Reese said from the back of the group. He had his hand perched above his knife as they walked.

"Allow me to prove myself."

20

"It's about time you all got here," Vickie said.

"How did you know we were headed here?" Luke asked, getting out of the driver's seat. He moved to the back seat where Reese and Ai sat. He threw the door open and let the pair get out.

"It's the nearest farm by your signal. Now," Vickie brushed past Luke and walked up to Ai. "You're with me. You're going to show me how to disarm these things."

"You have experience?" she asked.

"More than these two. We need at least two to disarm them all. The police chief said he's sending the squad to the plant with our information. How many silos did you set to blow?" She followed Ai toward the nearby silos beside the small house. She raised a hand toward the house.

A middle-aged couple stood behind a screen door and were staring at the group.

"Luke, go explain to the couple why we're here. Avoid using the word bomb. A panic will help no one. Reese, catch up. You're with us."

Reese jogged to catch up to the two women while Luke trudged over to the small house.

Reese caught up with the two women and kept Ai in his sights.

"Each of these two," Ai pointed up at the two mammoth structures. "They each have one around the back. Follow me," she said. She led the group around the circular buildings. Sure enough, once they got around to the back, they could see a small blinking device near the base.

"Here we are." She got to her knees. "Now watch carefully."

Reese wasn't paying attention to the specifics of what the woman in front of him was saying, knowing it was futile to try to understand the technical jargon. He did, however, watch her hands deftly move around the structure, explaining the build to Vickie.

"Make sure to not use a radio anywhere near these," she said. "The detonator I have should be inactive, but it's better to be safe. These are on a timer, all set at the same time. So long as you remember this, you should be able to take them offline."

Reese found his eyes glued to the flashing device beneath her hands on the cool grass below. He felt the wind blowing against his face while watching the two women work on something that, in his mind, could easily explode, killing everyone here with just a single mistake.

"Next, you need to remember this step or the whole thing goes up," Ai said. "I mean that literally. There will be a pressure wave carrying you and what's left of you up in the air."

"How delightfully descriptive." Vickie's attention was focused squarely on the explosives in front of her and Ai

Xiao's hands as they did their work. "Do not quit your day job to be a comedian now, Ms. Preacher."

"There is only one more safeguard you need to look out for."

Reese looked over to see Luke scratching the back of his head as he gestured over his shoulder with his thumb in their direction. *God knows what he's telling them*, he thought. He snapped back to attention with a shake of his head and returned his attention to Ai in front of him. He watched her grip a wire attached.

"With this," she pulled the wire free of its prior home, "it is disarmed," Ai said. The nearby screen showing a timer disappeared to a black screen. The blinking of the device ceased. "Now let's go to the next one, and we'll see how much you absorbed. I'll do it for safety's sake, though."

"I'd appreciate another run through." Vickie motioned for Reese to follow behind. She took the disarmed device from Ai and handed it to Reese. "Hold that. Don't worry, it's disarmed."

"So she says," Reese bobbled the catch but eventually kept it from falling to the grass below. He inspected the explosives in his grasp when he heard an unfamiliar sound.

Ai giggled. "I could have left right there, solider boy," she said, looking over her shoulder at him with a smile. "You're lucky I was telling the truth, or you'd both be screwed."

He quickly gripped the knife at his side until his knuckles were white. "You wouldn't have gotten far. Trust that."

"Now this time I'm going to ask you what to do and see if you remember, or if you'd have killed all of us. If you get more than one thing wrong, I insist on doing the rest by myself."

"Fine by me," Vickie said.

Reese watched the two find the next target. This time it was affixed high up on the silo, out of reach for normal people.

"They had a ladder nearby last time for some reason or another. Look around, it should still be here," Ai said.

"She'll look for it," Reese said, stopping Ai in her tracks. "You stay still right where I can see you."

Vickie ran around the silo until she came to the space between them. "I found it." She picked up the climbing aid and carried it back to the tense duo. She set it up underneath the flashing timer of death.

"This will be an excellent test." Ai climbed up until she was at the appropriate height. "First step?"

Reese looked around at their surroundings. The land was flat, and a barbed wire fence ran around the property for as far as the eye could see. Lines of trees were in the distance, obscuring further sight into the darkness. He held the ladder, keeping it steady.

"Keep it steady. I am beginning the process." She looked down at Reese.

"You just focus on that please," Reese said. "I've got you." He looked over and saw Luke approach. He waved him over and kept his voice low to not disturb the ladies once he got close enough. "What did you tell them about what we were doing and who we are?"

Luke leaned closer to Reese as the women continued their technical back and forth. "A bit of the truth, a bit of lies. I told them we were sent here to investigate a person reported being seen here. The dude was on board then. Apparently he called the night she planted those here. Are they almost done?" He looked up at Ai, working on the ladder.

"I'm more concerned with keeping my eyes on her and not on the blinking death surprise she set up," Reese said.

"So I see." Luke noticed Reese's hand near his weapon. "I don't think she'll run."

"No sense getting complacent."

"Can you two shut up?" Vickie asked in a sharp tone. "Next, you double check the power source."

"Very good."

"Then you finally unplug it from the package."

"I see you're a quick learner," Ai said. She plucked the wire out and the screen showing numbers shut down. "Good, you are ready to disarm them yourself now." She climbed down the ladder and hopped down to the grass as the group walked back to the cars. "Every single one of them are built like this one. Now all that remains is to get it done."

"You two can go with her," Vickie said. "I'll get the ones further south while you finish the ones up here."

"I'll go with you," Luke said.

Ai tossed the dismantled explosive over to Reese and tried to stifle another laugh at his alarmed wide eyes as he caught it.

"Up to Reese here. Can you handle her all on your own, big man?" Vickie asked as they walked.

"Of course I can," Reese said.

"Sure?" Luke asked.

"I never said I should, but I certainly could."

"Can't you take a hint?" Ai asked as the group passed the house toward the two vehicles they came in. "He's worried about her. They're obviously together. Stop being difficult and chaperone me, soldier boy."

"You've got quite the mouth on you now that you're helping us. You know that?" Reese asked.

"Maybe I'm in a better mood to be undoing this evil, or

maybe I joke to hide my tears." She opened the door on the car she arrived in and climbed into its back seat.

"She is so full of shit," Reese said, planting his hands on his hips.

"Best you go with him. He'll kill her otherwise," Vickie said. She wrapped her arms around Luke and leaned her head into his shoulder. "You can fuss over me all you want tonight after we finally get to bed."

"You're damned right I will." Luke returned the embrace before getting back in the driver's seat he arrived in. "Come on, everybody. We don't have all night. We have less than an hour to disarm how many more?"

"Four more bombs, three more locations," Ai said from the back seat with Reese..

21

"Pacing around isn't going to change anything," Reese said. "She's fine. We haven't seen any news reports of a random explosion on the south side of the city."

"We wouldn't until tomorrow morning anyway," Luke said.

"Let him walk," Ai said. "I would if I were him. You made him accompany you while babysitting instead of being with his woman."

"You be quiet." Reese pointed at her across the room. "Besides, why are you always annoying me and not him?"

"Because you are the guy who kept treating me like garbage and calling me a liar. He was the one who led me to make my choice to not murder countless innocents in some fool's errand to save my family. They wouldn't have wanted to be saved like that. I knew that from the beginning. Part of me couldn't accept them dying if I could do anything to stop it, though."

"I get that part," Reese said. "If my wife, Angela, or my daughter, Evangeline, was being held hostage, I know what I would do."

"Hold someone at gunpoint the first time you meet them?" Luke asked.

"Oh right, that was how we met, wasn't it?"

"He held your family for ransom?"

"Not so much," Luke said. "I was sent there to recover a debt he owed. Come to find out later it was because he illegally smuggled his wife into the country. However, because of his threatening to kill me on first sighting, Vickie tricked him into thinking she had explosives under his house and threatened to blow it up if he squeezed the trigger."

"Yet here you both are," Ai said. "You two seem friendly now."

"I ultimately helped him get his family back," Luke said. "This guy acts like an asshole, but deep down, he's not really that bad."

"The hell you say," Reese said. "I just get things done at the cost of other people's feelings is all that is. What are you going to do now, anyway?"

"I suppose that is up to your friends, David and Vickie. They are the leaders here, yes?" Ai asked. She sat at the foot of the bed and looked up at the muted television. "I would like to defect, but I don't even know if your country would take someone like me."

"Defect as in leave China forever?" Luke asked.

"It is as you say," she said. "Come tomorrow morning, I will have nothing left for me in China. My family will be executed, and I will be wanted for dead. My life there is over, through and through. Now my path is to make a life in this new land if given the chance."

"David, buddy." Reese raised his voice. "You almost done in there?"

The nearby bathroom door was closed and locked. "Give me a minute, for goodness' sake," his muffled voice said.

"I told you to not eat that pizza that was left over since yesterday," Reese laughed.

The bathroom door opened to reveal David holding a hand over his stomach with a disgruntled look on his face. "I wouldn't wish this on my worst enemy."

"How nice to hear," Ai said.

"Did you hear what she said while you were in there?" Luke asked from near the motel room's door. He peeked out of the blinds, searching for any sign of Vickie, to no avail.

"I was preoccupied with something else," David said. "What was it?" He gingerly sat down on one of the few remaining seats.

"Go for it, Ms. Xiao," Luke said. "Make your case. He's the man to talk to, not me or Reese here. We're just grunts."

"I know you and whatever organization you work for probably have plans to imprison me for the rest of my life, yes?" she asked.

"I do not know," David said. "We assumed you'd never help us with those bombs, and that you'd be like your old partner Zhang, fighting to the death. Why?"

"I have been thinking ever since we got back, and the word defect has been playing in my mind," she said. "I have nothing left for me in China. The government will soon kill my whole family for this, and I will be wanted for treason. I would like to start a new life, and the only option I see is to defect."

"Defection?" David asked. "That's above my paygrade. We might recommend that leadership consider it, but you'd have to know even if they accepted it, they'd require long-term service. I'm talking working with us for years or even decades. That's if they even consider it."

"I am prepared for that," she said.

"Yeah, well, don't go getting your hopes up."

Luke stayed looking out the window while this entire conversation was happening. He saw a familiar car pull into the motel parking lot and threw open the door. He slammed the door behind him and disappeared outside.

"Where's he going?" David asked.

"To embrace a loved one," Ai said. "He was worried she was dead, but she is a quick learner."

Reese tried to sneak to the window and peek out. He saw Luke envelop Vickie in a warm hug before he decided to stop watching and returned to his original seat in the cramped room. "It makes me miss Angela and Evangeline even more," he said.

The door opened. Vickie and Luke entered the room with a swagger.

"Mission accomplished, boys and girls," Vickie said with a proud smile on her face. "We got all the explosives disarmed and dismantled. No innocents will die via explosion in this small town because of us."

"That's nice and all, but what about pulling this out by the root?" Reese asked.

"Meaning?"

"Meaning we know who is funneling money to agents of China now, or at least one of them. Remember Eric Griswald?"

"I had almost forgotten." Vickie plopped down on the bed and laid down. "I was so busy with getting those bombs taken care of, I almost let it slip my mind."

"There's also the matter of what we're doing with Ms. Xiao here," Luke said.

"What about her?"

"I want to defect," Ai said in a matter-of-fact way. "I can divulge information that your agencies would love if a trade is required. I did not kill anyone on this operation, and I helped you stop the explosions. That should count for something."

"I do not need another headache." Vickie reached up and rubbed her temples. "You're serious? You're not just saying this to escape punishment? I ask because this is not a trivial thing you're suggesting. This is above even my or David's paygrade. The only thing we can do is make the case to the higher ups, and I have to say, lady, you have bad luck. We don't have the best rep."

"Hers is a clown show, and mine is checkered at best," David said.

"All I ask is that you try. It would be helpful to you and your country if they said yes."

"What does that mean?" Vickie sat up.

"It means I am willing to aid them. I can lead you to Eric Griswald and give you the evidence you'd need to make a big arrest. That should help with your reputation."

"You're referring to a tit for tat?" Vickie asked. "Yeah, that could work."

"She's got that look on her face again," Luke said.

"She's scheming alright," Reese said.

"It might work, but you'd have to give over every scrap of material you have," Vickie said, "including your phone. We can get you some photos printed out beforehand, but we'd definitely need it."

"Whatever has to be done," Ai said.

"As we were saying before your explosive entrance," Reese said. "What are we going to do about Eric Griswald?"

"We don't know it was him," Vickie said. "All we have is a known foreign agent's word against a countryman's word that most of the country thinks is an upstanding patriot. That's not actionable intelligence. We'd need more."

"I can get you direct evidence linking him with the

Chinese government." Ai reached into her pants pocket and pulled out her phone. "It's all on here."

"He gave you his first name?"

"No, he's not quite that stupid," Ai said. "He did use a phone, but wasn't very thorough in his cyber security. I simply back traced where the money came from and, sure enough, there was his name. It's all in this. Would this help with the defection?"

"More than you know. If you have actionable intel that could result in eliminating a traitor, it'd be an enormous show of goodwill. That, combined with the help in disarming the bombs, and I'd say you have an excellent shot, despite my reputation there. This might help both of us, as a matter of fact. Let me see that and corroborate this, if you don't mind."

Ai tossed Vickie the device. "Catch," she said.

Vickie caught it and got to work straight away with no further words. Her eyes were glued to the tiny screen as her thumbs moved nonstop.

"Look at her go," Reese's sarcastic voice said.

"What would even happen to this guy, Griswald, if this turns out to be true?" Luke asked. "He's a billionaire. The dude has pull with people in government, I'd bet. He's got to be insulated."

"If you're right," David said, "it would represent a huge national security threat where part of our government is compromised."

"It would be the story of the century," Vickie said. "That's what it would be. I know he schmoozes with members of the House and Senate. There's no telling how far this rot has permeated. Ah," she said, "here we are. Let me double check your homework, as they say." She looked over toward Luke and snapped her fingers. "Hand me my laptop if you would, babe," she said. "It's behind you charging."

Luke turned around and saw the device plugged into a small cord. He unplugged it and turned around, handing it over. "Here," he said.

"Thank you," she said. "Now it looks like you were paid via cryptocurrency. You back traced the transaction through the chain, I'm assuming."

"Then I checked the exchange he bought it from. With a little creative browsing, I discovered what credit card bought the funds that were in my newfound wallet. He didn't even bother mixing the transaction. It made it very easy."

"He probably had an aide do the dirty work," Reese said. "No rich man is going to do this tech nerd shit himself. No wonder it was sloppy."

"It's not like we can just travel halfway across the country and ask the guy ourselves," Luke said. "He lives in Los Angeles, I think."

"He loves to attend those Hollywood Premieres," Reese said. "My wife loves watching that tripe, and he's always there."

"Son of a bitch," Vickie said after a final key press. "You're correct," she said. "The credit card matches the one found on Eric's account. I see the Chinese taught you how to infiltrate sites at will, too."

"It's a nice skill to have. I admit it took me a little while to perfect it. Our internet is structured differently than yours."

"The good old great firewall of China," Reese said with a laugh. "What do we do now, boss lady?"

"I'm calling our handlers and reporting our progress is the first step. While I do that, I'll see what the higher ups want us to do with this information." She pulled out her phone. "Everyone stay quiet," she said. She dialed a number and cleared her throat.

"Hello," a familiar female voice said. "How can I direct your call?"

"I'm checking on the babysitter."

"What is the name?"

"Vickie Jones."

"Acknowledged," she said. "Please wait one moment for your call to be connected." The line cut off to elevator music.

"Babysitter?" Reese whispered to Luke.

Luke didn't answer with anything but a shrug and a single word. "Code?"

"Probably."

The line came to life with a sudden stop to the music. A male voice came on. "This had better be good news you're bringing me after all this crap," he said.

"Indeed it is," Vickie said. "We defused all the bombs she planted and saved the food processing plant. Well, the local bomb squad saved the local plant because of our intel, but we personally got rid of the explosives on the corn silos around the town."

"At least that's some good news."

"We also have a shocking development, sir."

"I don't like the sound of this," he said. "What on Earth are you yammering on about?"

"Ai Xiao wants to defect to our side, sir."

"Does she now?"

"She helped us defuse the bombs herself, sir, and she also told us where all of them were. She was instrumental in stopping all this senseless death. I believe she is genuine. She also has led us to a huge revelation."

"I'm getting tired of all these surprises. What is this one about?"

"We know who was paying her - an American. She says he's in league with China himself. They give him an order on who to pay, he does, and then they pay him. He's a stooge, but he's still working against us in wartime."

"Who is it, for goodness' sake?"

Vickie looked down at the laptop. "It's Eric Griswald."

The line went silent for a few moments. "Tell me you're joking."

"I am dead serious, sir," Vickie said. "This is huge. She gave us hard evidence linking him to this in good faith for her defection. She's serious about this."

"What evidence could you have to justify going after one of the biggest names in the country?"

"One, phone records. There's also the payment. We back traced it and, sure enough, it leads right back to Eric himself. There is no mistake, sir. I'm sending you the details, encrypted of course. It should be in your email within the next ten minutes after this call."

"How do you manage to take a good news report and still fill me with dread?"

"What do you want us to do?"

"Give me a minute. I'm thinking," he said. "You realize this will be both our asses if you're wrong, yes?"

"I am not wrong, sir," Vickie said. "I've done the digging myself. I've verified it. You know how good I am at back tracing."

"Son of a whore," he said. "Alright, listen up. I want you and your little merry band to go to Los Angeles and find someplace to stay. Do not, for the love of all that is good, do anything. I repeat, do nothing until I call and give you official orders. This is above my head. I have to take this to my boss, and he probably to his. Do you understand me? Be ready, but do not engage or even breathe in his direction without my say so."

"I understand, sir. Does that include Ms. Xiao?"

"She helped you with the bombs, she gave you the evidence, and she wants to defect," he said. "She's not going to run. Bring her along. I can leverage that with the higher ups and try to push that through. Have her help you however she can."

"Alright then," Vickie said. "Have a great day, sir."

"Fuck off. You made my life ten times worse with this phone call." He paused for a moment. "Great job, agent." The line went dead with that compliment.

"I think that's good news," Vickie said. "He said you're coming with us, and that it'd help strengthen his case on convincing the higher ups that you're serious and not working as a double agent. We have an even bigger job now, boys and girls, as the consequence."

"Woe is me," David said. "Another job with you animals?"

"I'd hate to be bored," Reese said. "Are we going after the son of a bitch?"

"Kind of," Vickie said. "Our orders from on high dictate that we drive to Los Angeles and wait for further orders. He doesn't have the authority to call for such an operation. He's bringing it to the higher ups, and he'll call us soon he said."

"Nice to see hurry up and wait infiltrated your organization too. Here I thought it was only the grunts and jarheads that had to put up with it."

"LA?" Luke asked. "That'll be a nice long drive. How are we splitting up the car rides?"

"I'll give Reese here a break. I'll drive with him. You take Ai here, darling. You two seem to get along well enough. As for room arrangements, we're going back to the high school days. Boys in one room, girls in the other. This is the girls' room now, so you two get your crap and get to the boys'. We leave at five in the morning. Do not be late."

"You heard her," Luke pushed Reese, causing him to take a step back. "You've got a new roomie."

"Joy is me," Reese said.

"Wait, you were including my car in those calculations, weren't you?" David asked. "I don't want someone else driving my car."

"It's happening. Deal with it," was all Vickie said.

22

"At least our accommodations in this place are pretty swanky," Reese said from the glass table in the room's corner. Luke sat across from him, with Vickie sitting next to him. Ai was standing beside the large sliding glass door leading to the balcony. The metropolis outside looked small from their elevated room.

"We're just to sit here?" Luke asked. "Where is David anyway?"

"He's too good to be in here with us. He's getting a massage in that spa this place has. To answer your question- that was the orders," Vickie said. She reached over and poked Luke with the eraser of her pencil. Leaning over, she showed him the book in her hand. "What's eight down?"

"Betting on the first and second place in a horse race," Luke said. "I believe that's exacta. It fits."

"Thank you." She scribbled the answer in the boxes.

"Shouldn't you know that?" Reese asked. "You taught him how to collect, didn't you? It's a family business to know gambling, I'd have thought." He looked down at the tabletop filled with phones in front of their respective owners and looked at his own reflection on the glass table. "I mean, your dad owns a betting place."

"A girl forgets things when she picks up dozens of new skills." Vickie paid him no attention, still looking at the puzzle book in her left hand.

Ai pushed the glass door to the side and stepped out onto the balcony.

The noise of it opening and closing caught everyone's attention. They saw her leaning against the rail, staring out over the bustling mass of humanity below.

"Poor girl," Luke said. "She's all alone in the world now."

"Yeah," Vickie said.

Reese didn't add to the exchange, only looking at her. His eyes softened. He pushed his seat out from the table and got up.

Luke saw Reese was staring at Ai before glancing over at the obviously downcast woman outside. He knew better than to speak or goad his friend right now.

Without words, Reese walked over to the glass door and went outside. He kept his distance but stood at her side. He placed his hand on the rail and looked away. "Am I intruding?"

"I'd like to be alone right now," she said. "I'll need to get used to it anyway."

"Look, I noticed that you've followed through with what you said before. I'm sorry for how I treated you, but I had my reasons."

"I was a dangerous threat to your countrymen and women," Ai said. "You were not wrong. I was a threat. Not anymore."

"I just wanted to say that," he said. "If this all pans out, do you have any plans on where you're going to stay?"

"I had not thought that far ahead," she said. "I was more

concerned with proving my worth for your group. I assume you're CIA by the way. Am I correct?"

"Me personally? No, I'm more of a boots on the ground kind of guy. No, I'm just an army grunt. I do what I'm told."

"You've killed many in this elongated war, I assume?" she asked. "It is ridiculous the number of lives lost that this war has caused."

"War has always been this way," Reese said. He took a step back from the rail. "Some think the more lives lost, the quicker the end of war comes. I think General Sherman in the civil war said that or something to that effect. I don't know if I believe that, but I have the feeling this war is coming to an end soon."

"I hope you're right, Mr.?"

"My name is Reese Hilton."

"In the grand scheme of my life, the war is no longer even something I'm concerned about if I'm honest," Ai said. "I'm more concerned with what's going to happen to me."

"I get that," Reese said. "If I'm correct, and I might not be," he said, "the way I understand it is you'd be doing similar things but for us. I don't know how free you'd be, but you wouldn't be locked away, rotting."

"I appreciate the attempt at cheering me up, Mr. Hilton, but it didn't work."

"I didn't figure it would." He turned and reached for the door. He opened it and came back to the two other occupants ogling him. "What?" he asked after slamming the door shut. "I just wanted some fresh air is all," he said. "I'm getting a shower while we wait." He gathered another outfit from the already opened suitcase on the other bed in the room. He stormed off into a room down the hall.

"I won the bet," Luke said. "You owe me."

"You'll get your winnings later," Vickie said. The sound

of nearby water falling became audible. "The call or text should come soon. He's always been prompt. It's his thing."

"I'm sure the paper pushers are really considering this," Luke said. "The man's net worth is more than I can imagine. Even if we get the go ahead, they could never suspect it was us, or we're fucked. They're not going to cover for us."

"We just wouldn't screw up. Whether they want him for questioning or if it's a more permanent solution impacts how we'll approach this."

"Isn't that illegal even for them?"

"It's adorable how you think that matters to them in the least, sweet thing," she said. She reached over and grazed his cheek with the palm of her hand. She gave him a playful, gentle slap to the face. "It'll be fine."

"Alright," Luke said. "You know that political landscape better than I do. We'll do it your way."

The phone nearest Vickie vibrated on the glass table. She grabbed it in a flash and read the message aloud. "You have authority."

"Authority?"

"It's code," Vickie said. "We have authority to kill him; and, in fact, are being ordered to do so. Apparently, selling out your country still has the death penalty. Who'd have known?"

"This isn't going to be easy," Luke said. "Someone that rich probably has private security."

"It was never going to be easy," she said. "Thankfully, we received another operator." She looked over toward Ai, still out on the balcony. "She could have insights that we do not. You never know."

"She's never killed anyone. You're aware, yes?"

"She won't have to. We have someone here that's emotionally constipated that fills that need."

"Reese?"

"Who else? He's our muscle here. We just need to get him in position and get him out. We're a team here, sweetness. We'll come up with a plan when he's out of the shower and include Ms. Xiao. For now," she said, "we'll do some research on where he is, where he frequents, and brainstorm how we'll do it, so we have something to offer when the time comes."

That night in the hotel room...

"How long do we have to do this?" Reese asked.

"No time limit, but we have to remain undetected, or we'll be disavowed and screwed sideways in the legal system. We have no protection from the men upstairs on this one. That's according to the code we received earlier. If we'd had a time limit, there would have been a second sentence," Vickie said. "Now we've been doing some research on our target." She placed two stacks of papers on the table as Luke did the same. "Everybody take one of each and familiarize yourself with him."

Ai, David, and Reese reached out and took one of each page.

"This guy has crazy private security," Reese said. "Impervious Shield is no joke. I know a guy who got a job there after he got dishonorably discharged for smuggling back home."

"Sounds like they hire real winners," Ai said.

"He was the best fighter I'd ever seen with my two eyes. The man did not know fear, and he did not miss. Do not mistake his morality for his skill, Ms. Xiao."

"Noted," she said.

"He's not lying," David said. He reached down below the

table and tried to scratch the cast in futility before abandoning it. "These guys are ex-military special forces - well, a lot of them anyway. The ones who want nothing but a pay day for their skill set."

"His security is beefy to be sure," Vickie said. "So why don't we avoid them entirely?"

"How so? These are not guys who slip up and leave him exposed. He is under watch from every angle when he is in public, and I bet you anything they keep men on his house premises," Reese said.

"We do not have to be quiet, though we do have to remain unfound. That gives us options," she said.

"You know, I've been wondering something," Luke said. "Do you think his security knows what he's doing?"

"Irrelevant," Vickie said. "We're to work around them."

"Quite the optimist I see," Reese said. "I'm sure these guys have cameras everywhere. If any of them go down, hell rains down, and they will swarm the place with men. These guys are the cream of the crop when it comes to security. Even if we have your little spy toys, we'd have to pull everything off perfectly."

"Then we'll do that," Ai said. "I can help with this more than you give me credit for. If you need someone to do things quietly, I'm your girl."

"First, we need to decide where we're doing this," Reese said. "Our choices look like it's either his Beverly Hills mansion or when he's out in public. I don't relish trying to escape from police in a metropolis like this, so we either need distance or a foolproof way of poisoning him, as I see it."

"A rifle would work, but we couldn't guarantee a civilian wouldn't get winged," Ai said. "All we need to do is get close enough to jab him with a needle and disappear into a crowd. It says here he's going to a newly opened nightclub tomorrow night. That's the place, if you ask me."

"His men will be all over the place," Reese said. "They'd never leave him alone in such a crowded dark space."

"Luckily," Ai said, "I'm just a tipsy girl who wants to get lucky with such a rich young stud like him. He'll make his guards let me through. I can play the drunk party girl better than you give me credit for. I just get close, jab him when I pull him in for a hug, and then excuse myself to go to the little girl's room. Before his men realize what's happening, I'm long gone. As for my face on cameras, leave that to me. I have something from my country that will help with that."

"What's that?" Vickie asked.

"You'll see soon enough. Don't you laugh when you see it, though."

"Now I can't wait to see this," Luke said.

"Go ahead," Vickie said. "Go gather this thing that will keep your face obscured from cameras. You have it with you?"

"It's in my suitcase that one of your men packed for me. Might I add, it was all just thrown in. Not one thing was folded. It's almost like they didn't care."

"They probably didn't."

"Be right back with it." She got up and hurried off to an adjoining room.

"It's not a thing where you can wear a device and have it blur your face, is it?" Reese asked.

"No, that's not a thing," Vickie said.

They heard Ai call out from the other room. "I found it. Let me get it ready."

"Are we alright with letting her do it?" Reese asked. He leaned forward toward the center of the table. The others followed suit. He lowered his voice. "She doesn't enjoy killing people, right? Should we put that on her?"

"How awfully nice of you, Mr. Hilton, concerning yourself with her wellbeing," Vickie said. "I can't do it. I'm legally not even supposed to be helping with all this. It's all unofficial. I cannot be the one to do it. Neither of you two would get anywhere close to the guy in a nightclub, and we all know a direct assault on his compound is a suicide mission. It's our only choice here."

"Here it is," Ai said, opening the door. She stood there in a bright pink hoodie with exaggerated cat ears sitting atop it. The sleeves had a graphic of cartoonish fur. A mask of a digital depiction of a cat's face and whiskers covered her face. She lifted a fist and imitated a cat. "Nya, what do you think?"

The three sat there in silence, taking in the absurdity in front of them.

"I want to go back in time to my sixteen-year-old self and bash his head in," Reese said before he burst into uncontrollable laughter.

"This is what kids wear nowadays," she said. She lowered both her fists to her side and narrowed her eyes at the laughing fit Reese was having at her expense. "I'll be able to get close like this. Trust me. The weirder I look, the more I'll fit in with those hipsters."

"With all due respect, Ms. Xiao," Luke was visibly trying to hold in his laughter, but was sadly failing. "I just can't," he said.

"He's trying to say you look like a fool," Vickie said.

"Where did you even get that?" Luke asked.

"I bought it online. Look, I can pass by the cameras and get inside. I head to the bathroom, change into something a bit more dignified, and then I can approach their party. It'll be easy. I'll just be another young patron that was in the establishment when I leave before he dies."

"Where would we be during this, exactly?" Luke asked. "You're not going in there alone."

"A pair of girls going into a club together would be less conspicuous than a lone one," Ai said. "Come on, who doesn't like a good girls' night out? It's either that, or I take one of the guys here as my," she raised her hands and air quoted, 'date for the night'."

"If it's about getting close to the guy, two women have a much better chance of getting close. Rich spoiled jerks like this love having threesomes, foursomes, and any kind of orgy. He'll let you in," Reese said.

"Because you know so much about that scene," Vickie said. "I am not wearing anything like that abomination." She pointed at Ai.

"Surely America doesn't make such squeamish agents?" Ai raised a finger to her mouth and tried to act cute. "Right? It's just some fabric and some acting. We can be two coming of age girls having a big night on the town. Picture it with me." She pranced around in an animated style in the lavish room. As she turned, it showed that the hoodie even had a matching cat tail accessory behind her.

"You going to take that from her?" Luke asked. "I believe you could do it."

"Of course I could," Vickie said.

"Good, then it's settled," Ai said. She pulled down the mask to reveal a smug smirk. "We need to go shopping right now and get you outfitted for tomorrow night. You two boys get up, because you need a makeover too. Those clothes you have won't work for what I have in mind. We also need to go to the drugstore and mix up a little concoction to get this done. You have money, yes?"

"It's in my purse here." Vickie barely had time to grab her purse before she was dragged out of her seat by the animated Ai. She pulled her through the hotel room and eventually the pair exited via the door heading outside.

"She's quite good at hiding those emotions," Luke said. "The fact she can even crack a smile shows her inner strength."

"I wouldn't even be able to get out of bed if my family had died this morning, and she's here just trying her best."

"If I didn't know better, I'd say you were starting to like her," Luke said.

"Me?" Reese asked. He looked over toward the glass door leading to the balcony where he'd shared a chat with her earlier. "How old was she, anyway?"

"She's like twenty-two," Luke said. "Why do you want to know that?"

"Nothing creepy or anything like that. I just wondered where her sense of blending in came from. I suppose I am getting older if that's the style the younger generation considers hip. She did say hipsters, didn't she?"

Luke grabbed a nearby bottle of water and unscrewed the top before taking a good, long drink. He placed it down. "I don't know what that get up was, and I'm just fine living my life that way."

"I dread when Evangeline gets older. Is that what she's going to dress like, or will it be even worse?"

"Probably worse. Now let's go catch up to them, or we'll never hear the end of it."

"Joy of joys awaits me..."

23

Luke and Reese had giant smiles on their faces as they looked at the two young female spies. Apparently, Ai had not been content to simply copy what she had donned before they left for poor Vickie. She had gone above and beyond with both of their apparel in the past motif she'd so proudly displayed the previous day.

Both girls were wearing oversized hoodies with the same ears on top. Now Ai's was a dark blue color and Vickie's was a rich purple. Both had a mask that had a digital depiction of a cute emoji along with some whiskers. The pants, however, were brand new. There were color matching socks that went up past their knees, almost to their matching miniskirts. Even the shoes were new and the same color.

The men comparatively had gotten off easy. They wore jeans, and their shirts were replaced with stylish brand-named ones. They looked slightly different compared to before as opposed to the other two.

"Do you like it?" Ai asked. "We had an argument about who should represent which color. I told her that blue would be better for the likely candidate."

"Does that actually matter?" Reese asked. He shifted his weight and placed a palm on the nearby wall.

"Of course it matters," Ai said.

"It does not," Vickie said. Her voice was docile, almost as if she'd had this argument a dozen times the previous day.

"You be quiet," Ai said with a quick turn. "The one who gets picked by our Eric will be the one to jab him. I even taught her all the movements using a pen."

"It's not like the movements are all that complicated," she said.

"No, but fumble even a little and the whole thing goes to pot. If you drop the syringe and they see it, it all goes tits up. Are you getting me? Hopefully he'll pick me. I'm good with my hands and quick on my feet."

"So, where would you want us tonight?" Reese asked, gesturing to himself and Luke.

"I doubt you two will even be able to get inside," Ai said. "This place is high end, and it takes a certain dress code."

"Like you'd know," Reese said.

"I was here two months ago, buddy," she said. "I know the local club scene. You'd be amazed at what you can find if you lurk in the dark areas of this place's night life."

"Was that before or after you went north to Humboldt and exploded a bunch of weed farms?" Reese asked.

"Weed farms? Who grows weeds on purpose?" Ai looked genuinely confused. "I was at the ports disrupting ships delivering food across the ocean. Well, to be more precise, I was sabotaging them, so they were not seaworthy. You'd be amazed at what you can accomplish with an O2 tank, a dive suit, and some explosives. I remember because it was just after...." Her eyes fell to the ground and her voice grew softer. "It was just after my mom's birthday."

"I think we've missed the cannabis joke here, so let's

move on," Vickie said. "You know this place and its fashion atrocities of the younger crowd, so let's focus on the logistics - the men behind the action, so to say."

"Mr. David can probably oversee the technological side from a nearby location," Ai said. "I say we have Reese and Luke go in before us and blend in as best they can. We can use a distraction at the right time, and that'll enable us to get it done."

"You want us to put on a show?" Luke asked. "Would staging a fight do the trick?"

"So long as you do it relatively near Griswald, I don't see why it wouldn't. His bodyguards are going to swarm you when you do. Try throwing something nearby. That'll get them good and pissed."

"I always love pissing off trained bodyguards that can kill me inside of a second," Luke said. "We can handle that, right?"

"Obviously," Reese said. "I'm more worried about you two. How are you two going to get near him? You know there's going to be gaggles of young women who want to get near him. It's going to be survival of the fittest."

"It'll be fine," Vickie said. "We can be very convincing. It won't be so bad."

"He has money?" Reese asked. "Yeah, it will. Mark my words now."

"He's right," Ai said.

"You were supposed to call that sexist," Vickie said.

"Why? If he's right, why lie and dance around the truth?"

"I love that honesty," Luke said with a shake of his head.

"You have a lot to learn about being a modern American woman."

"What is a woman according to your modern ideas then?

Why lie and make things more complicated? I don't understand this place sometimes."

Reese couldn't hide his grin. "Don't ask that question. It boggles some idiots' minds. They can't explain it. Let's get off of politics and focus on the job, boys and girls."

"David," Vickie said, "I assume you're still comfortable performing the digital overwatch role?"

David reached out toward Luke, who grabbed his hand and pulled him up to a standing position. "It's like riding a bike. You never forget."

"I'm going to trust that you also remember how to turn off cameras. You're going to need to take the one that overlooks Griswald's position out when we get there. We'll have to take our masks off if we want to flirt as much as we'll need to, and we don't need to be seen on camera."

"Loop or full-on crash?"

"Crash," Vickie said. "With all the people dancing, the DJ, and everything else, a loop wouldn't work. Now worst-case scenario, people," she said. "If everything falls apart, we will not force this. We can try again tomorrow. Do not force anything. That's how you get caught, and then we're all fucked. Is that understood?"

"Crystal clear," Luke said.

"I get it," Reese said.

"Yes," Ai said.

"Good," Vickie said. "You two will get a signal from David on when to cause the distraction. Make sure you only tell them to when we're close to him. I mean, at his side close," she said.

"I think I can handle that, boss," David said. "I just wish I was going in with all of you. I could use a drink and some music."

"Not with that knee, you're not," Vickie said.

"Sorry about that, by the way," Ai said with a wince. "I was just trying to get away and didn't want to kill you. You know how it is."

"Sure, I do," David said. "That doesn't mean I have to like it, though. I just wish you'd hit me in the chest and made me lose my breath or something. This makes getting around tough."

"Stop rehashing the past and focus on the here and now," Reese said. "We have the easy job. I do not envy you two ladies. I think you're underestimating how many young nubile women the dude is going to have clawing to be at his side. He doesn't go out in public often, and he's going to be swarmed."

"You two have the syringe on you, yes?" Ai asked.

"Why did you give these to us, exactly?" Luke asked, reaching into his overcoat pocket and pulling out a covered syringe.

"Call it a contingency," she said.

"Contingency for what?"

"In case he's gay or bisexual," Ai said, as if this was as simple as a walk in the park.

"No one knows his preferences," Vickie said. "It's not like the dude lives on social media and rambles about such nonsensical things."

"He could be searching for a husbando and not a waifu," Ai said. "We need you two to be ready."

"Was that English?" Reese asked.

"None of you know internet slang? How old are all of you?"

"Too old to know what those mean, though I have a good guess," Luke said.

"Let's get out of here," Vickie said. "The club opens in

five minutes. We need to get there before he does so we can scope out where he sits."

Later in a very loud, dark club...

Luke looked over at the bartender at the busy bar. "This brings back memories," he said.

Reese leaned over and almost yelled in his ear. "What was that? I can't hear anything in here with this noise." The constant bass being blasted by the club music nearly drowned his voice out. Not too far away was an enormous swarm of people on the dance floor, twisting, moving, and otherwise contorting their bodies to the beat of the music.

"Nothing important," Luke said loud enough for Reese to hear.

"This place is popping off," Reese said, taking a swig from the glass he had ordered previously.

"Don't drink too much now, buddy. You want to remember tonight, right? The grand opening of the hottest new club in the city doesn't happen every day."

"I'll be fine, you wuss." Reese upended the drink and let out a breath. "It's my only drink for the night. Stop worrying."

Luke looked up to the second floor of the large room and could see two outlines up there. One wore blue and the other purple. His gaze fell to the stairwell below. It had a large man standing in front of it. A small sign to his side read 'VIP area'. He leaned over to Reese and talked into his ear. "We need to figure out a way to get up to the VIP area. I'd bet anything that's where he'll be."

"We could always pay," Reese said. "That's the standard way of doing it, you know."

"Do you have a spare ten grand? Because I do not," Luke said.

"Then we'll have to get creative."

"Good luck with that," David said into their ears. "I'm looking at all the security planted around the place. They have every entrance to the upper floor guarded."

"How many have you seen?"

"The main stairwell, for one," David said.

"Look at the others and stop being lazy," Reese said.

"I don't have to take orders from you," David said.

"Do it," Vickie's voice said.

"Fine. Alright already," David said. "I was going to. I was just giving him a hard time. You know me."

"I wish I didn't," Reese said.

"Okay. I found a way up there, but you two are not going to like it."

"Lay it on us," Luke said. He looked over to a young man who was staring at him. "Can I help you?"

"You're cute," he said with a smile.

"Uh, thanks," Luke said. He turned back to Reese.

"Is this your boyfriend?" he asked. "Sorry, I didn't know." The young man took the drink and wandered off from the bar.

"Son of a bitch," Reese said.

"Let it go," Luke said. "When in Rome, do as the Romans do - even if it annoys you. Besides, I'm secure enough in my sexuality. Aren't you?"

"Do not ever ask me a damned thing about my sexuality unless your name is Angela."

"How do we get up there?"

"You two need to head to the north side of the room," David said.

Luke looked over. "That's near where the DJ is set up.

We can't get up there. Are you nuts? We'd be tackled before we got anywhere near it."

"I didn't say walk up to the damned DJ. I said go to the north side. There's a stairwell over there leading up that doesn't lead to the VIP area. It doesn't connect directly, but you can still get there if you're brave enough."

Luke looked over and saw the stairwell leading up and followed its path upward. He noticed that the railing and the VIP railing area were very close together, maybe only a few feet. The only catch was the chasm below if they failed the jump. They'd land near the DJ in full view of everyone should they fall.

"You're kidding." Reese was now following the line of thought as he stared up at the gap between the safety rails. "We'd be escorted off the premises if we tried that stunt."

"Then use that as the distraction if you like," Vickie said.

"They would take that seriously," Reese said. "Two guys jumping over the railing toward their client."

"We got our distraction then," Luke said. "Two drunk guys being idiots and playing Parkour simulator in their nightclub. Guess I'll need a drink or two so I can sell this."

"Check it out," Reese patted Luke's shoulder. He pointed toward the front door of the club.

Luke turned and looked where he directed. A large group of tough-looking men were surrounding someone they couldn't see. "That's him alright it looks like." The group pushed their way toward the stairwell leading to the VIP area in a hurry.

They could hear a few of the nearby patrons who raised their voices. "Oh my God," a female voice slurred. "That's him."

"He knows how to make an entrance, that's for sure,"

Reese said as he watched the bodyguards push back the throngs of people now flooding their group.

"Get ready up there," Luke whispered.

"We see it," Vickie said.

The group of men pushed through the crowd until they got to the VIP stairwell. The guard stepped to the side after a brief exchange from the lead guard. The group they escaped from were stopped by the guard after they'd passed.

"That poor bastard has quite the job," Reese said. "Come on, let's get a better view," he said.

Luke walked with Reese away from the bar and toward the stairwell that David had pointed out earlier. They reached the top and saw the night club from a whole new vantage point. It was much easier to see Vickie and Ai from up here without appearing suspicious. There weren't nearly so many people on this upper level.

The pair meandered over to the railing and looked down at the place side by side.

"Let's see how those two get on. We may as well get comfortable," Reese said. He leaned on the guardrail and looked down at the mass of likely intoxicated youth below.

With the girls...

"Get your game face on," Vickie said. "We need to make our approach."

"Let me take the lead on this," Ai said. "I can get in there - maybe both of us. Just play along and do as I do. If he's straight, he'll want us in there."

"I'll believe it when I see it. Most guys don't want desperate women to sleep with, especially when they have that much money."

"I didn't say go over and flash them. Now let's go before

too many women get the same idea. I can see some already eyeing him and trying to figure out their approach. We need to seize this opportunity while we can." She looked over at the group sitting down at a large, lavish table.

"You're lead on this, so I'm with you," Vickie said.

"Now take my hand." Ai extended a hand toward Vickie. "Just trust me."

Vickie reached forward and grabbed her small hand before feeling herself getting dragged off in Griswald's direction. "Let's do this."

As they approached the table, a large man walked in front of them with his open palm out toward the women. "I'm sorry, ladies. This is a private table. I advise you to move along and enjoy your night." He tried to wave them along past the table.

"Aw," Ai whined. "We just wanted to say hi to Mr. Griswald. We're huge fans." She accentuated the words in verbal honey. "Surely you understand?"

"Sure, I understand," he said. "You and every other young woman in here. You're not getting to this table, regardless."

"Hey," Eric called out. "Let them in," he said.

"Sir, I must protest." The guard turned around and tried to protest, but his employer cut him off.

"A man wants some pretty girls on his arms when he comes to a place like this. You heard me, let them through. Now."

The guard turned around and looked at the two girls with a sour look on his face. "You heard the boss. Just know if you try anything, and I mean anything, your head will spin with how fast you're out of here. Do you understand? Now, before we let you through, we need to give you a quick pat down."

"We went through a metal detector when we arrived, though," Ai said. "If we're going to get felt up by anyone, make it him," she looked past the guard at Eric and winked at him. She pulled down her mask temporarily and made sure he saw her lick her lips before raising it back to be in place.

"You want by me? I'm making sure you don't have weapons." He frowned. "This is not a negotiation."

"Okay, big man," Ai said. "Don't have a stroke now. You're too young for that."

The middle-aged man grumbled as he stepped forward and patted them down from their shoulders to their miniskirts. "You're clean. Go ahead." He backed off and resumed his watch.

"Ladies," Eric gestured over to them, "come, sit down. I have champagne on the way."

"That sounds lovely." Ai tossed the hoodie back and removed her mask before sitting down at his side. "I can't believe I finally get to meet you," she gushed.

"I'm the lucky one getting to meet you two," he said.

Vickie removed her mask and gave him an alluring smile as she sat on the other side of him. She could feel his arm over her shoulder. She gave a momentary glance over at Luke before returning her attention to their mark. "You know, you're more handsome in person," she said.

"Totally," Ai said. She leaned into Eric's side and placed her hand on his thigh. "I couldn't believe it when I heard you'd be here tonight. With all the good you do, we thought you'd be working. I guess even big men like you," she trailed her hand up and down his thigh with a featherlight touch, "need some rest like everyone else, huh?"

"Probably more," Vickie said.

A worker from the nightclub came by with an expensive-looking bottle and multiple glasses. He placed them on the table in front of them with a nod.

"What do you say to a toast to the opening of this fine club, ladies? It's my treat."

"We'd love to," Ai leaned forward with him, staying close.

Eric looked up to see his security having to keep a small group of women from approaching. "Let them through. We're having a party over here."

"I was just telling Valerie here that we needed a new place around here. Now is the perfect time and place."

"Go now, boys, and Godspeed to you," David could be heard in Vickie and Ai's ears.

"Alright, you're clean. Don't try anything. Do you understand me?" the guard from before asked the new girls.

Vickie looked over to where the two upper levels nearly conjoined and saw Luke and Reese standing a fair distance away. *Come on,* she thought. *Before they sit down would be nice. Don't be afraid. It's like a two-feet gap at most.*

The two men finally looked like they worked up their nerve, and both took off into a dead sprint. Reese ended up being the first to try. He used a nearby seat from a table by the railing and used it to springboard himself up. He placed a foot on the narrow guardrail and jumped, soaring over the gap with the DJ below.

Luke followed behind and made the jump. His landing was not nearly so graceful though, as he ended up slamming into Reese after he'd cleared the distance. Both men ended up on the floor.

"We got two!" A nearby man behind them yelled at the top of his lungs, barely piercing through the audio of the club music playing with its intoxicating beats. They could hear the clattering of footsteps along with the beat as a group of men charged away from them toward one end of the raised floor.

"Hey, who do you think you are?" Ai slapped the nearing women.

The young woman did not take this laying down. Ai and the young woman were suddenly in a no holds barred good old-fashioned cat fight, hair pulling included.

one of the few remaining guards behind the table rushed forward and got to work separating the two women.

"Girls, settle down," Eric said. "It's just two morons trying to kill themselves. Let's not lose our tempers here," he said, pouring the second of the glasses.

Vickie reached into her miniature purse and pulled out the syringe. She used her other hand to place her hand on Eric's nearest arm. Her syringe holding hand was fast as a blur as it moved toward his side. She pinched him as hard as she could while her other hand pierced the needle through his side and pressed down on the home-made concoction the pair of spies had prepared earlier. She stashed the needle away just in time before he jerked his head in her direction.

"Easy, love." He rubbed his arm. He raised his voice. "Get them out of here now," he said, gesturing to Ai and the new girl. The security forces from before were coming back now, having subdued Luke and Reese, and the venue's security could be seen escorting them down the stairwell they came up on, no doubt escorting them off the premises.

"Angie, I told you that you're too much of a hothead!" Vickie cried out, waving at Ai. "What did she say?"

"On second thought," Eric said, taking a second look at Vickie. "Why don't you go with her? You two are together, right?"

"I'm totally not her, though."

"Time for you to move on, girl." Eric motioned to one of his returning security. "She's moving on. Escort her, won't you?"

"Fine then," Vickie said as a muscled hand gripped down on her wrist. "No need to sick the wolves on me."

"Sir, we should head home," the senior guard said while she was being escorted away. "It's too dangerous here. You might be compromised."

She couldn't hear anything more as the man escorted her down the stairs and let her go on the main floor. She saw Ai nearby and approached her.

"Is it done?" Ai asked.

"It is," Vickie said. "Let's get out of here."

"Aw, alright then. It was a fun night, though," Ai and Vickie walked toward the exit.

24

———

Vickie and Ai sat in a small non-descript room of the giant building they'd found themselves in. The drive to Langley had flown by faster than either had anticipated. A young woman was sitting at a nearby desk in the cramped office. She was typing away at a blistering pace, totally deaf to the world around her; that is, until the little intercom on her desk came to life with a male voice.

"Send them in, please," the male voice said.

"You can head on in," the woman said. "I'd be careful. He's grumpy today."

"I can hear you," the man said.

"I'm not wrong though."

"Just send the two in already."

The two girls got out of their seats and entered the next room. This office was much bigger. It had windows lining one side of the room that went from the floor all the way to the ceiling. The view was gorgeous, showcasing the massive parking lot outside and a distant tree line. There was a nameplate perched on top of the desk that read 'Junior Director Fredric Shea'.

"Well, look who it is." The man placed the pen down to the side and slid the nearest paper he was working on away. "I assume you are Ai Xiao?"

"Yes, sir," she said. The pair of women stood in front of his desk with their hands at their sides, in a formal position.

"Sit down," he said, pointing at the pair of chairs in front of his desk. "You're making me uncomfortable just looking at the pair of you." He watched the pair take their seats before cracking his knuckles. "Now," he said. He reached up and ran a hand through his thick beard with a grunt. "I want you two to know how miserable you made my life the past week. Especially you." He took the nearby pen and pointed at Ai with it. "Now, is it true you wish to defect?"

"More than anything, Mr. Shea," Ai said. "My family has been executed because of my actions."

"Your family?" Fredric asked. "I don't follow. Were they using them as leverage over you or something?"

"That is how your Luke convinced me to change. My handlers took me when I was a small child and molded me into their idea of a perfect agent. They held my family over my head. Normally they'd have been eliminated, but they kept them alive so long as I did as I was told."

"You said Luke?"

"He is the one who questioned me and got the locations of the bombs and convinced me my life was on the wrong track."

"Isn't that the name of your asset?" he asked.

"He's also my boyfriend, if you remember, boss," Vickie said.

"Right. I remember that fiasco that you two put Maddie through." Fredric couldn't hide a laugh. "That woman deserved that mess with how much of a cocksure bitch she is. Right. So your brawler boyfriend is worth more than some muscle. Who'd have thought? Hmm..." He leaned back in his huge office chair with a squeak. "You're aware if we granted such amnesty, you'd have to work for us in exchange."

"I'd expect nothing different," Ai said. "I am a hard worker, as your team can attest to."

"She was pivotal in defusing the explosives and taking care of the other thing afterward."

"So I saw on the news this morning," Fredric said. "The news says he died in his house in the middle of the night. Unknown causes, they're saying. Apparently, he had a heart attack, and his security was left scratching their heads. Now, know that if you ever spill any of this to anyone, you're in deep shit. We take confidentiality very seriously over here in America."

"I once witnessed a man gossiping in training about something that was confidential to his friend. They dragged them both away, and we never saw them again. I know what keeping a secret entails, Mr. Shea."

"Good," he said. "Now you should know this decision was not made lightly. Many here did not want to grant such amnesty. They believe you're acting as a double agent. You will be under scrutiny far more than anyone else. Are you alright with that? Your digital activity, any letters you send, and anything else will be monitored as a matter of safety."

"Okay," she said. "If I dared to return home, they'd kill me; so, these terms sound better than that if I'm brutally honest. I am used to being monitored, so that's not a real change."

"I expected a little more push back if I'm honest," he said. He scratched his brown hair atop his head. "Would you want to be reassigned to a different team, or are you happy with this one?"

"I get to choose?" Genuine confusion washed over Ai's face.

"Not a choice, per se," he said. "More of a what's your preference?"

Ai looked over at Vickie at her side who'd remained quiet and then back to in front of her. "I'd like to stay with Ms. Jones and her friends."

"Friends, huh?" He glanced over at Vickie. "Good to see you and the infamous David Heron work well together. I admit I was in disbelief when I saw your request for his transfer. As unorthodox as your little team is, I cannot deny the efficacy of your results. Not a single explosive went off, and that little town's food supply has remained uninterrupted. You eliminated a traitor silently. Along with that, you got us another tentative agent in the process."

"We are ready for another job whenever it is needed," Vickie said.

"That will come in due time," Fredric frowned. "This whole revelation has started a shitstorm in the agency. One that is needed funny enough. We cannot have corruption where we suspect there is. Mr. Griswald had friends in high places in government. That is all I'm able to say right now. I don't have new orders for your team right now, so take a little time and rest after this job well done. Now as for you, Ms. Xiao."

"Yes," Ai leaned forward. She had her hands clasped in her lap.

"On your way out, you need to grab the essentials. Vickie will guide you. You'll need a driver's license, a birth certificate, and a social security number. Mind you, these are temporary and at our discretion if we withdraw them, but you'll need them to function in society. You'll receive a stipend to pay for lodgings you need as well. Do not take this generosity for granted. It took a lot of favors to make this happen."

"For real?"

"For real," he said with a slight smile. He saw her face light up in pure joy. She reached over and gave Vickie a small hug before the American woman pushed her away in a hurry. "You won't regret this."

"It wasn't my decision at the end of the day. I was just your arbiter. Don't fuck me over. If you turn out to be lying, you're on the chopping block; and I'll be right there with you. You should thank Vickie here. She was the one who convinced me."

"Do not hug me again." Vickie cut her off at the pass and stifled the attempted embrace.

"Always wanting to be so professional," Fredric said. He got up from the desk and wandered over to the large, pristine, clean windows. He had his hands behind him with his legs wide beneath him. "Sometimes I wonder if your unorthodox methods are the key to your success. No other agent would have wanted a civilian asset to assist on a mission as important as this one was. Whatever you're doing is working, so I won't get in the way."

Ai ambushed Vickie while she was looking over at her boss and gave her another quick embrace.

Vickie was going to grumble when she saw the look of unadulterated joy radiating off Ai. She swallowed whatever words she was going to say. She couldn't bring herself to be gruff now. For some reason she couldn't put her finger on.

"Now do not get complacent." Fredric stared down at the parking lot. His voice grew serious. "The next job will be even more difficult and risky. As one of you no doubt knows, and possibly even Ms. Xiao, technically, we are not allowed to operate on domestic soil; but what the public doesn't know won't hurt them. I recommend you keep your team together. It won't be long. Continue training, keep ready, and above all, be prepared for my call. Something big is rumbling in the pipeline, and you may be called to gather intel for such a mission. It will take all your cunning, wisdom, and creativity."

"We'll be ready, sir," Vickie said, finally peeling Ai off her just in time for her boss to turn around and return to his desk.

"You'd better be," he said. "God save this country. We're going to need the help, especially if people like you two are our best hope." He couldn't help hiding a smug look. "Now you two have a lot to do. Get out of here and remember what I said about staying ready. Go get her everything she needs, and get her some housing. We can't have her home-less, can we?"

"Right away," Vickie said. She stood up.

Ai followed suit and stood.

"Now get out of here. You're dismissed. I have work to do and can't have you two taking up my precious time." He shooed them out with his hand.

The pair exited the room and the small adjoining room. They found themselves in a long hallway.

"Follow me," Vickie said. "It's easy to get lost in here if you don't know your way around. I'm convinced they did it on purpose. They had unlimited government spending, and boy, did they justify it with this place."

"I am just happy I am not to be imprisoned for life or killed."

"I would be too if I were you," Vickie said. She turned a corner and headed for a group of elevators. "I suppose you'll be staying near the rest of us then, as far as housing goes. We need to be able to gather quickly, so that'd be helpful." She pressed the down arrow after they arrived at the elevators.

"Is there a church wherever that is?"

"There is," Vickie said. "There's both a Catholic one and a Protestant one, so you get your choice. If you're willing to drive further out into the country, you have even more choices in smaller villages. I wouldn't do that, though. That's like a half hour drive - but you're not me."

The doors opened in front of them, and a few people filed out. They gave Ai dirty looks as they passed by, one even pushing her using his shoulder without an apology, making her take a step back.

"Watch your step, asshole," Vickie called after the retreating man.

He didn't answer back, but flipped her off.

"What a dickhead." Vickie got into the elevator with Ai and pressed the desired floor. "That's probably something you'll have to get used to. Just don't ever strike them, or they'll cry to the higher ups. Then you're well and truly fucked."

The elevator doors closed, and they descended with the relaxing music in the confined space.

"I don't have much of a temper, but thank you for the warning. Our countries are at war," Ai said. "I expect to get some nasty looks, considering who I am. I forgive them."

"You are too nice for this profession."

"Better too nice than the other choice."

The doors opened, and they stepped out to another group of people, some of them giving the same nasty looks to Ai as they passed by. This time nobody made physical contact as they cleared the area.

"It's close by now. Let's get you all the paperwork you need. Such a thrilling part of the job, wouldn't you say?"

"Enthralling," Ai said.

25

"Y ou're sure about this?" Ai asked. She looked at where she'd be staying temporarily. "It's too much for someone like me."

Luke and Vickie were nearby. He wrapped an arm around Vickie, who curled into his chest. "We'd been meaning to move in together, anyway. This place will treat you well - it did for me. You need somewhere to stay while you look for your own place."

"Thank you very much." Ai turned and bowed.

"Please," Luke gesture upward, trying desperately to get her to stop the overly formal bow. "You don't have to do that."

"I will treat the place with the utmost respect." She finished the show of respect and looked at the loving couple. "It will be as you left it. I swear this to you. "

"Now that this is settled, let's go introduce you to Reese's family. We're trying to start a tradition after a successful mission, apparently." Vickie looked up at Luke with a playful smile. She turned her attention back to Ai before speaking again. "I'm sure they'll love you."

"She's an easy-going lady, and their daughter, Evangeline, is a little angel, despite her father's shortcomings," Luke said. "It's close by. Ride with us, and we'll drop you back here afterward. My stuff's already moved out - well, most of it."

"Sounds good to me," Ai watched as the pair turned back to their car. They got in the front while she got into the back.

"You should know before we get there that she and her family are from the Philippines," Vickie said. She started the engine and got them moving toward Reese's house. "She's not the biggest fan of China's government."

"That makes two of us," Ai said. She leaned her head against the window at her side. "I regret what my country did to all those countries, including her homeland. I only saw what they put on the news, which was mostly propaganda."

"Let's try to steer clear of that whole subject," Luke said. "I'm more interested in how he's going to introduce you, if I'm honest." He reached over to the armrest on his right and pressed a button. His nearby window rolled down. It let in warm air along with a strong gust of wind.

Vickie negated that by using the control to her left and rolling it back up. "Sometimes I wonder if you still have a grudge against him for almost stabbing you the second time you met. Oh, oops, I'm wrong. For him slashing you to ribbons, I should say."

"It's a guy thing to fight each other from time to time," Luke said. "I don't make the rules, I just follow them."

"You do a lot of things, but following rules has never been one of them, and we both know it."

"Maybe beating up debtors isn't following the law, but

it's honest work," Luke said. "Which reminds me, I have my first day back tomorrow night at the storefront."

"You run a store?" Ai asked.

"He works in my father's illegal gambling den."

"It's a book making place, not a den."

"They're illegal in this state, so it's a den," Vickie said. "It's a charming one, no doubt. We have lots of memories there, but I'm glad to be out of there. When I got out of there, my clothes stopped smelling like stale cigarette smoke. Besides, how can you stomach bartending and going out to collect from low lives?"

"Compared to this job, those sound like paradise. It's not nearly so stressful. Yeah, someone may want to try you, but I've got a reputation around here. Most just pay up, so I just drive around collecting."

"Until someone new wants to prove themselves and pulls a gun," Vickie said, clearly not amused.

"I'm honored you're worried. You're always welcome to come with me on the job, you know."

"I have slightly more important worries than people owing my father money for their gambling addiction. Thank you though. That chapter of my life is behind me, thankfully."

"I did not expect to find out you were in such seedy work," Ai said.

"It's not like I go around beating people up for fun. I don't want to hurt anybody, but people's memories tend to forget and then magically remember when I'm there."

"Which is why you were the one to talk to me. You did not question me how I imagine you normally do to your debtors."

"I had a hunch that wouldn't work as well after listening to you talk," Luke said.

"We're here," Vickie said. They pulled up to the house.

Evangeline was outside in the front yard with her mother nearby on the front porch. She was jumping on a large trampoline with a huge smile on her face as the vehicle approached.

Angela looked up from the book she was reading and raised a hand, along with a greeting. "Hey you two!"

The three got out of the car. Luke and Vickie both waved. Ai gave an awkward wave as the trio approached the porch.

"Oh, who is this?" Angela pulled off her sunglasses and looked at the three. "You're new," she said. "Are you Ms. Xiao that my husband told me about?"

"I am," Ai said.

"He said you were being used by the Chinese – that they were holding your family over your head." She saw Evangeline coming closer, near within ear shot. "Is that true?"

"Yes, ma'am."

"You poor thing," Angela said. She approached the timid Ai and gave her a warm hug before backing up a few feet. She gestured to her daughter who was approaching after getting off the trampoline. "I want you to meet our daughter, Evangeline. Say hello, Evangeline."

The young girl climbed up to the porch and spoke in a loud, confident voice. "Hello Luke, Vickie, and other lady."

"Her name is Ai Xiao," Angela said. "We told you last night. Try not to forget people's names, dear. It's rude."

"Sorry, Mom. Hello, Ms. Xiao," Evangeline said.

"It's a pleasure to meet you, Evangeline," Ai bent over, trying to get to the small girl's eye level.

"Daddy said you were a nice lady last night," the girl said.

"Did he now?" Vickie asked.

"He told us the entire story after he got back last night," Angela said, "leaving out certain parts for security. He did tell us about the new girl, though."

The nearby front door opened, and Reese stepped out. "My ears are burning. What did I do?"

"Nothing important, dear.

"Everyone come inside out of the sun. We'll get you all some drinks and have an enjoyable time today. It is the start of a new friendship, after all."

"That sounds lovely," Luke said. He, Evangeline, and Vickie followed Angela inside, leaving Reese and Ai outside.

"Come on inside," Reese said. "She'll yell at me if we don't."

She carefully followed Reese through the door and gently shut the door behind her. She immediately took her shoes off and placed them near the door before continuing toward the sound of lively chatter.

"I hope you all like take out," Reese said as they entered the living room. "That's the plan for tonight."

"We should get Lou's," Angela said. "You all have been gone for a while, and his sub sandwiches are legendary."

"It has been a while," Luke said. "I could use a Philly Cheesesteak."

"Let me get a pen and paper, and we'll get it ordered," Angela said.

Ai chose the only remaining seat, which was at the end of the sofa by Luke, who was beside Vickie. Her thoughts wandered as she listened to the chatter. Evangeline pestered her father with something or other. The two who'd helped her find her new residence whispered to each other, and for the first time in a while, she felt something she hadn't felt in a long time. *Acceptance,* she thought. *I forgot what this feels like.*

"What would you want, sweetie?" Angela looked at her. She had the pen at the ready, about to write her order. "Oh right," she said. "You probably don't even know their menu. That's not a problem. Do you have a phone?"

"I do, but it's unnecessary. I'll have the Cheesesteak," she said. "It's been too long since I had a good one."

The afternoon gave way to evening as the group enjoyed the rare moment of rest they treasured. For them, it was just another happy day. For one among them, it was the start of a new life.

26

Ai woke to the chirp of her phone at her bedside table. She rolled over with a grumble and grabbed the infernal device that woke her. She saw a text message from Vickie saying she was bringing guests over to her house that morning, and that she had something important to tell everyone. She had an inkling as to what the job was as she climbed out of bed.

She quickly changed clothes and headed downstairs. She got herself a drink from the kitchen and a small breakfast. She had finished her meal when she heard the doorbell for the first time in her new place. She placed the dishes in the nearby sink before heading over to open the door.

She opened it to see Reese, Luke, Vickie, and David all outside. She stepped to the side and welcomed them all in. "Come in," she said. "Everyone's up so early."

"It's like ten in the morning," Reese said, closing the door behind him. "You just got up?"

"Some of us sleep in, Mr. Hilton. Not as if I need to ask, but what's happening that we're all here this fine morning?" Ai asked.

"Word from on high has come down," Vickie said. "We're to head the team to investigate for corruption in Congress."

"You're shitting me," David said. "Who are they even wanting us to look at?"

"We're going to be doing a lot of digital surveillance to start with," she said. "We're going to be looking at bank accounts - payments coming in and out for every single sitting representative, senator, and possibly even higher up the chain. We have full authority to carry out these operations."

"We're being disavowed if we get caught I take it?" Reese asked.

"More than likely," Ai said.

"We won't be going after anybody physically unless we have rock solid proof they're either cooperating with China, or they're bought and paid for. Uncle Sam's shady brother wants a purge of all the traitors."

"We're calling the CIA Uncle Sam's shady brother now?" Luke asked. "That's generous and a little terrifying all at once. They're more like that shifty guy who makes people disappear and manipulates people."

"My point," Vickie leveled a glare at Luke, "is that this is an official order from the higher ups. This isn't just Fredric's thing anymore."

"It's going to take months investigating hundreds of people like that," David said. "Never mind that even if we find corruption, what do we do then?"

"Take a guess," Vickie said.

"You're not serious? This is historic shit. Surely we can simply send them to prison or something. Bodies dropping in Congress will cause a political earthquake. We'd be lucky to finish the war if that happens."

"Management thinks that getting rid of a traitor would be a net gain. If a little upheaval occurs, it's an acceptable price. Mind you, we're not cleared to just start blasting. We have to send all of our proof up the ladder, and they make the final decision. It's not like we're going to just go rogue and start neutralizing people."

"Killing you mean," Reese said.

"Let's not church it up," Ai said. "This is going to be a lot of work."

"It's necessary," Vickie said. "We cannot allow our country's leaders to prioritize their own checkbook over the welfare of the country."

"Are you new here?" Luke asked. "That shit's been happening since the dawn of the nineteenth century. It's just recently they've stopped trying to hide it so much since they think we're all idiots - ironically, usually presenting themselves as the biggest morons."

"Let's pass on the history lesson and focus on the damned gravity of what she just said." David pointed at Vickie. "Surely there are other teams that are going to be on this case as well. Yes? It's not all on our shoulders, is it?"

"I am not privy to that," Vickie said. "Just focus on our jobs. We're all in this together for the next few months. Now we're going to have to teach you two how to do this." She glanced at Luke and Reese. "We need everyone to pitch in on the research. That means we're going to have to make sure Ai here is up to speed. I'm not sure how much digital training she has."

"I did back track the payments to Griswald, but I'm always up for a brush up on my skills," Ai said.

"So that's that," Vickie said. "We're all clear on what we're doing the next few months then?"

"Why am I here?" Reese asked. "I assumed I'd be back overseas next week. I'm not a computer whiz. I'm just muscle."

"I don't know if you've been paying attention," Vickie said. "We're going to need just that."

"I don't know about doing that to an elected official, man," he said.

"Think of it as when George Washington would shoot deserters who wanted to defect to Great Britain. It's the same concept."

"Jesus." Reese shook his head. "It's going to take a while to wrap my head around that."

"This is no doubt going to be a major event for the country by the time we're done," Vickie said. "History will never know our names, and it must be that way. We won't be heroes. We're toiling away, doomed to never receive credit for what we do. However, if we do not do our jobs, this country will fall to corruption, greed, and ignorance."

"You should have been a politician with speeches like that," Ai said, cracking a smile. "I've heard worse speeches from elected officials."

"She is climbing the ladder," David said. "Or at least angling for it. Office politics are still politics."

"Are you all done wisecracking? I know you all are nervous about this, but be serious for a minute. This isn't fun and games. This is an incredibly serious responsibility we've been given. The men and women we investigate have personal security. They are careful, and they don't want to be caught."

"There's nothing more dangerous than a cornered rat," Reese said.

"Precisely," Luke said. "This is out of my ballpark, but

you know I'll help you however I can. I always will. I have since childhood anyway. That's not going to change."

"Aren't you just precious?" David sneered.

"You got a problem?" Luke asked.

"My problem is they handed me this shit sandwich of a mission that's akin to career suicide. You think they're going to give this kind of job and leave us alive to tell the tale of how they hired us to investigate and neutralize any traitors in Congress? You're nuts if you think they want that. We'll be retired ourselves."

"Retired?" Ai asked. "Does that mean killed too?"

"Yes," David said.

"You still believe in the Barnes rumors?" Vickie asked.

"What?" Luke asked.

"The story goes that Barnes was an agent in the nineteen seventies," Vickie said. "He was a regular prodigy of an agent. They gave him a key job during the Korean Gate investigation. Now at this point rumors abound."

David took over on the storytelling front. "Rumor is that he was the one who secured the intel that clenched that investigation via, shall we say, illegal means. He was put down for working on this job, since they were afraid it would reveal their own misdoings. Same as will happen here. They won't want evidence of their work."

"Allegedly," Vickie said. "We'll be fine. We're doing our jobs to the 't'."

"So was Barnes if you read the mission reports, which I know you did if you went through the same training that I did," David said. "He eliminated who he had to and was hanged for it, if you'll recall. The only bright spot is we would get two to the back of the head."

"Aren't you just a ray of sunlight?" Vickie stood up and

walked to the middle of the room between everyone who was sitting. "We don't get a choice, so preaching doom and gloom is counterproductive. I will tolerate no more of that kind of talk. Besides, if we stay out of the limelight, they won't have a reason to kill us. We all took a vow of silence regarding this thing at one time or another."

"As I recall, Barnes took the same vow of silence. Though I hope you're right," David said.

"I always am."

"Moving off of his fears," Ai said, raising her hand. "Can I ask a quick question?"

"Go ahead."

"Are we staying here or heading out to do this?"

"We're going to pack our bags, boys and girls," Vickie said. "We're heading to DC."

"I always wanted to go there at least once in my life," Ai said. "That was always a no-go zone for me before. Is it true that it is its own province?"

"I'm surprised they didn't send you there to really sow chaos," Reese said. "One explosion there and you'd send the country into a panic."

"They were worried it would send a wave of patriotism through your population if an attack occurred there," Ai said. She pulled out her phone and pulled up a message she'd received years ago. "You can see here." She tossed the phone to Reese.

He studied the message. "They really sent you messages on your phone?"

"It was encrypted originally," Ai said. "Give me some credit at least."

He tossed the device back and leaned forward in the seat, planting his elbows on his legs. He looked around the room at the different occupants. "This will be a war, you know. We got around Griswald's guards because of where he was. These tight asses in suits, they will not do that. They're going to be on Capitol Hill, maybe give a speech or two, and then head to wherever they're staying. You know that."

"We've risen to every challenge thrown at us so far," Luke said. "This one will be the same. We even have new talent to keep us honest."

"Isn't this just a lovely peace and love vibe we've got going on?" David trudged forward, his tone not matching his words. "This is bordering on treason - the job we've been given. She's putting a pretty bow on it, but that's what this is. These are elected officials that the people themselves voted on."

"I can always relieve you if you'd like and get a new member if you'd prefer," Vickie said.

"Really?"

"No."

"Damn you. Why me?"

"You're a valued member of the team, little buddy," Vickie said. "You know your way around a computer, and that's all we'll need you for. God knows you're not going to get your hands dirty." She paused. "Well, not again anyway."

"That was not my fault. I keep telling you, he did that to himself!"

"Because of what you did."

"Did I miss something?" Ai asked.

"She's digging up my history," David said. "Which is supposed to be private, by the way."

"Can I ask what that was? If we're going to be partners, I like to learn a bit about them."

"Let them tell you," David said. He got out of his seat.

"They're going to tell you anyway. It's not like I have a choice in this, apparently. I'll be the good little soldier and march toward death with all of you, sure." He made for the door. "When and where are we meeting for the drive?" He asked this from right in front of the door.

"Come on," Luke said. "Just sit and calm down."

"Calm down? No offense, but you and Reese over there shouldn't have even been involved in this last job. You're not trained, and the only reason you were is because she," he pointed to Vickie who was giving him a dirty look, "she decided to utilize the good will of Mad Maddie and used that clout to pull you in. As a response, they saddled her with my ass. I was supposed to be the one keeping this whole thing from turning into a circus with her clown world reputation at the agency."

"Is that right?" Vickie asked.

"It is."

"It's a good thing the circus did an even better job than management expected then." She showed off a smug smirk.

"Fuck you," he said.

"We're going in two cars tomorrow morning," Vickie said. "Who wants to be in which?"

"I'm with you," Luke said.

"Agreed."

"I'll go with Ai," Reese said. "Someone's got to acclimate her to American society, and you all are not shining beacons I'd choose for a tutor.

"That leaves you," Vickie said, looking at David. "Who are you going with?"

"Can't I just drive my damned self and listen to music on the way?" David asked.

"If you insist on alienating yourself, but I would like to

incorporate you with the team as much as possible. You'd have to undergo team-building exercises. Is it worth that?"

David narrowed his eyes at her and just stared her down. "I'll go with the soldier boy and the Manchurian defector over there."

"It's settled then. See you in the morning..."

THANK YOU FOR READING!

Luke and the gang will return next year for another adventure. If you'd like to support this work, please consider leaving a rating or review on Amazon. Thank you and have a great day!

ABOUT THE AUTHOR

Alex J Fischer has been writing for close to a decade and has won six National Novel Writing Month challenges in a row.

Alex grew up in a small town in Ohio and still resides there. Hobbies include writing, video games, and watching crime shows.

ALSO BY ALEX J FISCHER

Morris Crime Family:

Welcome to the Family

The Silver Lining

Any Means Necessary

The Fourth Bullet

A New Generation

Full Circle

Order of Vengeance Motorcycle Club:

The Order of Vengeance

Vengeance Above All

Masked Justice:

The End of Innocence

Masked Justice

Blind Justice

The Collector:

The Debt Collector

Pawns on the Hunt